Molting

Book Three of Feathered Dreams

By Brittany Putzer

Molting

Editor: Kat Pagan

Cover by: Rae Lumpkins

ISBN: 978-0-578-99280-8

Published in the United States.

Dedication

To God, who gave me this wonderful imagination and stubborn, strong will to conjure this book series. Also, to my amazing family and friends. All of your love has helped me soar to unimaginable heights. I will be forever grateful for your love and support.

#LiveLaughRead

Contents

Masking the Pain

"Thank you all for coming today as we gather to say farewell to our dear friend, Jack Wilfred Gable."

Jab. Jab. Hook.

"Jack was a wonderful husband and an incredible father, and he will forever live on in the hearts of those whose lives he has touched."

Jab. Roundhouse.

"As you can imagine, Lady Ann is very distraught and has requested that I come up and say a few words about her father. Jack was a gentle spirit, who constantly took care of those in need..."

I drive down the haunting memories as hot sweat slides off my chin, and stare at the slim figure in front of me. "Stop dancing around. Come on, don't hold back this time, Sam."

Before the words escape my lips, I am on my back, blinking at the training room ceiling. I squeeze my eyes shut as pain throbs from my mouth.

"Not again, Ann. I told you, you need to duck when you see my fist coming." Sam offers a strong hand up as her black braid falls over her shoulder.

I slap her palm away. "You did that on purpose."

She cocks a hip while her emerald eyes glitter. "And risk having the King bite my head off, *again*? You may enjoy his tongue lashings, but I do not."

I accept her arm and she yanks me forward. I rub my fingers across my face and sigh when scarlet paints my

1

wrist like a blank canvas.

Christian is going to give me hell for this.

"That's enough for today, Sam. Go clean up," Vinny grumbles from the corner of the room.

A towel hurtles towards my face and I catch it with ease.

"King Christian's going to chew me a new one for this. Ann, please stop bleeding during your training sessions."

"You're the head of his guard and I know he trusts your judgement. Stop being such a baby."

"Don't you think this has gone on long enough?"

I run the towel across my chest and still at his words. My hazel eyes shimmer, narrowing at him as I recall the series of events over the last few months. My dad's body was found shot in an abandoned lot, and since then, I have secluded myself from the world.

During the day, I work as a silent office slave alongside Prince Ryan, with Christian as both my King and self-imposed dictator. Then, at night, I travel to the training room with Vinny and Sam to practice self-defense.

"I won't stop until I find out what happened to my dad. I've told you that. And I will do whatever it takes. So, suck it up, buttercup."

I slap his cheek before brushing past him to shower, but before I can get too far, Vinny snatches my wrist.

"Your dad wouldn't want you seeking revenge like this. He would want you to live your life and settle down."

I arch a brow, knowing exactly who he is referencing

when he suggests *settling down*. Before my dad's murder, Ryan and I had talked about traveling and building a home together. Since then, I have been pushing him away and focusing on physically exhausting myself day after day.

"Not everyone wants to get married, have kids, and *settle* down like you and Karen. So, just drop it, before I drop you, pretty boy."

"Aw, you think I'm pretty?"

Vinny collects me in an embrace and ruffles my hair. I shove him away, give him the bird, and saunter off.

"That isn't very ladylike. Sam is teaching you bad habits."

I roll my eyes, fighting the urge to dropkick him. I know I would lose but that's okay—the pain would be better than the numbness.

I run my hand over the steamy mirror in the bathroom and look down at my black and blue arms. Maybe I wasn't cut out for combat? I tug at my wet chestnut hair as memories overtake me.

The people I love are withering away, especially when they are around me. First, my mom to cancer when I was ten, and now, my dad.

When I enter my room, I smile at my maid, Karen, and her ever-growing belly. Even pregnant, there is not a single hair out of place or stain on her starched uniform.

Her beautiful smile melts into a scowl. "Ann, we need to ice your lip. Sit down."

I wave her aside. "Don't you start fussing over me too. I got enough of that from your husband in the training

3

room. Do you know if Detective Mack has called?" I ask, referring to the investigator Christian has assigned to my dad's case.

"Actually, I was just coming to get you. Mack walked up the stairs a few minutes ago, and he is in the office talking to King Christian."

"Thank you, Karen."

I rush out the door before she can respond, praying I haven't missed Mack's report.

"Lady Ann, I thought you promised me you would call before you and Sam sparred?" Tim, Christian's assistant, teases.

"Tim, you know you are always welcome to come and watch us; we are down there every night."

"Oh, I bet you *are* down there every night." He winks before knocking on Christian's door.

"You may enter," booms Christian in his all-business tone.

My eyes rake over the man behind the professional voice. He is my age, tall, and has dirty blonde hair. But his most swoon-worthy feature is that set of piercing blue eyes. I could stare into them for hours. And beyond his physicality, he is confident and one of the smartest men I know. But outside of that, the man is nothing more than a control freak in a suit. Whenever he speaks, I'm reminded of the many reasons we never worked out.

My head pivots as the other occupant clears his throat. Detective Mack is an older, shorter man with hazel eyes and dark hair. He smirks as he extends a hand to me. "Good evening, Lady Ann, I see you are still training with the guard."

"And I see your efforts on finding anything useful are just as successful, Mack."

I can tell I hit a nerve when he squeezes my hand, but I hold my own. It has been far too long since my dad's body was found. There should have been more evidence or leads by now, which means Mack is either lying to me, or incompetent. Regardless of his motivation, I'm getting restless waiting around to find out.

Christian rubs his face then frowns at my fat lip. "Ann, is there any way you could actually *avoid* injury during these instructional sessions?" He dabs my swollen lip.

I hiss at the sting and snatch the handkerchief from him.

"Christian, stop babying me. I am trying to improve my abilities, but it isn't as easy as it looks."

"What was I thinking, permitting this nonsense?"

There he goes again, trying to run my life as if he owns it *and* me.

I ignore him and turn back to Mack. "Are there any new details?"

He shuffles some documents and places them in my hand. I clutch the pieces of paper as if they are a lifeline. Finally, some answers.

Maybe Mack isn't so useless after all.

I scan quickly and read that the murderer left behind a boot print with foreign pebbles embedded inside the indentation, as well as a single bullet casing. The report continues to state that the body positioning suggests the victim was shot from behind.

The blood drains from my face, and I collapse in one of the vacant chairs as I attempt to imagine why somebody would shoot my dad in the back.

"I am compiling responses from local store owners and recovering video footage of that night." Mack stands to leave, looking from me to Christian. "I will report back when I have more information."

"Thank you again for coming, Mack," Christian says, escorting the older man through the door. My mind runs over the new data Mack presented. How can we possibly find the killer with just a stupid boot print? This is ridiculous. We aren't getting anywhere.

When I look up, I see Christian sitting next to me as he eyes me carefully. Our relationship's complicated at best. When Christian turned twenty-one, he had to pick his future wife from a selection of ten women, and I was one of those girls.

Even though he chose Mary, I have no hard feelings. Because of our differences, we are better as friends and work well together in the office. I can trust that he has my best interests at heart. And he can trust that I will always be a pain in his side.

"Ann, you look pale. Have you eaten anything today?"

"Yes, I have."

"Have you consulted with Ryan?"

"I have been busy."

"Stop behaving like a two-year-old and communicate with him. The quicker you do, the better you will feel."

I refuse to let him talk to me like this, so I decide to change the subject before I strangle him.

"I need to travel to the location where my dad's body was found."

Christian stops in his tracks.

"Why would *you* do that? That is why I hired Detective Mack."

"But his progress is slower than a snail's crawl! And I believe he missed something."

"We have discussed this at length. Mack's the best in the country. Let him do his assignment. That way, we can keep you protected."

"Christian, I am done with hiding!"

"Ann, you must remain calm. We are not concealing you. We are trying to protect you, while also finding Jack's killer."

I turn away, as I feel tears brimming my eyes. He wraps his arms around me, hugging me tightly.

I pull from his grasp before I lose hold of my emotions. "You can't keep me here forever, Christian."

"You are not a prisoner, but a valued member of this Monarchy. And we are attempting to..."

"Defend me. I get it."

I shake him off and stomp towards the haven of my room, before he can continue his endless prattling about how important I am, and how unsafe it is outside of the Palace walls.

I couldn't care less. I need answers.

When I enter my room, I find Karen dusting the pictures on the wall.

"I can tell from your tears that there was no good news from Detective Mack."

I run my fingertip across the most recent picture of dad and me at Christian and Mary's wedding. Our smiling faces bring back so many memories. And when I close my eyes, I can still hear his contagious laughter as he twirled me around the dance floor.

A knock pulls me out of my memories. I look towards the door and see Vinny kissing Karen and talking to her belly, while she giggles and ruffles his hair.

"The King has called me to his office. Any ideas as to why that is, Ann?"

"It's probably because of my stellar attitude and quick reflexes."

"Yes, that must be it. I'll see you guys later."

Vinny gives Karen's belly one more rub before walking out, passing Ryan as he goes.

"Prince Ryan, how nice it is to see you again." Karen offers Ryan a hug, and he too rubs her belly and talks to it, reminding the babies inside that he is their awesome, self-proclaimed uncle.

I wrinkle my nose. Why does everyone feel the need to touch her belly? Is it good luck? I wonder if all that rubbing could harm the twins?

When I look up from Karen's belly, I see Ryan's brown eyes resting on me. I tilt my head, as I notice the tips of his dark locks touching his eyebrows. I clench my fists as I ache to run my hands through his hair again.

"Well, chica, I'm off to meet Vinny for dinner." Karen envelops me in a hug as best she can. "But I'll return with cookie dough and whipped cream, and we can watch *whatever* you want. Even if it's *Gilmore Girls* for the hundredth time." She rubs my arms. "Chin up. Things are going to be looking up soon. I can feel it."

"Thanks, Karen. Just leave the pickles behind. They ruined the whole feast last time."

"Oh, you are no fun! Taking my long, thick pickles away." She winks at me before she turns back to Ryan. "Good luck."

Once the door clicks closed behind her, Ryan directs his attention to me.

"Christian gave me the update from the detective. Are you okay?"

"Yes, thank you for inquiring."

"Ann, come on, talk to me."

"We are talking, Ryan."

He sits on my comforter and pats the edge of the bed, but I stand where I am. I need to focus on my mission, not play feathered princess.

"What are we doing, Ann?"

"We are communicating. Isn't that what you wanted?" I back pedal as he advances towards me, until my butt hits a hard surface. Soon I am pinned between his arms and the wall.

Ryan gently grabs my chin and forces me to look at him. "I love you, Ann. That's no secret. I know this is a hard time for you, and that's why I have given you space, but I need to know that *we* are okay. I need to know that you still love me too." He rubs his thumb over my swollen lip.

My body ignites as it responds to his familiar touch. My brain becomes fuzzy with desire and I lean in to kiss his lips, but at the last second, I shake my head and chastise myself.

"Ryan, I do love you. But finding my dad's murderer is priority right now."

"Ann, Jack is gone." He clasps my hands in his. "You know he would not want you to continue this way. He would want you to start a family and carry on his memory."

"My father meant everything to me! He was the *only* family I had left! And someone took him away from me! And they need to pay."

"You can't do this on your own. Please do not shut me out. Confide in me. Let me help you."

"I have been allowing you *and* Christian to help me, but we are not getting anywhere with the investigation! I understand you two have a country to run, and that's why I need to find out more information on my own."

"You are right. We know little of what happened that night. But we are doing our best to find out more." He sighs. "Have you even considered the possibility that *they* are after you now?"

"If they are, then we can utilize that to our advantage and toss me out as bait."

"Are you even listening to yourself? We can't do that!"

"Why not? Risking my life to bring down a killer, that

seems like a fair trade to me. Who knows who else they have slaughtered, or are planning to kill? We could save multiple lives."

"Ann, you can't keep doing this to yourself."

I cross my arms over my chest. "What am I doing, exactly?"

"You are acting like a lone ranger when we are all hurting."

I shake my head and walk away from him. I cannot imagine anybody hurting as much as I do. The pain burns so deep; it is an inferno slowly devouring me.

"Listen, I am tired. Can we talk about everything I am doing wrong some other time? Like the day after never?"

"That's not what I meant."

Each syllable he utters is laced with agony. I resist the urge to comfort him as I swing the door open.

"Good night, Prince Ryan."

"I love you, Ann." His eyes speak all the things I have always wanted from him and now, cannot have.

"I know you do."

I watch his slumped frame as he brushes past me. I never meant for him to get hurt, but I cannot let another person I love die.

Once I am alone, I lay my head in my hands and tears spring forth, until all my strength is sapped.

I am a farm girl, striving to become a warrior, and failing miserably at both.

Let the Games Begin

His breath is labored, his legs continue to pound the asphalt as sweat beads and stings his pores. He turns the corner and prays for shelter. A hooded figure cackles, aiming a gun at his exposed back. I scream out for my dad to dodge the bullet, but my words float to the ground. His body crumbles and I am powerless. My tears fall like feathers while I cradle him in my arms, watching his life force stain my white dress.

I wake up dripping in sweat and gasping for oxygen. I vigorously rub my eyes, freeing them of my nightmare. Then I lean against the soft, plush pillows before glancing at the clock.

"That's it. No more late nights filled with sweets and pickles."

I toss my legs over the side of the bed and aim to get ready for the day. Once I'm in the office, I fall into my chair and pout at my empty to-do list.

I crane my neck towards Ryan's workstation and my lips pull back. He has *plenty* to do. I tiptoe closer and run my fingertip over his list. I grin and chug away. By the time the office staff flocks in, I am cleaning his filing cabinet.

"Well, someone is up early... again," Ryan comments.

"Yes. You've got to love those little nightmares that keep you going," I retort.

"Ann, the doctor offered to prescribe you a sleep aid."

"Ryan, I *am* sleeping. It's what happens in my sleep that keeps me up."

"What about Christian's suggestion, some counseling?"

"No, thank you."

"Ann..." He stops short as he scans his area. "Did you clean my desk *again*?"

"Yes, I got bored and ran out of things to do. You're welcome."

He begins to leaf through his files. "I have a sorting system, and now it is messed up."

I throw my hands in the air. "I'm sorry I screwed everything up."

Ryan rubs his face, looks around at all the head shakes of the other workers, and frowns at my departing figure as I stalk out of the office.

In the hallway, I swipe at my annoying tears as they blur my vision. But I am too late, and I run into a hard chest.

"Oh, I am so sorry. I wasn't watching where I was going."

Once my eyes can focus, I see a man with brown hair and green eyes. I tilt my head at Queen Mary's little brother. "Max? What are you doing here?"

He gives me his cute, boyish smile. "Lady Ann, it is nice to see you again." His lips brush my knuckles.

"Mary never mentioned you were coming for a visit."

"Does a younger brother need a reason to visit his sister and cause trouble?"

"Max? I thought I heard your voice." Mary pops her head out of her room and embraces him. "I missed you.

13

We were just heading to breakfast. Are you hungry?"

As he exits his room, Christian wraps an arm around Mary's waist. "Good morning, Maximus, it is nice to see you in good health. What is on your itinerary for this *unannounced* excursion?"

"There's my favorite brother-in-law." Max shakes Christian's hand. "Well, if you must know, I was in the city conducting some business and I thought I would stop in to say hi. If that's okay with you?"

"Of course it's okay." Mary locks arms with Max and pulls him towards the dining room.

Mary is an odd ball, and the more I get to know her, the more I loathe her presence. So, normally, I wouldn't stick up for her or her kin, but Max should be allowed to visit his sister without the third degree from his highness.

I shift my arched brows towards Christian to judge his emotions. But his handsome face is as stoic as ever.

"Christian, what was that about?"

Christian walks away but I stand my ground.

"Why are you acting like that towards him? I thought you liked Max."

"I do not ask a great deal from you, so please heed my request. Stay away from Max."

"Why do I need to stay away from him? Are you playing the jealous boyfriend card again?"

"Ann, please do what I expect, no questions asked."

"How long have you known me, Christian? It's been what—two years? You know I don't follow commands blindly."

14

"I cannot answer at the moment." He rolls his eyes when I tap my foot. "How about we convene later and discuss it?"

I know he won't give me any more information, by the way his vein is sticking out in his neck, so I drop the subject for now while we walk.

"Fine, have it your way. But if you don't talk to me, I'm running to him in the dead of night and becoming his new BFF."

I can't suppress a yawn as we take our seats in the dining room. In the corner of my eye, I watch Ryan peer over at Max before turning to me.

"Do you have any idea why Max is here?"

Max meets my gaze and winks before returning to his conversation with Mary.

"I honestly have no clue. I tried to make Christian squeal, but he is lockjawed." I start on my eggs. "I think you are just jealous of him because he was hitting on me at Christian's wedding."

He disarms me with a charming smile and my heart aches.

"You have got to be kidding me, Ann. Me, jealous? Of him? Max knows where he stands."

He leans in and kisses my cheek while watching the subject of our debate.

Oh, yay, a cock fight.

I shoo Ryan away and grumble at his possessive actions. That move *never* worked for Christian when we were together. I don't know why Ryan thought I would let *him* get away with it.

Elizabeth clears her throat as she sits next to me. "Ann, would you like me to return Snowball to you?"

I smile, remembering the fluffy hen Christian bought me last year. While she's been a great emotional support animal for the Queen after the loss of her husband, I don't require that. I need answers. Ones that, unfortunately, Snowball cannot provide me.

"I appreciate the kind offer, but no. Thank you."

She places a hand on mine, pulling my eyes to her icy ones. "Ann, sweetie, if you need someone to talk to, you know I am always here for you. I miss Jack dearly, and I can't imagine how you are feeling."

"Thank you. I'll keep that in mind."

I poke at my breakfast sausage while emotions rise up in my throat. After a few minutes, I chug my coffee and excuse myself. As I walk out, I feel everyone's eyes on my departing back.

I am sick of being treated like a fragile child.

I chew on my lip as I figure out where to go. Now that my office work is complete, I have extra time to refine my defensive skills. And if I hurry, I can catch Sam and Vinny before they get ready for their patrol shift.

I quickly return to my room, throw on my chicken-print yoga pants, and grab a scrunchie. As I pull my hair up, there is a knock at my door.

"Ryan, why you insist on knocking, I will never know. This is *your* house. You can just walk right—"

I stop short and my eyes widen.

"Max, you do know this is not Mary's room, right?"

He makes no attempt to hide his searching eyes as they run over my tight workout pants and tank top.

"Are you preparing to go jogging?" He leans against the door frame, blocking my exit.

"Yes, now watch me jog away from you." I brush past him and head downstairs.

"Ouch. My dearest Ann, what happened to the sweet girl I knew and loved?" He steps next to me.

"She died alongside her father." I pivot on the balls of my feet, towards Max. His rock-hard chest collides with me. "What the hell are you trying to do?"

"I am trying to catch up with an old friend."

"We are not friends. Do us both a favor and go spend time with your sister. She needs all the friends she can get."

I turn away, and to my dismay, he follows. He is like an annoying gnat, buzzing obnoxiously in your ear. Why doesn't he take the hint and leave me alone?

"I'm sorry to disappoint you, but I can't hang out with her right now. I'm all yours, *sweetheart*."

I arch a brow but continue my fast pace. "And why not?"

"Well..." He rubs his neck and blushes. "I just can't at the moment."

I pinch his cheek. "Aw, wittle Maxy, are you afraid she may put you in a dress and paint your fingernails, *and* that you will like it?"

17

He chuckles as he massages his jaw. "If you must know… apparently… she is ovulating, and she and Christian want to be alone to take advantage of it."

I stagger as I trip over my own feet. Mary and Christian haven't been married very long, and they are already trying to have kids?

"Aww, is little Annie jealous?"

"Of course I'm not." I shake off my ruffled feathers. "And if you know what's good for you, you won't call me sweetheart again," I hiss.

Now I regret sticking up for him earlier. I keep the silence as I move to the training arena.

I allow myself to relax as I breathe in the familiar, musty smell and hear the soft thuds of fists on punching bags. It is still early, and there are a few guards training inside. They nod in greeting, as I enter and move to a punching dummy in the back before beginning my routine.

In the corner of my eye, I see Max surveying the equipment. It is hard to concentrate when it feels like I am babysitting. I slam my fist into the tough exterior and grumble.

I turn to yell at him, to order him to go find someone else to bother, but my mouth goes dry.

"Max, what are you doing? This is a sanitary training area. You are required to wear a shirt."

My eyes are glued on him as he continues his strip tease. His gaze never leaves mine as he starts to unbutton his collar. He smirks at me before he throws his shirt aside. I tear my gaze away from his bare chest, but it is increasingly hard to do as he struts towards me.

My stupid hormones better get ahold of themselves, because Max is too young and worse yet, he has Mary's blood coursing through him.

Think of something else, Ann. Like butterflies, chickens, chickens with round, hard breasts...

I shake my head to dislodge all of my impure thoughts.

"Since I have a few hours to kill, I might as well burn some calories." He grabs a pair of gloves. "How about you take some of that pent-up rage out on me?"

"No way. With my luck, you will go back to Mary crying. Then I will have to deal with her griping." I resume punching the bag, instead of his face.

Suddenly, he strikes my shoulder, using enough force to make me lose my footing. I glare up at his grinning face. "Come on, Ann, don't be afraid of me. I will go easy on you, just like everyone else around here."

His comment strikes harder than his jab.

I scowl as he continues to bait me. "They are babying you, sweetheart. They are trying to help you move on and away from your pain." He smacks his gloves together, his muscles rippling. "But do you want to know what I say? Don't lose that fury. Use it to fight. Fight for your dad's memory. Because if *you* won't fight for him, then who will?"

My eyes narrow, not sure how I feel about his taunting. He is right. Everyone is coddling me when all I want to do is avenge my father's death.

I put my gloves up and roll my shoulders. This is either going to be a really good idea or a really bad one.

He cracks his neck from side to side. "Just nothing below the belt."

"Do you really think I play dirty?"

"Yes, I do. But it's nothing I cannot handle." He winks. "Come at me, little *chicken*. I am ready for you."

We dance around each other with our eyes locked on to our opponent's gloves. He swings, but I sidestep and land a punch hard on his left shoulder. He shakes it off before he dives at me with a newfound vigor. I yelp at the crazy look he is giving me, then I drop, roll, and get back on my feet swiftly before he can land another blow.

By this time, a small crowd is gathering around us. They watch Max, carefully assessing his every movement. And I know they won't let Mr. Macho hurt me. So, I hurl fuel on the fire.

"I thought you weren't going to baby me."

"Wow, someone's overly confident."

He hooks a punch at my nose. I duck and thump him in the stomach, making him bend over. Then I jam my elbow into his back, causing him to kiss the floor. He lies there, his mouth in the shape of an 'O' as the air is forced out of him. Once he catches his breath, he reaches for my hand. "Ann, will you marry me?"

I can't help the laugh that escapes, as I slide my gloves off and offer him a hand up. Max groans as he grabs it. Then a slow grin spreads across his face, and he tugs me on top of him to commence a wrestling match.

We roll around on the mat, each trying to pin the other in a jumbled mess of body parts.

"What the hell's going on in here?" Vinny's voice blares

over the rumblings.

We both lie there panting, unable to speak. I stare at the ceiling, trying to suck in air. When we don't respond, Vinny stands over me, glaring.

"Both of you, on your feet!"

I rise unsteadily, feeling sore all over. "I'm sorry I didn't wait for you, Vinny, but I completed my work early and started some light cardio. Then this jokester came in here, egging me on. So, I put him in his place."

I smirk in Max's direction.

"What are you talking about? I believe I was the victor." Max offers Vinny a hand. "I don't think we have officially met. I'm Max, Mary's brother."

"I know who you are. What I don't know is who gave you clearance to be in here? This is for authorized personnel only." Max brushes past Vinny and towards his shirt. "It looked like Ann needed someone to chat with."

Vinny narrows his eyes. "She has plenty of people to *chat with*."

"But no one as charming as me."

Vinny steps in front of me. "Find another way to pass your time while you are here, young man. And stay out of my training areas."

Vinny puts a protective hand on the small of my back and guides me out the door.

"Ann, what are you doing? You shouldn't be rolling around with him like that. Christian only cleared you to train with Sam or me."

"I don't know which one of you is being more

judgmental! Christian or you! Max is only trying to help. And besides, it was nice to spar with someone who doesn't play by the rules. I learned a lot from his moves."

Vinny mumbles under his breath while shoving me forward. Once we get to the top of the stairs, Vinny turns towards the office and Max catches up to me. Before Max can say anything, we stop and watch Mary giggle against Christian's neck as they emerge from his room.

"Well, that was quick." Max wiggles his eyebrows, getting Mary's attention.

"Max, I was just coming to find you." She grimaces. "What happened to you?"

"Ann beat me up."

My mouth falls open, then I close it.

"Ann, why in the world would you do that to him? Max is a guest in *my* house and will be treated with respect." Mary calls out to my departing figure, "Get back here. I'm still talking to you."

Max pats his sister's back. "Leave her be, sis. You know me. I asked for it."

Mary's *holier than thou* mindset is grating on my *last* nerve. I slam my door on her high-pitched whining, but before it shuts, Christian pushes his way through with gritted teeth.

"What were you doing with Max?"

I grab a towel and dab my lips, suppressing my scream of annoyance.

"Don't give me that look, Christian. Max was the one who followed me to the training arena. How was I supposed to stop him? Then he taunted me into sparring with him."

"Ann, I informed you earlier that I didn't want you around him."

I roll my eyes. "Christian, haven't you been listening to me? Max followed me. Plus, you heard what your wife said. I am supposed to *treat him as a guest and with respect*," I say in my best mock Mary voice as I bat my lashes and sway my hips.

Christian rubs his face, obviously not entertained with my behavior, so I change the topic.

"So, Christian, Max informed me that you and Mary are trying to conceive." I elbow him as I make my eyebrows dance.

"That was never Max's business to discuss."

"But Mary told him, and it was her business to talk about. So, it is true?"

He shifts his silver tie around, clearly not wanting to broach the topic. "Mary's insisting that we become pregnant by the end of the year. I am just along for the ride, as they say."

I snort. "Did you just say 'along for the ride'? Doesn't that go against proper etiquette?"

"Please cease your teasing. Marriage is not effortless, and we have been attempting to become with child for some time now."

I hold a hand up. "Now, *that* is too much information."

He cocks a brow at me and his eyes twinkle with a playfulness I have not seen in a while.

"Are you absolutely certain? Because I could offer you a play-by-play?"

I groan and fall back on the soft covers. Then I reach for a pillow and toss it in his face.

"I can't believe you are stooping to such *crude* behavior. Besides, that is my job."

He catches the pillow. "It was worth it to witness you cheerful again."

"I think that is a matter of opinion." I mutter and guide the conversation away from me. "Christian, why do you think Max can't be trusted?"

"Can't you, for once, just *trust* me? Why are you always cross-questioning me?"

"Come on, you can't blame me. I mean, you forgave Mary and Ryan for what they did to your dad. Surely, Max couldn't have done anything worse than what *they* did." My face pales at his solemn expression. "Do you believe he knows something about my dad?"

"Ann, I *in no way* said that."

"You didn't have to. It is written all over your face."

Finally, I have a lead to go on. I jump up, ready to act.

"Just give me time, okay?"

"Only if you let me assist you. I mean, I can even lure him out for you."

"Absolutely not! If he believes we are onto him, he might run. I want you to act natural, but don't travel anywhere alone with him. Vinny's attempting to keep tabs on him discreetly, but it is difficult, especially with Mary everywhere."

24

Christian is right. Now that Mary is Queen, she is actively involved in everything inside the Palace. It is part of her job description.

"Christian, you do realize you may very well be sleeping with the enemy's sister."

"Mary's my spouse and Queen, and I am confident that she has no knowledge of this."

I clench my fist. "If she has anything to do with this..."

"Please remain rational." He grabs my balled hands. "Ann, swear to me that you will not do anything irrational. Or so help me, I'll lock you up and throw away the key."

"I think we both need that advice."

We simultaneously get lost in thought, likely trying to imagine how screwed we are if we really do have a murderer walking the Palace halls.

Christian softly brushes his fingertips down my cheek before dropping his arms to his sides. Then he grabs the door handle. "Did you actually defeat Max?"

I puff out my chest like a noble rooster.

"Yes, I did."

He displays a rare grin, which reminds me how young he really is underneath that 'stoic businessman' façade.

"You know, maybe the training is aiding you after all. Fantastic job, Ann." The pride in his voice ignites a spark of hope in my heart.

When the door closes, I replay our conversation in my head, as I hold the pillow to my chest and pull at its corner. I hope he'll continue allowing me to train with

25

Vinny and Sam. I stare down at the map of bruises on my arms. I need all the help I can get.

At the sound of my door closing, I look up to see Ryan sitting on the edge of my bed.

"There is a rumor going around that you disrespected the Queen's brother, by leaving welts on his body. Is that true?"

"Not intentionally. But, yes, Max followed me to the training arena. Then he started a fight that I finished."

"Did Mr. Manners lecture you for your bad decorum?"

"Yes, Mr. Pain-In-My-Butt just left."

"So, you will be careful around Max, right?"

I shrug. "I told Christian I would, but I know I could get answers faster than he can, if I had the right opportunities." I watch Ryan's frown deepen, but before he rains on my parade like his brother and Vinny, I continue, "Ryan, I know you care for me, but I am a grown woman."

He runs his hand through my hair to my scalp.

"Trust me, I am very aware that you are a grown, *beautiful* woman. But maybe *you* need to be reminded that I am also a grown man and miss you like crazy." He massages the nape of my neck. "And I don't want to suffer any longer. I need you."

I open my mouth to protest, but he crashes his lips onto mine and my resolve crumbles.

The embers of passion ignite and burn brightly as his tongue caresses mine, and I'm lifted up into his strong arms. My hands greedily travel over his stubble, then through his hair without breaking our embrace. I tug at his long strands before running my fingertips up and down his biceps.

Ryan catches his breath and grins down at my messy braid. "You are breathtaking."

"Ryan, please. You mean *everything* to me. I can't lose you too. It will shatter my very existence, and I'm barely holding it together as is."

"Hey, look who you are talking to? I have the means to procure an endless supply of duct tape to keep you from falling apart. Come on, you aren't going to lose me."

"Ryan, you can't promise me that. I *need* to do this."

"Do what, exactly?"

"I need to dig deeper into Max."

"But Christian is doing that already."

"And how good of a job do you think he will do? I mean, Mary is his wife… he has to be a little partial to all of this, whether he says it out loud or not."

Ryan shakes his head. "No, I trust Christian."

"Did you know they are trying to get pregnant?"

"No, he never said anything to me." He rubs a hand over his chin. "That does complicate things, doesn't it?"

"It most definitely does. When she becomes pregnant, I doubt there will be a fair trial or even a thorough investigation. Time is not on my side."

"But what can we do?"

"What do you mean 'we'?"

"I told you I am here to assist, duct tape and all."

"Oh, no, you don't. I need to get close to him while gaining information." My eyes brighten at the thought. "Maybe I could get invited to his home and check things out."

"Weren't you just listening to our warnings? No, absolutely not. You can't get *that* close."

"Well, do we know anyone else around here that could possibly get close to him?"

"I can use the whole brother-in-law position as an excuse to hang out with him."

I quirk a brow. "Nice try, but Max knows how you feel about him."

"I do not like your strategy. We know next to nothing about Max. And after I overheard the guards talking about his fighting skills..."

"What if we sneak off to his house while he is here and snoop?"

Our conversation ceases as Karen comes in with a food tray. Ryan leaps up with a scowl.

"Karen, you shouldn't be carrying this heavy thing."

She laughs as he grabs it from her. "You are worse than Vinny." She sits on my bed and smiles. "So, guess who just got spa resort gift certificates!"

"Please tell me it's the Queen," I grumble. "And her shady brother."

"Pfft. She doesn't deserve that. No, I did. Vinny bought them for me for a weekend of peace and quiet."

"Oh, really? That's a nice surprise." I glance towards Ryan. Is Vinny trying to keep Karen away while Max is visiting?

"And afterwards, he is sending me to my mom's house for a pre-baby vacation."

"That is sweet of him." I paste on a smile and hug her. "Although, I'm going to miss our late-night pillow fights."

"I'm sorry I will be away for a while, but I know a great replacement maid…"

"Oh, don't worry about it! I only keep you around because I like you. I don't need a maid. I have been cleaning up after myself for years."

"I have seen your definition of clean. And trust me, girl, you need help." She pats my hand. "Well, enjoy the food. I need to get packed because I leave tonight."

Karen blows kisses before closing the door behind her.

I turn to Ryan. "If Vinny is this worried, we have a problem."

He grabs a pastry and paces. "Do you remember that bowling alley in the basement?"

I grab some of my cherished red velvet macaroons off the tray.

"Sure, I do. As I recall, I wiped the floor with you last time we played."

"The only reason you won was because I tripped over my laces and made a gutter ball. What if we play a family game of bowling tonight? Then I can examine Max's shoes and compare the sizes with the prints we received from Detective Mack?"

"Ryan, that is a brilliant idea! Why didn't I think of that?"

"Well, I am the brains of the operation." He shoves the pastry in his mouth. "So, how badly did you beat Max?"

"He has a few bruises, but he plays dirty so I got some too."

Ryan runs his fingertips over a bruise on my arm.

"You have to be more cautious. Who knows what he has up his sleeve?"

"And what about Mary? Shouldn't we be keeping watch over her too?"

"I overheard Christian talking to Vinny, and he mentioned he had Mary's room searched the other day while she was in the city. He even has her phone tapped."

"Really?" I arch a brow. "Yet, he is trying to have a baby with her. Something isn't adding up. I feel like we are missing a huge piece of the puzzle."

After we eat, Ryan goes to plant the idea in his mom's head about a family game night, while I change into something more revealing to capture Max's attention. As I glance into the mirror, I glide my fingertips over the feather necklace my dad gave me for Christmas, and I sigh. This whole thing is a mess.

There is a knock at my door as I put the cover on my lipstick. "Come in."

Max pops his head in, and his eyes wander over my tight jeans and blue tee shirt. "I came to make sure you didn't have any lasting injuries after that beating you got." He grins. "But I can see I may have bumped *my* head, because now you look like my dream woman."

I roll my eyes. "Does that pickup line actually work?"

"I don't know. Why don't *you* tell me, sweetheart?"

I throw my silky locks over my shoulder. "Not at all."

"You can't blame a guy for trying." He arches a brow. "So, where are *we* going?"

"Ryan invited *me* to go bowling tonight."

"I thought this boring event was a family activity?" He shrugs. "Well, at least now, I can have some eye candy while I am forced to play." He offers his arm to me.

I brush past him—playing hard to get like Ryan and I talked about. "How is your bruise healing?" I banter as we walk towards the office.

"How about I show you personally? We can play doctor," he purrs.

"No, thank you."

Ryan looks up from his desk. "Wow, you look absolutely breathtaking, Ann."

He wraps his arms around me as he kisses me passionately. Then he slips his hands into my pockets, massages my backside, and presses me into him. "I told everyone to meet us down there, but we have a few minutes to spare." He grins at me, before he turns to Max with feigned shock. "Oh, I didn't see you there."

Max purses his lips. "Of course you didn't. I wouldn't want to keep royalty waiting, shall we?"

All three of us walk down to the bowling alley and meet up with the rest of the family. We grab our bowling footwear, and then break off into teams: Mary and Max, Christian and Ryan, and me and Elizabeth. As I lace up my shoes, I watch Max change his. Once he's done, I raise my chin towards Ryan, who approaches Max's boots slowly. I then strut forward to choose a ball. Max gawks as I bend at the waist, trailing my nails over the round, glossy finishes before making my selection. And he is so distracted by my performance that he doesn't realize what we are up to. Once Ryan goes to inspect the stolen goods around the corner, I grin at Max.

"Looks like it's you and me." I bat my lashes.

He visibly swallows. "For what?" he squeaks out.

I giggle and pat his arm. "To bowl against each other."

He glances at the screen. "Oh, well, then let the games begin."

He walks over to his bowling ball to make the first move.

Ryan sneaks the boots back under the table, unnoticed, and he gives me a thumbs up. Then I narrow my eyes at Max's back.

"I *agree*—let the games begin."

Losing the Battle

Unfortunately, the bowling game concludes with Ryan and Christian the victors. After the game, everybody eats together, then we go our separate ways.

Ryan ushers me into my room. "Well, that was entertaining. I never realized how awful you were at sports."

"You shouldn't be surprised, Ryan. You know I'm not very good at group activities. Were you able to get the shoe size?"

"I did one *better* for you, and collected these from the crevices." He pulls out a baggy of pebbles from his jacket pocket. "*And* he's a size thirteen. Which, by the way, is pretty small in my opinion."

I stop untying my shoe and raise a brow. "Really, Ryan? You're comparing sizes?" I roll my eyes as I change the subject. "I think I am going to check Christian's office. Maybe my dad's case paperwork will have the shoe size in it." Then I retie my shoes and stand, but Ryan blocks my path.

"Woah, Ann. You can't just break into his office."

"I need to view those police reports again, Ryan. And I am not going to burglarize his precious space—I know his safe code."

"If you are going to break the rules, take me with you so I can be your lookout."

"Oh, no. I don't want you to get in trouble if I get caught."

"But I want to help you."

"How about you wait for me in my room? Then, if Christian catches me, you will still have his trust."

"If you are not back in five minutes—" he warns.

"Come on! Be more realistic! It will take me five minutes just to open the safe."

"Fine, just leave before I gain my sanity and change my mind."

I crack open the door and scan the dark hallway. I hold my breath as the guards pass by. When I see that the coast is clear, I casually stroll over to my desk. At the last second, I beeline to Christian's office entryway. I press my ear to the smooth wood, to make sure no one is inside. When all I hear is silence, I creak the door an inch, my palms sweating.

Once I am inside, I leave it cracked open so I can monitor the sounds coming from the hallway. I pull out my phone and light up the keypad. I have seen Christian do this hundreds of times. I gently punch in the code and it pops open without hesitation. I marvel at the organization of Mr. Perfect, then I snatch the folder with my dad's name on it.

I finger through its contents, and my hand stills as I look at a photo of a scrap sheet of paper. I squint as I see it has an address written on it in my dad's handwriting. I rub my chin as I scan Mack's notes scribbled below the picture. It reads: *found in front pocket of victim's pants.*

I bite my bottom lip tightly, trying to stop the tears that are welling up in my eyes, as I look at the images of my dad's bloody body lying face down.

I lean back against Christian's desk and rub my neck. Why didn't Christian or Mack show me this?

I yelp as I see a shadow dancing across the wall. I pivot towards the doorway, clutching the folder to my chest.

"Snowball? You scared me, girl," I whisper to the chicken in the threshold.

The white fluff ball struts towards me and stands at my feet. Her dark eyes judge my actions for a few moments, before she decides to join in on my act of treason, and hops into the safe.

I squeal as she scratches at the papers and they go flying all over the floor.

"Are you trying to get us caught?" I hiss as I collect her mess. "How can you pick Christian's side in this? Fine, fine, I get the hint! I'm leaving right now. Just stop making a ruckus."

Once her disarray is restored and the safe is closed, I collect her in my arms. Her silky feathers bring a warmth to my heart that I haven't felt in a long time. I place a kiss on her head while I squeeze her.

"Thank you for coming to check up on me, girl. But you really shouldn't be walking the Palace halls all by yourself. Christian may decide you are too naughty and turn you into Chicken Cordon Bleu. Then I would have to kick his butt."

I tap on Elizabeth's door and she answers immediately. "Oh, thank God! I was just about to send the guards out to find her. Naughty little thing." Elizabeth giggles as Snowball clucks softly in her arms. "I can't stay mad at you. Here—eat your dinner and get some rest."

"That new dress looks really cute on her." I smirk at Snowball's red silk ensemble.

Elizabeth embraces me and squeezes. "I've missed you. It was so nice to see you out and enjoying yourself tonight, Ann."

"Thank you for letting me tag along. It was entertaining, watching Mary and Max lose and throw hissy fits."

"You are always invited to our family events. And I agree. It was nice watching Mary get taken down a notch. Don't tell anyone I said that." She smirks and elbows me. "Aw, look at her getting herself all tucked in for the night," Elizabeth coos at Snowball.

"Well, it's getting late—I should get back to my room. Goodnight, you two."

My fingertips instinctively reach up, and I rub the feather necklace dad gave me for Christmas. As I walk back to my room, I recall what I found in Christian's safe. My dad had an address in his pocket. But why?

When I enter, Ryan looks up from his pacing with a scowl. "Thank goodness! I was beginning to worry." He stops as he inspects my pale face. "Did you get caught? How much trouble are we in?"

His hand moves up and down my back, and I look into his dark eyes as my heart splinters. "Christian lied to us, Ryan."

"Are you sure about that?"

I throw my hands up. "Yes! I saw the documents in the safe!"

"My dad had an address in his pocket! Why didn't they

tell me this information?"

"Ann, I am sure there is a perfectly good explanation."

I raise my chin. "I am going to check out this address." I grab a bag and load some essentials.

"Like hell! There *must* be a reason he kept this address a secret!" He grabs my shoulders and stares into my eyes. "Please, just get some sleep tonight, and then we can ask Christian about all of this tomorrow."

"Ryan, I can't question him about the papers in his safe. Then he will know I snuck into his office."

"What if we tell him we are going on a romantic getaway—like to the lake house? Then we can check it out together?"

"He won't let us leave without guards, especially right now."

"We can try, right?" He grabs my bag and stashes it in the closet. "We will think of something. *After* a good night's rest and our emotions have settled. Okay?"

I narrow my eyes. I need to act on this information before Christian can stop me.

"How about a compromise? Why don't we search the address up? Then it will *prove* that you are overreacting," Ryan offers.

From my phone, I zoom into the location on the map. Staring back at me is a large white mansion. "It's a house? But it makes no sense." I detour to the mailbox image, read the gold lettering, and feel the blood drain out of my face as I crash on my bed.

"What is it, Ann?" He grabs the phone, leaving me in a

haze. "But there must be a mistake. That's Mary's house."

"Well, now we know why Christian's keeping it a secret. He already knows who the murderer is. He is just protecting her."

He shakes his head. "No, there has to be another reason. Mary would never do this."

My eyes drift to my nightstand, where my dad's watch now rests. When the officer handed it to me after dad died, it was covered in debris. And Christian had insisted that a jeweler clean it before giving it to me. I collect the cold metal, and run my finger over my dad's name inscribed on the back. Maybe that is what Christian is doing now? Removing all the grime of the *what ifs*, so that he can present me with the cleaned truth.

Ryan sleeps in my room to make sure I don't sneak off in the dead of night. While we settle under the blankets, we agree to think of a cover story to check out Mary's house. That night, we hold each other close, both of us unsure of what tomorrow will bring.

The next morning, I stretch out my limbs but Ryan's arm is draped over my stomach. "Ryan, move your arm. I am trapped underneath it."

He laughs into his pillow. "Nope. You are forever mine." Then he moves his warm lips to the nape of my neck.

I run my hand through his hair. "Ryan, you need a haircut."

He mumbles as he leaves the bed. "Yes, *mother*."

I mutter and toss a pillow at his departing figure before he can close my door. When we convene for breakfast,

I can't help but watch Mary and Max over my waffles. What are they up to? Was it just Mary involved? Christian catches my wandering eye, and I quickly look away.

After we eat, I try to escape quietly, but Christian grabs my elbow. "Ann, we need to speak privately." Then he guides me into his office and slams the door. "What is going on with you today?"

"What do you mean?"

"Why were you glaring at Max all morning? I told you to leave it alone, that I was managing the situation."

I cross my arms over my chest. "Really? Are you sure?"

He blinks, looking surprised, but quickly regains his composure. "Why are you questioning me?"

"Because I know you are protecting other people."

He sits behind his desk, watching me. "You know me better than that, Ann."

"Do I, Christian?" I glare at him, trying very hard not to tell him what I know, but I feel it boiling up in the back of my throat and threatening to choke the life out of me.

"Stop being so dramatic. We have always been honest with each other."

His lie knocks the breath out of me. I can't believe, after everything we have been through, he is again choosing to protect Mary—even though all the evidence is pointing to her. "How dare you sit there and lie to my face," I spit at him.

Mr. Stoic actually pales. "Ann, what are you prattling on about?"

There is a knock at the door, and we turn to see Tim.

He stops in his tracks as the tension in the room hits him. "Uh, sorry to interrupt but Mack is here, my King."

Christian rubs his face, returning some color to it. "Thank you. You may send him in."

Mack shakes our hands and sits down. "I'm sorry to disappoint you, but there is not much to report. However, we did find the shoe size."

"Let me guess, size thirteen?" I retort under my breath.

He raises a brow. "Yes. How did you know?"

"Lucky guess. Now, if you'll both excuse me, I have work to complete."

"Ann, we aren't done with our discussion," Christian roars.

I stomp out of the office in a huff. I'm done waiting for someone to actually do something about my father's death. It's up to me now.

I snatch the bag I packed last night and sneak into the kitchen for some sustenance. I freeze as I hear someone coming around the corner.

"Lady Ann? I thought that was you." Jock wipes his hands on his chef's coat. "You haven't come to see me since your father's funeral. How are you, my dear?"

I witness the pity flash across his face, and I tear my eyes away.

"I'm feeling better. Thank you for asking. Actually, I am on my way to the stables to take Frenchie an apple. You know—get some air and go on a trail ride to clear my head."

There. That should buy me some time if anybody

comes looking for me.

"That sounds like a wonderful idea! Here, why don't I pack you some sandwiches? That way, you can stop at the meadow and have a picnic."

"Oh, I appreciate the offer, Jock, but I don't want to trouble you."

And I don't want to waste any more time. Who knows how long it will take Ryan or Christian to notice I'm gone?

"It is no trouble at all."

"Well, you see, I wasn't planning on being gone *that* long. I still have tons of paperwork to do in the office. So, the ride will be super fast."

Jock nods. "As you wish, Lady Ann. Here is some fruit for your ride, and please, visit again soon."

I sneak out the back door and jog to the garage. Once I am in my car, I set up the GPS. I groan at the six-hour drive, but I know it will be worth it. I will find something, especially with Max and Mary occupied at the Palace.

Once I am on the road, my cell phone clucks—it's Ryan. I bite into a crisp apple and tap the steering wheel. I don't want him to find out where I'm going, because he will choose to be my knight in shining armor. And, inevitably, he will get hurt and it will be all my fault... *again.*

The ache in my heart persists, and I pull over to catch my breath. I swipe my cheek. If I would have just told my dad about Mary—damn it. I'm always messing everything up.

Once I collect my emotions, I get back on the highway, and by the time I drive through the elegant neighborhood, velvety darkness covers the pristine lawns. I park on the

41

side of the road and turn off the engine. Good thing I drove the car Christian bought me for Christmas, or my old farm truck would be sticking out like a sore thumb.

My gaze wanders over the mansion looming in front of me—it's pitch-black inside. My phone clucks again, and I glance down to see Christian's number. I better get moving before he crashes the party. Because I wouldn't be surprised if Mr. Control-Freak placed a tracker on my vehicle. I grab my flashlight and push open my door. I stretch as I step out into the warm night air.

I place one foot in front of the other while my conscience screams how dishonest this feels. I swallow its protests and stand taller. I wiggle the doorknobs and the windows, but they are all secure. I groan at myself for not thinking this through. *Come on, Ann! Think!*

I spot a large white shed in the backyard. I tilt my head—*bingo*. Maybe there is a key hidden under a planter? I push open the door and cough at the musty odor. In the corner, there is a small desk with a lamp, accompanied by shelves laden with various objects, including some dried blossoms. I flip on the light and run my hands over the book sitting on the table. I flip through the pages slowly, taking note of the subject matter: *herbs and ancient spices.*

Suddenly, I hear grass crunching. I flick off the light and poke my head around the corner to peek into the night.

My hand flies to my frantic heart as a cottontail rabbit soars in front of me, before making its way to the woods behind the shed.

That was close. Trying to catch my breath, I lean

forward with my hands on my thighs. I have officially lost my mind. I laugh until tears slide past my chin.

"What the hell am I doing *here*?" I chastise myself.

Am I really *so* desperate that I've resorted to prowling and breaking and entering?

I stand straight and close the shed.

My dad would be so disappointed in my actions tonight.

I trudge back to the car and vow to not participate in any more crazy, illegal stunts. As the car door closes, I lean back against the headrest and rub my hands down my face, pledging to cooperate with Christian, and continue to investigate lawfully from here on out.

"Well, here goes nothing."

I pull out my cell phone and groan at all the missed calls flashing. My finger hovers over the screen as the hairs on my neck stand up.

Instinctively, my gaze darts to the rearview mirror, and I let out an ear-piercing screech as a pair of emerald eyes stare at me. Before my brain can register what is happening, a cold blade presses against my neck, silencing my cry.

The Real Enemy

My life flashes before my eyes, while my phone slips from my numb fingertips and lands with a resounding *thud* on the floor.

"Hmm, clever and gorgeous," the silky voice says against my ear while adding pressure to the knife's edge.

"Why are you doing this, Max?"

Max cackles as he runs a hand over my jawline. "Don't worry. You will get the answers you are searching for, sweetheart. But first, I need you to drive to where I tell you. And if there is *any* funny business, I will knock you out and drive myself, understand?"

"Just tell me—is Mary involved?" He puts more pressure on my neck. I squeal as I feel a jolt of pain before blood trickles down my shirt.

"Don't make me kill you now, without the answers you want. That would be a complete waste. Now, do what I asked you to do."

How did he know I would be here? I stare into his dark eyes weighing my options.

A wicked smile spreads over his handsome face. "Let's go, Ann."

I swallow loudly as I start the engine. While I pass tall oak trees, the temptation to hit them head-on overcomes me, but I can't command my hands to do it. Because as much as I would love to end this nightmare, I need to know what happened to my dad and why.

"Max, how much further are we traveling? I am nearly

44

out of fuel."

"We are almost there."

I look around unsure of where *there* is. The town around us is deserted.

I steal a glance at where my phone landed, under my seat. When I dropped it earlier, I called my last missed number and purposefully said Max's name loud and clear, knowing Christian would hear me.

Once we get close to a shopping plaza, Max instructs me to park in the back, next to a black SUV.

"Are you going to be a good girl and get in willingly, or do I need to carry you?"

I narrow my eyes at him. "You can keep your hands to yourself."

He opens the passenger door silently and I get in. When he climbs in, he side-glances my untouched seat belt. "Ann, buckle up."

I snort. "You're joking, right? After all of this, you are asking me to be safe. Which is it? Do you want to kill me, or save my life?"

He glares and reaches behind his seat for duct tape. "You know, I think I prefer a silent Ann at this point." I grumble while I slam my buckle into the receptacle. I shoot him a glare before he grabs my wrists and wraps them with duct tape. When his warm fingertip traces my lips, I pull away from his touch. What is this guy's deal?

His smirk melts into a mischievous grin while he places a small piece of tape over my mouth and slaps it for good measure.

When he punches the gas pedal, I blast back and pinch my eyes closed as I try to think of anything but being abducted by a madman. So, I take inventory of my body: I'm starving, have to use the bathroom, and feel my adrenaline wearing down and exhaustion taking its place.

Max slams on the brakes at a red light and my eyes shoot open. Arrogant jerk! I wish my mouth wasn't taped, so I could blare out a terrible *Fast & Furious* joke. But instead, my mouth becomes parched as I watch him twist open a bottle of water and chug it. I moan as I observe a few lost droplets slither down his neck.

He turns to me and side-glances the empty container. "I guess I should have saved you a sip, huh?"

I scowl and face away from his feigned innocence.

When we finally pull into a driveway, I am fidgeting in my seat as I attempt to hold in my bathroom emergency. I blink up at the building. How the hell did it take this long to circle back around to Mary's house!

As the garage door closes, he gets out and opens my door. Then he places his hand on my back and guides me inside. When he stops walking, I step away from him until my back hits the wall. He smirks and rips the tape off my mouth. I lean forward as I feel a layer of skin detach.

"Is that better?" I glare at him, refusing to respond. "So, it's the silent treatment for me, is it?" He shrugs. "Well, it's not a great plan—especially if you want the answers that I know are eating away at you." He stares into my eyes, daring me to prove him wrong.

"Max, I need to use the ladies' room."

"This way, my Lady." He bows before walking off.

I follow him downstairs to the basement. It's cold and dark, but it has a small bed and a bathroom in the corner. He motions towards the bathroom with a nod. I roll my eyes and raise my hands with the duct tape still applied.

He arches a brow and crosses his arms over his chest.

"Come on, Max! Please?" I beg, not wanting to have to explain why I need my hands.

"You have five minutes, *with* the door open. If you try anything funny, I won't hesitate to punish you."

"Whatever, Max, my hands, please."

Max cuts the tape off my wrists, his eyes never leaving mine. "You don't think I'd hurt you, do you?"

I rub my wrists. "Max, I know you *could* hurt me—easily. But I am not sure you would."

As I use the restroom, I think of a game plan for my predicament. If Christian received my call, he will need some time to get to me. So, I have to keep Max's interest on me while I get the answers I want.

My brows crease. What if Christian doesn't want me found? Then no one would know about Mary's involvement. And he can continue to live the lie he's living. I snort. But surely Ryan will come. Or will Christian not tell him where I am? I take a deep breath as my five minutes are up. I need to concentrate on keeping Max distracted.

Okay, first plan of action is to buy some time. I look down at my growling stomach—and *maybe* get some food. I wash my hands, trying to remove the sticky tape residue. When I look up, I squeal as I see Max right behind me staring at my reflection.

Well done, Ann. That's a great way to start off your plan. Keep your cool if you want to make it out of here in one piece.

I force myself to look at Max. He really is quite handsome with his brown hair and dazzling green eyes. I turn to face him and he brings his hand up to my neck. I flinch as he runs a finger along the cut he inflicted earlier.

"How about I get you something to eat?" The way he huskily purrs into my ear makes me think he is *not* talking about food. "What, Ann, you do not trust me?"

My mind races. I am trapped between his arms and the bathroom wall. In all the dark romance books I've read, this is the moment when the girl swoons into the bad guy's arms and shreds her clothes.

But in real life, it is the complete opposite.

I swallow the uncertainties and clear my tightened throat. "Well, you did kidnap me and threaten me more than once. So, you haven't given me any reason to trust you, Max."

At a leisurely pace, I feel his fingertips untwine my braid. Then he runs a hand through my loose locks. "You really should have just listened to Christian and stayed away from me."

"How do you know he told me that?"

"I was eavesdropping. Then when I saw the way Christian looked at us while we were talking—that idiot. Thinking he can *love* another woman while he is married to my sister."

I try to take a step back as his tone gets higher and his eyes darken. "No, Max, Christian loves Mary."

He cackles. "Keep telling yourself that, sweetheart."

"It's the truth."

He grabs a fistful of my hair and tugs. I groan in pain as he bores his eyes into mine. "Good," he hisses. "Then Christian won't mind seeing your dead body on the side of the road. Just like your nosey little father."

His words rip through my fear, and my eyes burn. I bring my knee up and straight into his groin. Then I shove him away. "How dare you talk about my father like that!" I ball my fists. "So, it *was* you who killed him!"

Max coughs and groans before glaring at me. "Your dad came here, snooping around too. The old man found the herb book and put two and two together. But the fool thought *Mary* was the mastermind behind it all."

"Why did you do it?" Tears well up. "He was my father! Surely you knew I would come after you!"

"I didn't think you would be clever enough to piece it all together. Let alone, beat me in a boxing match. But here we are. So, what do you think will happen next?"

I wipe my eyes. "I don't care. I got the answers I came here for, and justice will inevitably be served."

"Oh, really? Do you honestly think Christian is going to let the blame fall on his beloved wife or her family? She is our Queen. And soon-to-be mother of his child. Do you want to know what I think will happen? He will just let this all blow over. *Boohoo*, an old man was murdered—it happens every day. Then a distraught Lady Ann took off from the Palace and overdosed on pills. *Whoops*, that depression moved to suicide."

"Well, I guess you have it all figured out. The question is: what are you waiting for?" I step forward in his face. "Do it already."

49

His eyes soften as he strokes my arm. "How about I grab you some food?"

I narrow my eyes. "What's the catch?"

"That brain of yours is working overtime. I can see smoke coming out of your ears." Then he moves his hand to my heart. "I hear your stomach growling over your rapid heartbeat." He leans in and whispers as he massages my chest, "How about I make you some food and, in exchange, you give me a kiss?"

I step away and bite back the urge to slap him. "You just informed me that you killed my father! Now you expect me to kiss you. You are out of your mind!"

"Fine. Then starve." He stomps out, and the basement door shuts behind him.

There are no windows to crawl out and no weapons to grab. I rub my sore scalp. Then I walk to the mirror to examine my neck. It is red and swollen, but not bleeding anymore. I sit on the little bed and lie back, digesting Max's words.

He killed my father because he was trying to investigate Mary's intentions. I need to get back and talk to Christian. He needs to know what Mary and Max are up to—before it's too late.

My growling stomach pulls me out of my thoughts, and I wonder how long I can live without food or water.

I doze off and on, and after a while, Max strides back in with his hands full. My eyes grow wide as I see him carrying a sandwich and a bottle of water.

Max smirks as I eye the food. "So, Ann, have you changed your mind?

I tear my gaze away. "How about I kick your butt and get it from you?" I retort.

He glances down at his pocket as it starts to buzz. "What?" he says, answering his phone. "Yes, I know… Mary, you worry too much… No, don't get them involved. I'll take care of it… Yeah. See you soon." Then he hangs up. He runs a hand through his hair. "Well. Mary sends her love. She wants me to kill you immediately and return to the Palace."

"Well, you can send my hatred right back to that little twit. Max, are you always going to be her little slave and do her dirty work for her?"

He thumbs the tip of his blade. "I volunteered for this job because you hold a very *dear* place in my heart." He sends a grin my way. "Ann, ever since you turned *me* down at the wedding, then started dancing with Ryan and even Dan… You treated me like I was beneath you—that hurts."

"You were drunk, Max. Plus, at that time, I didn't know how *charming* you were."

"Well, now you do know me, and you won't even exchange a simple kiss for a meager meal?" He pouts.

I watch him tighten his grip on his knife. If I get too close, he could easily slice me. Therefore, I try to keep him talking. "Did you say you were the brains of this operation? I do love intelligent men."

He arches a brow and puts his knife back. "Of course, I am the brains. When King Mark was threatening us, I had to find some way to keep Mary at the Palace and get rid of the King." He sighs. "And since Christian was falling for you, I had to make things happen fast."

51

"What things, Max?" I stutter.

"You remember Cherie, right? Ryan's fiancée and the *love* of his life? Who do you think threatened her? Then made her lie to him about having a guy on the side. I found her weakness and exploited it. And since you seemed to care for Ryan from the beginning, it was easy to push you two together."

"How did you know I was interested in Ryan?"

"You are an open book! Plus, Mary would call me, I would see it on the news, and when we came to visit before Christmas, I saw it firsthand. So, I guess you can say thank you."

"Thank you! What am I thanking you for, exactly?"

"I made Cherie leave the picture, so you and Ryan could finally be a couple."

"No. Ryan would still have chosen me either way," I whisper to myself.

"If Ryan ever finds out the truth, what do you think he will do? Ignore it, or go back to Cherie?"

He walks over and sits next to me. "When your dad was in the hospital, who do you think pushed the notion that you *had* to go to him as soon as possible? It pulled you away from the Palace, didn't it?"

My mouth falls open. "But then I returned."

He rubs his face. "Yes, that *stupid* chicken project! It kept you close to Christian. He even proposed to you instead of Mary at the announcement party. But the King stepped in," he says with a smirk directed my way. "And Mary had the opportunity to use the herb to kill the King while also pretending to save you. She even got Ryan's support, which was brilliant." He leans back, proud of himself.

My stomach rolls at the information, and my brain tries to comprehend everything he is telling me.

"So, I was right all along. Mary is not innocent in all of this."

"Mary helped but I did most of the legwork, and apparently, I still am." He grabs his knife again, but I put a hand on his.

"I'll take the sandwich deal if it is still on the table?" I say, trying to sound eager.

"I am not sure. Mary was pretty adamant about me killing you and getting back to the Palace."

"But, Max, I thought you were the mastermind? What do *you* want?"

His eyes rest on my lips. "No funny business? A kiss in exchange for food?"

I play laugh. "Have you seen me eat? I take it very seriously."

Before he can think too much about my motives, I close the gap between us and slam my lips against his. Despite the evil permeating from him, his lips are soft and warm.

He moans against my mouth and runs his hands across my backside, before he yanks me to him and deepens the kiss. When he finally withdraws, I sigh with relief.

"I can see why your love spell is still enticing King Christian." He runs a thumb over my swollen lips. "And a deal is a deal."

I eat the peanut butter and jelly sandwich and wash it

down with the water. It's not my preferred snack, but it'll do for now to regain my energy.

"I wish we could have tried to make *this* work between us. Ann, you really are a beautiful, intelligent woman."

"Max, try *not* to kill your crushes family next time, if you want it to work out."

"Yes, you are probably right." He shakes the empty bottle in front of me. "And *you* should have checked the water before drinking it, sweetheart."

I put my hand over my mouth as it dawns on me. "It was already opened," I whisper to myself.

"Yes—and unfortunately for you—laced with a sedative."

"You *tricked* me!" I blare.

"Come on, you started all of this. Remember that taunting bowling match, where you agreed to let the games begin?"

"Me? You think I started this? You were the one who killed my dad, tried to get on my good side, and drugged me! I only wanted to find out what happened to my dad!" I rub my temples, desperately trying to work out a strategy. "Now that I am on borrowed time, what are you going to do next?"

"Well, once you are out cold, I will push pills down your throat. Then I'll bring you back to your car and leave you inside, with the pill bottle. Eventually, someone will find you, and by that time, it will be too late."

His words rest heavy on my chest. "How long do I have?"

"It depends on your metabolism. But, considering your full stomach, at most? Four hours. Or as few as one."

This jerk has another thing coming if he thinks I am going down without a fight. With all my strength, I slam my head into his gut. He crashes to the floor and we tumble towards the stairs. I get back on my feet and glare at his coughing figure.

Once he catches his breath, he grabs for my wrist but I jerk back and swing, giving him a fat lip.

A manic sound leaves his mouth as he spits crimson. "You are a fighter till the bitter end, huh? Well, a little entertainment before your demise is fine with me." Then he dives towards me. I roll again, but he anticipates it and slams his body on top of mine. As we crash to the ground, my breath is forced from my chest and I gasp for air. I swing my hands and legs wildly, trying to get him off. But I fail.

"Come on, Ann. Do you give up yet?" He positions his face inches from mine.

My vision swirls and I let my head fall back. I stop fighting, knowing that it's just making things worse. "Get off me, Max."

"No. I like you in this position."

"How can you seriously be flirting with me, while planning my downfall!"

He tilts his head. "I am very talented, in many, many ways. I can give you a few more examples if you want?"

I roll my eyes. "What I want is for you to get your lard butt off me, and allow me some peace for the last hour of my life!"

"Why should I?"

"Because even though you are under Mary's command, I know in some sick demented way, you do care for me."

"I am not under her command! It is the opposite!"

"Really? Then what's that vibrating in your pocket? I bet she is calling you, *again*."

He rolls off me to answer his phone. "Yes!... I did!... Soon!" Then he throws his phone against the wall, smashing it to pieces.

"Why, that is some control you have, Max. I mean, I love the way you really stuck it to her and fought her demands."

"Shut up!" he snaps at me before he slams the basement door.

I look around the room, desperate to find some way to escape. When I come up empty-handed, I climb the stairs. I turn the doorknob, but it is locked. I side-glance the white bed sheets. Maybe I could just hang myself from the ceiling fan? I could foil his plans, and take away Mary's satisfaction of getting what she wants. I move the cold fabric between my fingertips as a tear moistens my cheek.

That little conniving witch! My dad was murdered by Max, and Mary knew the entire time. I pull at the blanket, trying to rip it to shreds. She has been playing with *everyone*—getting them to do exactly what she wants.

Poor Christian. After everything he has been through, he now has to deal with this? After he let her slide when he found out about the herb… And what about the lie detector test? How did she pass that?

Max strides in with a bottle of pills in his gloved hands.

His eyes wander over me and fall on the sheet. "Either you are trying to take a nap, or attempting to undermine my plan?"

"Both," I say as I lean my head against the wall.

"Well, I wouldn't expect anything less from you." He sits next to me on the bed and touches his fat lip. "I am going to miss our banter."

"No, you won't. You will just move on to your next victim."

"Yeah, you are probably right, and that would be Christian."

My mouth falls open. "Why?"

"He isn't as moldable as we had originally thought. But hopefully, once you are out of the picture, things will go our way. However, if he gets suspicious, we will have to do something with him."

"But Mary will never succeed Christian. Ryan will."

"Someone has done her homework." He tilts his head. "If Mary becomes pregnant, the child will reign once they are old enough. So, my dear sister has plenty of time to be an influence on her offspring. Or, if she isn't pregnant, she can just try to marry Ryan."

"That's ridiculous—Ryan would never do that; he doesn't even like her."

"Wouldn't he? He does seem to like his brother's exes." He smirks at me. "He has informed you they kissed, hasn't he?" My face pales, and I start to feel my stomach churn while Max's eyes grow wide. "No way! He never told you?" He rubs his stubble. "Let me see. It was after King Mark's funeral, when Mary was worried

57

that Christian might choose you. So, she started visiting Ryan's room in secret. Eventually, she had him wrapped around her finger too. For a while, I even thought they were sleeping together." He shrugs. "She never confirmed nor denied that much."

I sway in disbelief. Ryan and Mary? So, when I saw them together after the funeral in Ryan's room, they *were* about to kiss, even though they both denied it. Does this mean that Ryan is lying for Mary? She's covered all her bases. Both men are blind to her ways, while I am the idiot stuck in the middle, believing that either of them could ever really love me.

I dash to the bathroom and throw up my sandwich. As I rest my head on the porcelain, I begin to think… maybe this will pull the poison out of my system?

Surprisingly, Max gently guides me off the hard floor. "I wish it were a different time and situation. You don't deserve them, Ann. They are easily manipulated. First, by their father, and now, by Mary. You are stronger and smarter than that." He runs his hand over my back. "What I wouldn't give to have more time with you."

The lightbulb inside my head goes on. This could be the opening I was praying for. I step into him, pressing my body against his. "Then just lie. Tell Mary that I am gone. No one will know but me and you. You can lead the scheme, and let her think she has won. You don't need her. *We* don't need her."

I watch as he looks down at my lips again. "Nice try, Ann. But I can't. If I double-cross her, we won't be safe anywhere."

"Max, come on, think about it. If you keep me alive,

then you have something to dangle over Mary's head. I know the thought has crossed your mind."

"Why would I need anything to negotiate with? Do you really think she would betray me? Mary wouldn't dare double-cross me."

I arch a brow. "Are you really that naïve? She is used to getting her way. If she thinks they are on to her, she will easily drag anyone down, before allowing herself to take the blame."

I see his mind working, but he shakes his head again. "No way. Mary isn't that foolish. She needs me to do her dirty work. That is the kind of relationship we have." He glares at me. "Stop trying to manipulate me."

"Max, what do I have to lose? I have lost my father, Ryan's been lying to me, and Christian's wrapped around Mary's finger. Right now, you are the closest thing I have to a friend... or family." Then I force myself to hug him tight, trying to gain some sort of empathy.

At first, he tenses and guards his weapon. Then he wraps his arms around me and hugs me back. As we embrace, I falter and sway. Max strokes my hair. "It's okay, Ann. Rest now. I have you." He gently lifts me up in his arms and lays me on the bed. The last thing I see, before blackness swallows me, is Max towering over me with a frown.

The Agony of Moving On

Bright blinding light—that's all I can see. I shield my eyes as I blink and scream for help. Faint voices call out from the distance. I try to move but I am frozen in place. Where am I?

Soft feathery wisps stroke my arms before they flutter to the ground. Their familiar touch brings me comfort. As some float past my ear, I swear I hear my dad calling out to me.

I try to respond, but no words leave my mouth. I panic, realizing I am mute. Then I hear my mom's voice beckoning me—as sweet as a chicken's song. I relax, knowing that she is near, and my end is approaching. I am *finally* where I belong.

Once I surrender to the brightness, I become weightless and tumble backwards onto the sea of feathers.

Suddenly, I hear someone shouting my name. Is that Christian? I try to listen to him but the more I do, the more distant my parents' voices become—and the less clear.

"Come back to me! I cannot and *will* not do this without you, do you hear me! Damn it, Ann!" His voice is laced with agony, and each syllable splinters my soul. After everything that has happened in his life, this is the *last* thing he needs. "You cannot leave me, Ann! I demand you wake up this minute!" Then I hear him sobbing. I have never heard him cry before, ever. "I love you, Ann, please…" he moans softly.

As quickly as his voice came, it vanishes.

I shout to my parents, telling them that I need to check

on Christian and that I'll be back soon, but no words are emitted. Instead, I am sucked into an empty abyss.

The stench of alcohol burns my nose. I attempt to sit up but my body feels like it has been hit by a car. I groan and turn my head. My vision is blurry, and my mind feels fuzzy.

Is this hell? I shiver. Or maybe the morgue?

Once my eyes cooperate, I blink at Christian as he sits next to my bed. I frown at his hunched figure, curled into himself with his head in his hands.

"So, the little shit actually went through with it," I croak out.

Christian's head shoots up and I stare into his tear-stained face. "Ann?" He rubs his dark blue eyes. "Am I dreaming?"

I lift my hand to his face. "I am just following orders, my King."

Christian blinks back tears, as he gently rubs his hand down my face.

"I am delighted you listened to me—for once." Then he rests his forehead on mine. "Ann, I must insist that you don't *ever* go off by yourself again, do you understand me?"

"Yes, Sir." I salute his stern expression.

"Why are you always so challenging?" he says as he pulls back. "Now that you are awake, I'll retrieve the doctor."

He reluctantly releases my hand and walks out. I smile

as I notice Vinny, standing guard in the corner of the room. When our eyes meet, he steps towards my bed.

"Ann, I am so glad you are awake."

I lean back, feeling safer with him nearby. But then I remember Max and Mary and their long list of crimes. My eyes grow wide, and my heart rate monitor beeps. "Where are Max and Mary?"

He grabs my flailing wrist. "They are in jail, awaiting their trial. Don't worry about them. You did it, Ann. You caught your father's murderer." Then he arches a brow. "Do you think it was worth it?"

Before I can answer, Christian returns with the doctor and pushes Vinny aside. Christian watches me carefully as the doctor finishes his checkup.

"My King, I will run some labs to evaluate her organ functioning, but from what I can see, she seems to be responding well to the treatment." He pats my hand. "Welcome back to the land of the living, Lady Ann."

Once the doctor closes the door, I lean my head against the pillow and tears brim my eyes. "I am such an idiot. I should have listened to you when you warned me about Max."

"I agree—but, I should have been completely honest with you about all the events that were transpiring. That way, you wouldn't have questioned my actions when you broke into my safe." He grabs my hand and squeezes. "But you must understand I was only trying to protect you from additional misery. I had *everything* under control." He chuckles at my narrowed eyes. "Let me rephrase that—I had *most* of it under control."

"First of all, I did *not* crack open your safe. I punched in the code, and it magically opened." I yawn and my eyes slide to the door. "Are Max and Mary really locked up?"

"You are safe here, Ann. And we will discuss the situation in depth once you get some rest."

When he walks towards the entryway, I panic and clutch his wrist.

"Please, don't leave me."

His frown dissolves into a small smile as he lowers himself next to me. "Nothing would give me greater joy than keeping watch over you. Now, close your eyes—I will be here when you wake up."

"Thank you," I whisper as I drift off to sleep.

My bare feet pound on the hard surface as darkness envelops me. The next thing I know, I'm falling fast, down a pit, and flipping head over heels. I open my eyes and watch as soft white and blue feathers commingle all around me. I reach out, and just as my fingertips brush against them, a wind kicks up and throws my body around in a violent tornado. The feathers, once peaceful, now slice through my body.

My eyes dart around the room. Am I still plummeting? Or back in the basement, awaiting my untimely death?

My vision clears and my breathing slows as I hear Christian whispering to me.

"How are you feeling, Ann?"

I close my eyes for a second, then open them. "Better—I think. Now that I'm not falling or having feathers attack me."

Christian brushes my hair off my forehead, then he bends down to pick up some papers littering the floor.

"Oh no. Did I do that?"

He waves me off as he sits back down to reorganize them. "It is not a problem, Ann. I did not want to sign these anyway." He leans back while his eyes appear out of focus. "I feel like my life's collapsing. Yet, the country continues to command my attention. I adore my citizens, but it is frustrating, at times, being the only one they look to for guidance."

Soon his eyes refocus and he clears his throat, returning to his classic stoic look.

I throw my legs over the bed to grab a paper he missed, and I sway at the sudden movement. Christian steadies me, while my brows crease as I notice the dark circles under his eyes. Memories flood my mind.

"Christian, when you rescued me... were you *yelling* at me?"

"Yes, I was."

"I thought I was dreaming—I heard you."

"If you weren't dreaming, and it was real, where were you really?"

"I do not know exactly. I heard my parents talking to me, and it was beautiful. But then, I heard you, demanding I return." I smirk. "Now I am stuck here." I pinch and pull the grey hospital gown. "Wearing this awful thing—*again*."

"Now, Ann, don't be ridiculous—I have seen you wear worse clothing choices."

The doctor closes the door and taps on his tablet. "Well, it looks like your test results came back normal. You may return to your usual activities. Are you ready to leave the hospital wing?"

I offer a small nod and wrap my arms around myself, knowing that no matter where I go, the effects of those days will forever haunt me.

Christian rubs my back. "I know a well-qualified therapist that can assist you, if you want to speak to them. We will get through this. We always do."

I don't meet his gaze. "We don't have a choice, do we?"

"No, but we must remember to behave as the ducks do in the waterways."

"Did you just suggest we act like a *duck*? Are you feeling all right?" I place my open palm over his forehead.

He kisses my hand. "That statement simply means we should be calm on the outside, but paddling like hell underneath."

Has this been his life motto all along? That is a complicated way to live. And it feels like lying to me. What ever happened to honesty and empathy? How can you accomplish that if you are constantly *pretending* to be fine?

"I don't think that's a great way to live, Christian."

"Oh, and how do you propose we handle this?"

"Well, like the chickens do."

He quirks a brow. "How are they different?"

"Well, chickens are not afraid to show others how they feel. They run around, scream when they are mad, shout for help when they see a predator—they are honest with each other."

"I suppose I should observe your feathered companions more, prior to deciding which creature I would rather simulate: a chicken or a duck." He turns towards the doctor, who's standing by the doorway. "Can we procure a wheelchair to return Ann to her room?"

"Well, you can start by waddling like a duck, and see if you like it." I smirk. "And, Christian, I plan on walking out of here with my head held high, as the *llamas* do." I elbow him.

Christian rolls his eyes at my joke.

The doctor clears his throat. "Well, if you insist on walking, at least allow me to get a maid to grab you some clothes?"

"But where are the clothes I came in with?"

"They were disposed of. I apologize—we couldn't save you *and* the clothes," the doctor throws over his shoulder as he leaves.

Christian places a cold, metal object in my palm. "I convinced the medical professionals to keep your necklace safe."

I run my fingertip over the black feather charm my father gave me the last Christmas we shared together.

"Christian, did I die?"

"If you had, you wouldn't be here."

"You know what I mean—did my heart stop?"

His eyes glaze over and he swallows. "I made it to your car as swiftly as I could muster the guards. We had to airlift you here. And, yes, we did lose you momentarily. But that isn't relevant now. You are healthy, the tests

66

show positive results, and now we can move forward."

A maid brings in my clothes and I change quickly. Once we are walking out of the hospital, I clear my throat.

"Christian, I intend to go to the jail. I must confront them."

"Ann, I think you ought to take it easy."

"Please do *not* battle me over this, and *try* to understand how important it is to me."

Christian brushes past me silently, continuing towards the stairs. Did he hear me? Before I can question him, we round the corner, and all the servants stop in their tracks. They eagerly welcome me back, while I plaster on a smile and offer kind words in response.

I never realized how many people liked me at the Palace. I side-glance Christian as the crowd thins. "Does everyone know what happened to me?"

"There was significant chaos when they flew you back here, Ann. We have not witnessed that level of excitement in an exceptionally long time."

We make our way to the office, and Christian guides me towards his desk. In the corner, I watch as Ryan's head looks up from a stack of papers.

Once our eyes meet, Ryan leaps up and collects me in his arms. I return the hug, but I keep my distance, especially after everything Max told me about him and Mary. With all that information, and his secrecy, I don't know where that leaves us.

"Ann, I was so worried. Are you okay? I mean, of course you aren't *okay*... but physically all right?"

I clear my throat as I fight back tears. "Yes, I have the doctor's seal of approval."

I gaze into his soft brown eyes. How could someone I love so much damage me the most?

"Listen, Ann, about..."

"Not now, Ryan." I rub my temples.

He nods and turns to Christian. "I called Mack, like you ordered, and he is on his way here. Should we set up the conference room for the meeting?"

"Thank you, but prior to us setting up, I need to retrieve a USB microphone for Ann."

Ryan's eyes dart to me. "Christian, you cannot be serious—she *just* left the hospital!"

Christian narrows his eyes. "Ryan, I am completely aware of the situation. However, *Ann* demanded this—I am just attempting to assist her. Because if you recall the last time I didn't, she was kidnapped."

"She what...? Ann, are you sure?"

I raise my chin. "I need to see them after everything they have done to me."

"At least take Vinny with you?" Ryan grumbles before he departs.

Christian watches Ryan's every move, then he searches his desk. The anger in his eyes matches his actions, as he slams the drawers closed.

"So, I assume you know about Mary and Ryan?"

The tension thickens when he lets the words echo around us. Then he places the USB in the pocket of my sundress. "This is just in case they say anything we do not know already." He pauses and looks into my eyes. "Ann, bear in mind, you do not have to do this. We have all the evidence we need. And Mack said they will never see the light of day again."

"I have been lied to, cheated on, and poisoned—and they are the ones responsible. I'm doing this."

"If anybody understands, it is me." He turns towards the door, but I collect him in a tight hug, willing his warmth and strength to seep into me. He whispers in my ear, "We will persevere—one day at a time."

"Yes, we will be like chickens—one day at a time."

Vinny knocks and nods towards us. "I'm sorry to interrupt, but Prince Ryan requested a chaperone for Lady Ann."

Christian stands in front of me and raises his chin at Vinny. "You are required to maintain a close eye on Lady Ann, and make certain no injury ensues." Before Vinny answers, Christian turns to me. "Ann, I am sorry that I cannot accompany you. But I do not trust my actions around them because of my anger. Don't be long—we have a lot to discuss when you are finished."

I turn to Vinny, and we start our trek to the jail. "Vinny, is Karen back from her vacation yet?"

"No, and I don't want to worry her while she is away. We can catch her up when she returns."

"How awful was it after I left?"

"I have never seen King Christian that anxious."

"How did Ryan take it?"

"Ryan was extremely upset, and he begged Christian to let him accompany us on our rescue mission. But after Christian questioned Mary, he told Ryan to stay back and keep some normalcy at the Palace."

"How angry is Christian with Ryan?"

"I'm not sure how much you know, Ann, but Christian's calmer than he was."

When we near the jail, Vinny nods at the two guards standing watch. As I step inside, I see Mary sitting on her bed, away from the door. Max is standing in his own cell, with a smile on his face as he grasps the bars.

"Welcome back, sweetheart. I've missed you," he sings.

I pull off my shoe and chuck it at his pretty-boy face. It hits its intended target, making him stumble backwards. He falls on his butt, rubbing his red forehead.

"Ann," Vinny warns from behind me. "We aren't here for that. Now, be civil, or we are leaving."

Ignoring Vinny, I glare at Max. "I thought you said *you* were the mastermind. What happened? Lose control of your sister?"

"Max told you he was the mastermind? Give me a break." Mary snorts from her bed, shaking her head and sending the blonde tendrils bouncing around her neck.

Max rolls his eyes at her. "Who found the herb? Who brought it to you? You would be nothing without me."

"Max, sit down and shut up before you screw something else up." Mary waves him off with her polished hand.

Max tosses my shoe at Mary but he misses, and I grab it

off the floor.

"Thank you, Max," I retort as I pull my shoe back on.

"See what I mean? You cannot even aim straight, idiot," Mary grumbles.

Max frowns. "Can I have your other shoe, sweetheart?"

"Leave her alone, Max. Can't you see she is gloating?" Mary retorts, crossing her arms over her chest.

My mouth falls open. "You are joking, right? Your highness," I hiss.

She shrugs her shoulders. "Well, now, that title falls on you, Lady Ann."

I glance towards Vinny. "What does she mean?"

"Ann, Mary's toying with you. Let's go." He gently grabs my elbow and leads me towards the door.

"You know, I have had my fun with Christian," Mary purrs. "So, I guess you can have *my* leftovers. I mean, you are used to that by now, aren't you, Ann?"

Vinny holds on a little tighter. "She is not worth your time."

Mary chuckles. "Come on! Did you really think you would ever be their *first* choice? Look at you." She finally stands and stares at me with a fake pout. "Poor, little, naïve farm girl—she is trying so hard to be something she is *not*." She leans forward. "While the people she loves die, one by one."

"So, because I'm not a whore like you, I am naïve? You are nothing but a murdering liar—caught and trapped in a tiny cage. Even the Palace meat birds outside have a larger pen."

She clenches the bars. "You will *always* be second best! I got Christian first, didn't I? You *may* have received his first kiss in the competition, but I got the important firsts: his wedding... and don't forget the wedding night." She cackles. "Hopefully you can imagine *that* on your wedding night." Her eyes darken. "Our two bodies becoming one and... oh, well, I won't bore you with the details. You will know soon enough."

I snatch my arm from Vinny's grasp. "You are just spewing nonsense to get a rise out of me! But you know what? You aren't worth my time. You. Are. Pathetic." I spit the words out.

Mary is venomous and destroys everything with just the flick of her tongue. How could she have been hiding her true intentions for so long?

"Oh, and Ryan, can't forget sweet, innocent Ryan. You thought you had him wrapped around your finger, didn't you? Stupid girl! You should have taken the ones who actually wanted you—like Dan or even Max. Too late now. You are being sucked into this cutthroat world, and there is nothing you can do about it, your highness."

As she sinks her fangs into Ryan, my eyes flick towards Vinny's sidearm, before I snatch it and point it at Mary's head.

Gasps echo off the brick walls, while Mary steps away from my wild eyes.

"Set it down—you are not a killer," Vinny says as he moves towards me with his hands up.

All the pain from my father's death clouds my judgement, and I yearn to witness her perfect blonde hair turn crimson. I switch the safety off as I steady my trigger finger, prepared to end her pretty little life—no matter the consequences.

As the trigger pulls back, I am suddenly hit from the side, with the full force of Vinny's heavily armored body.

The gun fires into the air.

Vinny quickly handcuffs me. Then he yanks me up as the other guards rush in. "I can't believe you did that! What the hell, Ann?"

The right side of my body is scraped from the sudden force. I spit blood out on the floor, my eyes never leaving Mary's. I curse as I observe the bullet lodged in the wall, just above her head. It would have been a perfect shot.

Max claps wildly. "Great job, Ann. I never knew you had it in you. You know, Vinny, old boy? If you want to just toss her in here with me, I can punish her for you."

My whole body is aching as Vinny pulls me through the doorway and helps me maneuver the stairs in silence. By the time we reach the third floor, I hear gasps as we pass servants. Vinny enters the office and knocks on the conference room door.

Ryan stares down at us. "What the hell happened? I knew this was a bad idea!"

Vinny uncuffs me as the door closes. "I'm sorry, Prince Ryan, but it was necessary. Ann was out of control." He helps me into a chair.

I feel their eyes on me: Ryan, Elizabeth, Christian and Mack.

Christian is the first to speak. "Vinny, you have exactly two milliseconds to clarify why she's bleeding."

Vinny grabs the USB from my pocket and tosses it. Christian catches it midair with a frown. "I apologize for failing, my King. All of the answers you seek are on there." Then he walks towards the door and crosses his arms, daring me to make another move.

"Ann, would you like to elaborate?" Christian asks.

I look away from his stern expression.

"Well, then I guess we have the opportunity to hear what happened." He presses play.

Listening to the whole incident all over again makes me clench my fists as hot tears burn down my face.

"You attempted to shoot Queen Mary?" Mack asks as he rubs his hands over his face. "Well, Ann did get us some more confessions." He turns to me. "Ann, can you give us a rundown of what happened when Max kidnapped you?"

I fixate on a spot on the table and retell my story of that awful night, recounting every detail Max let slip—even how he threatened Cherie. After I finish, Mack grabs the USB from Christian and pats my arm. "I'll take it from here, Ann. Rest assured, they will pay for their crimes."

When the door shuts, Elizabeth looks at me with tears in her eyes. "I do not blame Ann for trying to shoot that evil woman! After everything she's done, she deserves that and a lot more!" She glares at Ryan and Christian. "You both should have listened to me when I told you something was off, and you should have looked into it!" Tears stream as she shakes her head and storms out of the room.

Ryan looks at the table. "I am sorry. I should have told you both about Mary and me."

74

"Damn right you should have told us! I can't believe you let me walk in there, without saying anything about you two." I glare up at Ryan. "After everything we have been through together… Did you *ever* love me? Or was it just a ploy to keep me busy so I wouldn't look into *her*?"

"That is not true. Ann, come on."

"*We* had a plan. We were going to get married and build *our* future together."

Anger rides up the back of my throat, and I grasp the edge of the table.

"Why her? It could have been *anyone* or anything else." I slam my hands on the table. "Look at me!"

Tears burn down my face as the sting of Mary's confession continues to cut me to my core.

"There is no excuse, Ann. I messed up. What more do you want me to say to you?"

"When did you guys kiss?" I swipe at my cheek.

"After dad died, after I told you we had no chemistry."

My mouth falls open. "I specifically asked you if you two were meeting secretly and you lied to my face!"

"I was only trying to protect you. And once everything was out in the open about dad, we stopped. I promise, Ann, while I was with you, it was only you. I never cheated on you."

"Why did you let your brother marry her after everything? Not only did you know she was a murderer, but you knew she was a cheater too. That should have raised a huge red flag."

I rub my temples and turn to Christian, who is

unusually quiet. "What was Mary talking about in there? Why does she think I am next in line to be Queen?"

"I briefly touched base with you about this, after dad passed—it is the law. If the first marriage is unsuccessful and the second choice is unwed, they are the next in line to be Queen."

Ryan leaps to his feet, toppling his chair. "Forget what the rules say! Christian, you wouldn't do that to me! You know how much I love her."

"Obviously, dear brother, you had someone on the side. So, you will have to forgive me, but I am questioning how much you really loved Ann to begin with."

Ryan pinches the bridge of his nose. "You would do that to your own brother?"

Christian jumps up, fists clenched. "How dare you accuse me of purposely harming you, when *you* did it to me first, *brother*, with my fiancée."

Their glares send daggers as they standoff, brother against brother. I glance back at Vinny and shoot him an SOS with my wide eyes. Vinny clears his throat and steps beside Christian. Ryan slams his fists on the table and stomps out.

Before he steps over the threshold, he turns to me. "Ann, I never stopped loving you and never will—no matter who you are *forced* to marry." He glares back at Christian before slamming the door.

Christian lowers himself into his chair and jerks at his tie. "If you would like to fight this, I will petition the people and have it go to a vote."

"How would you like to handle this, Christian?"

"Does it *ever* matter what I want?"

"Yes, of course it does."

"If you genuinely want to know, what I would like is for you to be happy. On your farm, with your dad, and another man who is comparable to you and can provide the life you deserve." He sighs. "That was my plan—always. And it broke my heart to see you with Ryan and then Dan. But I took the sacrifice, so you could be happy and have what your heart desires." He runs his hands through his hair. "But now that will never happen. Mary turned out to be a power-hungry temptress! And you..." He turns to me. "You lost your father to the same person who took mine. And now you are asking me what I want? After everything I have put *you* through?"

"Yes, I am. Why is that so hard to believe?"

"You deserve more than this... better than... *me*. I will always love you. My sweet, outspoken Ann. And I'll remain a loyal friend, but I don't want this life for you." He smooths the wrinkles in his suit. "I will have a press conference as soon as possible and call for the vote. After I update everybody on our situation with Mary and Max." He squeezes the doorknob then turns to me. "I hope you realize how sorry I am, especially for everything Mary said."

"I needed to hear it—don't be sorry. Mary was right about everything." I place my head in my hands.

He kneels beside me and snatches my chin. "Hey! You will cease believing those deceptions immediately. Do you understand me? Now, brush yourself off and let's get you medical attention and sustenance."

His icy eyes bore into mine as his words wash over me.

Why didn't I see it before? Mr. Perfect loves me, always has.

I clear my throat and change the subject. "What are you going to do to Vinny?" I say teasingly.

"I intend to promote him."

I swat Christian's arm before he continues, "Ann, it requires courage to confront your best friend." He pats Vinny on the arm.

"Thank you, Sir." Vinny nods at Christian, then sticks his tongue out at me once we pass him.

As we stride along the corridor, I watch as the servants shoot us questioning glances.

Do they know what happened in the jail too? I steal a peek at Christian, but his confident swagger doesn't miss a beat as we continue down the winding hall. The warm sunlight dances through the stained-glass windows, causing light prisms to gleam off the polished tile floor. And I begin to question: what will happen to us now?

Starting Over

I cross my legs in the green grass, while a warm breeze tosses my hair. I blow on my mug as the sun glitters above the tall treetops. This is exactly what I needed— to be surrounded by the only things that make sense to me and, bonus, can give me unconditional love. I stroke the black and white feathers of a Plymouth Rock as she stares longingly at my dark coffee. I offer her a sip, but she turns away from it and pecks at my hand. I smirk at her persistence—okay, maybe their love isn't always *unconditional*.

I reach for the sunflower seeds Jock gave me, and all eyes zero in on me. I sprinkle the goods around while they push and shove to get a taste. Once the treats are gone, they surround me, demanding more.

"Sorry, girls, that's all there is."

Once the little flocksters get the hint, I lean on the fence post and cringe at my body's soreness. Vinny is one *big* boy. I vow to never piss him off again, unless I'm willing to suffer the consequences.

The sun's rays reach above the tree line. The brilliant orange and yellow hues light up the world, kissing the darkness away with its warmth. The heat is welcoming, and the brightness soon has my eyes tearing up. My heart aches heavily for my father—each beat feels like daggers. My lips quiver and I squeeze my eyes to let the tears fall. The one man that I could depend on is gone *forever*. My body shakes with sobs as his face swims in my memories.

But his murderers are behind bars—I should feel better, right? Additionally, I brought justice to the country, so why does it feel like I am *more* of a failure?

The gate to the pen opens and then closes softly. I swipe away my tears and I blink at Christian's concerned face, then I sweep my gaze over his unusual outfit.

"Are you breaking in the jeans and tank top I bought you for Christmas?"

The gift was meant to be a joke between us, but look who's laughing now? That man looks yummy as a cowboy wannabe. Who knew *all* that muscle was hiding behind a suit? It is a real shame this isn't his everyday attire.

Christian leans his head back on the fence as the flock struts over to shake down the newcomer. His icy eyes wash over my skinny jeans, and he smirks.

"We are just two peas in a pod, huh?"

I clear my throat and offer him my cup.

"Here, take this. You have clearly lost your mind, wearing something that distasteful, my King."

"Thank you for the thoughtful gesture."

"Are you skipping work today?" I tease.

"How about skipping on life." He sips the coffee.

"You? Mr. Punctual?"

"Today I am just a normal guy, enjoying ordinary man things. Like relaxing in jeans and drinking coffee while watching the sunrise." His eyes dart around the grass. "While being surrounded by feathered raptors and most likely lounging in chicken poop." He lets out a long sigh. "I am living the feathered dream."

Hearing a King say "poop" sets off my exhausted brain and I begin laughing, really laughing, until I'm snorting like a spring pig.

Christian glances at me from the side. His eyebrow arches as he looks at me like I have finally lost my mind.

He is right—*I have.*

I gasp for air. "Did you just say the word *poop*?"

"I'm not permitted to say that phrase?"

"I have never heard anything like *that* come out of *your* mouth."

He runs a hand through my hair.

"I am delighted I could make you laugh again, Ann."

I finish my giggling fit. Then I rest my head on his broad shoulder. "What ever happened to our simple life?"

"Apparently, there is no such thing for us."

"What is going to happen next, Christian? To you, me and Ryan?"

"Life is full of uncertainties—our lives are no different. We will continue to take it one day at a time."

He kisses the top of my head before he plucks me into his lap. We watch the sun and chickens for a while. All too soon, he draws me up. We examine each other for chicken poop, then we move back into the Palace.

Elizabeth corners us and waves us into the office.

"Where have you two been? We have a press conference in an hour, and I need you two primped and prepared." She frowns down at our clothes as she plucks a feather out of my hair.

"So, there is no rest for the weary?" I return her frown.

"Ann, this is important. We need to get stability back. We cannot be viewed as weak or unbalanced. Now, get a move on young lady."

"Please, Elizabeth, we have been through a lot. Can't we just..."

"No, absolutely not—we need to settle this before the rumors spread like wildfire. Don't you agree, Christian?"

He looks up and nods. "Of course, mother."

"Great! Everything is all set. All you have to do is change and meet us in the gardens."

I pivot towards my room, but Elizabeth calls me back. "Ann, is it really necessary that we call for a vote over this? Can't you just agree to be Queen and drop it?"

"Elizabeth, this is Christian's decision, and he is very adamant that it goes to a vote."

"You two need each other. You always have." She purses her lips. "I have set out an outfit for you in your room and sent Adrie to assist you."

Even though I know Elizabeth is just doing her job, being dismissed like a petulant child doesn't sit well with me. With a roll of my eyes, I stomp off to meet Adrie in my room.

Adrie is a kind, older woman who normally assists Elizabeth in her daily life, but she isn't *my* Karen. She ushers me to my outfit laid out on the bed. It is a long pink dress with shimmering gold and lace flowers.

My fingertips glide over the fabric as I retain the urge to pitch a fit about the color. This shade was Mary's favorite to wear, and I am not amused. Is Elizabeth *seriously* trying to preen me to stand in Mary's place? Nothing can compensate for my lack of grace and obedience—not even twinkling Pepto Bismol colored gowns.

My eyes reflect in the full-length mirror and I barely recognize myself. I look beautiful, strong, and well rested—the perfect replacement.

"Thank you, Adrie, for your assistance."

"It was my pleasure, Lady Ann." She gives me a half bow.

When Adrie is out of sight, I adjust my cleavage— trying to shove some of my self-respect back under the fabric, but it's no use. I grumble and try to take in a calming breath, but the dress makes it impossible. I throw my gloved hands up in the air and stomp down the stairs in my glass slippers.

I spot Christian waiting at the foot of the stairs in a light-blue suit. When I am in his line of vision, his gaze sweeps over every inch of my body. I falter as I approach, and he captures my waist with a grin.

"Lady Ann, why am I getting this unexpected sense of déjà vu?" He runs his hand down my face. "I wouldn't want you to hurt your other ankle this time."

Before he rights me, he bends down to collect my fallen heel from the ground. I shake my head of the inappropriate thoughts fluttering around as his breath warms my ankle. Christian sets my foot inside my shoe and before he rises to his full height, he runs his warm palm up my calf, massaging as he goes.

"There, everything is as it should be. Are you ready?"

He offers a strong arm, and I watch him for a reaction or an explanation of his movements, but there isn't any. I arch a brow and open my mouth to demand one, but then I feel everyone's eyes on us and clamp my lips shut as scarlet rises up my neck.

I clear my throat and fix a matching confident smile across my face. "Let's get this over with."

The guards open the garden doors as we approach. And before we even make it outside, cameras are flashing and videos are recording. Blinded by the lights, I stumble towards the podium while I force a smile at Elizabeth and Ryan.

Christian clears his throat at the flock of people. "Thank you, everybody, for coming on such short notice. Please, take your seats and we will begin. As you all know, a lot has transpired over these last few days. We appreciate your patience and understanding as we sort everything out and resettle ourselves."

He then updates them on Mary and Max's malicious plans and how we thwarted them in the end, but unfortunately, I had been kidnapped and hurt in the process. Also, that we will have a trial for Max and Mary, but as Mary is no longer Queen, he will need the people's help in deciding what to do—either follow the law and marry me, or rewrite the law and have another group of women come from the states. The reporters go wild at this suggestion of rewriting regulations and start raising their hands with inquiries.

Christian points to a male reporter, who stands eagerly. "Why rewrite the law, King Christian? Is Lady Ann not a suitable replacement?"

Christian shakes his head. "Lady Ann is more than appropriate as a Queen."

A female reporter stands and meets my eyes. "But, Lady Ann, what happened with you and Prince Ryan? Are you two not seeing each other anymore?"

"We are not currently in a relationship." I try not to frown as I feel heat rise up my face. I *so* didn't want to talk about this right now.

"Ann, do you love King Christian?" someone shouts.

I glance towards Christian, then I return my attention to the reporter. "We are very good friends, who work very well together, and we even tend to balance each other out."

I do my best to glaze over the fact that I'm not sure if I do in fact love Christian—we have a very complicated relationship.

Another reporter raises their pen in the air. "Lady Ann, could you ever love the King?"

"If given the opportunity, I do not see why *any* woman, including myself, wouldn't love the King. Christian is strong, courageous, and well, let's be honest, very handsome."

The reporters laugh as they scribble in their notebooks. Then they follow up with Christian about new security measures to make sure this doesn't happen again. They also ask him when he thinks the next wedding will take place. He very gently answers as best he can. Then they turn back to me.

"Lady Ann, if you do not marry King Christian, what will you do next? Are you going to continue to bounce back and forth with the Princes?"

I clench my jaw at the wave of laughter and ignore the last part of his question.

"I am not sure what I will do. My life has revolved around the Palace for so long, and with my dad's passing, I do not see myself returning home anytime soon. I *do* have a friend who will be having twins soon. So, I am sure I will have my hands full, helping her and her husband with diaper changes."

They accept my answer, before they move on to some photo shoots of the whole family. Then they transition from the garden towards the patio for some refreshments. Once the reporters leave, I wipe my brow and go as fast as my heels will allow me towards the Palace.

Just as the glorious burst of icy air caresses my face, Christian presses his body against my back while whispering, "Well, I believe that went smoothly."

I stomp on his foot, forcing him to take a step away from my already heated frame.

"Maybe from where you were standing. But I am so shaky and I feel like I am going to throw up."

"Thank you for undertaking the press conference with me, Ann. I appreciate your show of unity."

"Not that your mother gave us any choice."

I grumble towards my room ready to rip off this horrendous fabric, but when I open my door, I am thrown backwards by Karen's embrace.

"Oh, Ann! I cannot believe all of this mess! Are you okay? I mean, of course you aren't!"

I squeeze Karen and breathe in her familiar floral scent. "Oh, Karen, I missed you so much. Don't worry about me. I'm dealing with the hand life has dealt me, as usual." I swipe my eye and put my hand on her round belly. "Auntie Ann missed you guys too. How was your little vacation?"

"It was so beautiful!"

She tells me about her mini retreat while I secretly wish I could have the luxury of that right now. Maybe I can pick up a new romance novel and get a mental reprieve?

"And you look absolutely radiant!" I comment as I watch her talk.

"Thank you, sweetie. And you look like... crap." She frowns as I remove the heavy makeup, revealing the bruises and small cuts from Vinny plowing into me. Her eyes start watering, and I let her cry on my shoulder.

Ryan pokes his head inside and gives Karen a pretty-boy grin, and then he kneels at her feet to talk to the babies.

As I watch him, my heart shatters with envy. I wanted that—him talking to our children. Now, with the lies between us, I know that can never happen and it hurts more than I ever thought possible. When he meets my eyes, he clears his throat and rises to his feet. While he strides towards me, Karen sneaks out the door with a grin and a thumbs up.

He squeezes my hand. "Would it be redundant if I told you again just how sorry I am?"

"Why didn't you tell me about you and Mary?"

"I didn't want to hurt you any more than you were

already hurting. And Mary is a great manipulator. She had a lot of people fooled. Including yours truly."

"What am I going to do, Ryan?"

"Just be yourself—strong, confident, loving, and compassionate." I move a lock of his hair out of his eye, and he leans into my hand. "You will make a great Queen, Ann. Plus, you know Christian has always favored you."

"Please, don't say that. You know that's not *who* I am, or who I want to become."

"Why do you think this country was set up this way? It allows the molding of royals and commoners to come together. That way, the kingdom is run as efficiently as possible, while representing both sides."

"What? Stop! You're supposed to tell me to fight for us! No, this isn't how it was supposed to go!" Tears start streaming as my sanity splinters.

The sudden urge to drop to my knees and beg him to do something, anything, overwhelms me. But to retain some form of dignity, I allow my eyes to do the pleading while I try to send him a telepathic message: *Come on! Don't throw in the towel yet! Fight for me!*

Surely, I'm worthy of at least a discussion between them?

Ryan looks away while he squeezes his eyes. "Don't you think I know that? There's nothing I can say to change anything. But you know, no matter what happens, I will always be here for you. You are too important to me. Plus, we have Karen and Vinny's babies arriving soon. I mean, did you get a look at Karen's belly? She is a whale!"

My eyes bore into his. Typical Ryan, cracking a joke to

lighten the mood. I mock disgust and play along. Because it's easier than the alternative.

"Do not let Karen hear you call her a whale! Or it may just be the last thing you do."

He laughs and straightens his tie. "So, do you forgive me enough to continue as friends?"

"If that is all I can have with you, then yes. But please, be honest with me—no matter how much you fear it may hurt me. Okay?"

His lips linger on my forehead before he ambles out without a backward glance, or an answer. When the door clicks, I drop my facade and crumble into a heap.

Is this really happening? Are Ryan and I over? How can he give up on me this easily?

I pull myself together and stand on shaky limbs. As I stare at my reflection, I remind the depleted woman staring back that nothing is set in stone; there is still a chance for my happily ever after.

"I see you and Ryan are conversing again."

In that moment of resolve, I didn't notice Christian enter with Snowball cradled in his arms.

"We are working on being able to be in the same room." I shrug. "Without wanting to kill each other." I look at his casual but dressy outfit. "No more jeans?"

He passes the hen to me. "The jeans are a little too restrictive for long durations of time. I need to practice before I can wear them more often."

"Yes, I guess they do take some time to get used to."

I stroke Snowball as she yawns and burrows.

"Just as I speculate gowns and heels were for you when you joined us at the Palace?"

"Yes, they took a lot of practice. And yet, I'm still tripping over myself in them."

"Listen, Ann. I am sorry for not being more patient with you in the past. I never comprehended how tasks, which I thought were uncomplicated, could affect an outsider. You have transitioned incredibly well here, and I applaud all of your hard work and dedication. I mean, facing those reporters was not easy but you did a magnificent job."

"Now just remember *all* of that the next time I show up to dinner in sneakers and my mother cluckers shirt."

He wrinkles his nose. "I thought I had Karen throw that shirt away after you wore it in front of the French Ambassador?"

"You did *what*?" I fling clothes out of my dresser like a mad woman, until I clutch my coveted shirt. I pivot on my heels and wave it triumphantly. "You are such a liar."

He snatches the shirt and raises it above my head. "I was not lying—I did ask her to remove it. But it must have slipped her mind. Don't worry, I'll take care of it."

"Now, wait just a minute. Don't do anything rash. Remember, you were just singing my praises a minute ago. Just hand over my shirt and no one will get hurt."

He arches a brow and scoffs, "You can't injure me."

"Now, Christian, you have seen me fight and shoot a gun. Do you really want the entire Palace to witness their King sobbing?" I tap my foot for good measure as I hold out my wiggling digits. "Just hand it over, Mr. Sassy-

Pants."

"You will remember to wear it outside only, correct? Or in the confines of your personal space?"

I leap up and grab the shirt. "Fine. Whatever you want, Old Timer. Geez, I can't even wear what I want. This is ridiculous."

Christian chuckles, then clears his throat. "The voting will take place immediately, and we will have an answer in a day or so."

"What happens then, to us?"

"It depends on what the verdict is, and what *you* want. You may continue to work here, return home, or do whatever you want." He collects my hands in his. "I will support you in any way that I can—I owe you a great deal. Even if you are not my wife, I will always consider you a good friend."

My throat tightens. I can't handle these "what ifs" right now, especially after Ryan *just* gave up on me.

"What's up with everybody being all mushy-gushy today?" I pull my hands out of his grasp.

Christian sits farther away from me on the edge of the bed, looking defeated.

Knowing Snowball can cheer him up, I shove her in his lap. Then I lower myself next to him, not sure what to say to comfort him.

This man could be my husband soon… the father of my children… but he is so broken and lost. I bite my lip as I consider this. We both are damaged. We make a perfect pair.

I place my hand on his knee. "I meant what I said at the press conference earlier—*any* chick would be lucky to have you as their rooster." I bump his shoulder, but when my joke doesn't turn his mood around, I sigh.

"What about you, Ann?"

"What do you mean?"

"Would *you* feel lucky marrying me?"

"Of course. Although you are featherless—" I smile at him. "Marrying my good friend is a bonus. But the wedding night will be a little awkward." I tease as Mary's taunting comes to mind.

"I seem to recall that we had *no* complications with the physical element of our relationship."

"You know what I'm trying to say. I have pressed those feelings down for so long, and I just don't know if I can easily have them resurface. Plus, with your history with Mary and mine with your little brother, you don't think that will make things… I don't know… awkward?"

"We may be worrying about nothing, but we'll take it one day at a time." His hand stills on my doorknob. "Ann, I have an appointment for you with my therapist later today. I know you said you were not interested before, but I'm putting my foot down. You must talk to a professional about everything. Especially about your father's death and Max's abduction."

I furrow my brow and stand to walk him out. "I can't promise you I will spill my guts to them, but I will at least attend the appointment."

Christian grabs the doorknob again but hesitates, causing me to run into his hard back. "Oof. Christian, what is wrong with the door?"

He pivots, his blue eyes sparkling. He sets Snowball on the floor and she ruffles her feathers while she explores. Then he runs his fingertips through my loose hair, making me shiver. He lowers his lips to mine and I freeze.

When I hold back, he tugs me against him with determination. The passion we once had reignites as he leisurely trails warm kisses from my fingertips all the way up to my ear.

My heart melts while I hum softly and arch my neck, letting him take control. When his mouth seems to touch everywhere but my lips, I push him against the wall and match his hunger with my own. When he moves his eager hands downward, I gently pull back, breathless.

"Christian? What... why?"

He leans his head on my forehead. "I just wanted to demonstrate a point." Then he nips my lower lip before pulling away from our embrace. "I will see you soon, Ann."

He collects the feathered princess and exits before I can respond.

What game is he playing? My hand rests over my racing heart, while I lean my head on the cold wall before banging it in frustration. What the heck was that? How could I go from one guy to the next so easily? Am I that shallow? I squeeze my lids shut and instinctively put my fingertips over my swollen lips.

I shake my head of the heated memories, then I stroll out the door, eager to receive my much-needed therapy session.

Next

After therapy, I am exhausted and tear-stained, but grateful. The therapist was wonderful, just like Christian said, but I wish it wasn't so hard and slow moving.

When I make it to the dining room, I plop down next to Christian.

"Could I have a glass of white wine, please? No, wait! How about you just bring me the bottle with a nipple on it?" I ask the waiter.

"Ann, did you have a good therapy session with Cindy?" Christian asks over the rim of his water with a smirk.

I throw back my cold glass of liquid courage before I respond.

"Yes, it was very eye opening—she suggested that I run far away from you and this crazy place before it's too late. And I agree. So, I'm packing and leaving tonight."

Water dribbles down Christian's chin and he scrambles to catch it. "What? That doesn't sound like Cindy to me. *Oh*, you are teasing me. Ann, what am I going to do with you and your sarcasm?" Once he collects himself, he whispers into my ear, his warm breath tickling my neck, "I would like to provide you with proper notice… Cherie is on her way to the Palace to pay Ryan a visit. She called the Palace the moment the press conference aired, seeking permission to visit. Apparently, she still loves Ryan and wants to plead her case to him."

I poke my roast as Max's words echo in my head—he was right. When Ryan finds out Cherie never deceived him, he will take her back with open arms.

"Ann, I am baffled by your reaction. I thought you would be delighted for them. They are making amends and healing wounds. Surely you know how refreshing that is, after putting Max behind bars."

I shove a potato in my mouth. "If I was really *that* mature, I would be happy for them."

Once we finish dinner, I go to my room and change into my workout gear. Then I make my way to the training area. When I walk out of my room, I collide with Christian as he goes downstairs. He looks me over in my tight gym pants and tank top and tilts his head. "Ann, where are you going?"

"To the training area to work out."

"Why would you need to do that? The threat you were training for is behind bars."

"Why not?"

"Ann, are you annoyed with me?"

"Not at the moment, but give it time." I scoff, "Do I need an excuse to want to punch something?" I arch a brow.

He furrows his. "That is a bit aggressive, don't you think?"

"Good night, Christian."

I push past him and stomp off. Why is he asking twenty questions? Mr. Control-Freak needs to take a chill pill.

I scan the mats and see a few guards working out, but no Sam or Vinny. Well, I guess I will just train solo tonight. I stretch my tight limbs then warm up on the punching bag, imagining Max's ugly face right in the center. All the horrible things he said to me, did to me—I pound my retribution into the sandbag until tears and sweat roll down my chin, but the ache still smolders.

I lean against the punching bag, gasping for peace.

There is a tap on my shoulder, and I swing at the shadow behind me. I stop inches away from his face as I realize I am no longer a prisoner in Max's basement.

"Oh, crap! I could have hurt you, Christian! What are you doing?"

"Can't I pummel an inanimate object too?"

I watch as he stretches in grey sweatpants, muscles rippling. Oh, boy. Not sweatpants—they are my weakness. And mix those with his icy blue eyes—I am in trouble.

Or am I?

"Let's see what you got."

He looks at the gloves then back at me. "Ann, absolutely not. I am not fighting a… you."

My mouth falls open. "You were going to say a girl!"

He shrugs, unashamed. "Well, it is not appropriate."

I punch him on the shoulder, making him take a step back.

"Ann, my answer is still no."

I leap forward in the defensive position, egging him on. When I punch again, he dodges.

"If physical exertion is what you require to move out of

your sour mood, then, fine, let's do this."

We dance around each other, taking swings here and there but not making a connection.

"Come on, Christian. I know you aren't this weak!"

I swing and connect with his stomach. He groans and holds his abdomen. I punch at his head while he has it lowered but then he charges me. We roll on the floor until we collide with the wall. Finally, tired and sweaty, we lie on our backs, breathing heavily while staring at the blinding white ceiling.

"Ann, I hope you understand that I went easy on you," he says through labored breathing.

"You are just mad that you got beat by a *girl*."

I roll over on to my stomach and push myself up. My muscles scream. Why do guys fight dirty when they know they are going to lose?

"Ann, are you yielding so soon?"

"Nope. I am just going for *heavier* arsenal."

I push open the double doors leading to the indoor shooting range as I sip my water.

"Where did you learn how to shoot? I don't recall granting Vinny authorization to instruct you on that."

"I have a farm, Christian. How do you think we fend off bears and coyotes? With sticks and pebbles?"

"I guess I never put much thought as to what a farmer actually does, other than gardening and collecting eggs."

When we arrive at the Palace's indoor gun range, we gear up and pick our lanes. I aim for the head of the silhouette, picturing Mary's pretty face, and I let round after round hit its target. When I run out, I set the gun down and look at my handiwork. I turn to see Christian staring, wide-eyed. I can't help the proud smirk I offer him.

"What? Never seen a *girl* shoot before?"

He shakes his head. "I never imagined a candidate for my future wife would know how to shoot or fight, but it does make me wonder."

"Wonder about what, exactly?"

"What other activities she could excel at." Then he winks in my direction as he grabs his target.

Is Christian flirting with me? I shake my head at his playful banter, then glance at the bullet holes in the head of the picture. I run my fingertips over the round punctures and sigh.

"Sometimes I really wish I could do this in real life," I whisper to myself.

"Well, you could join my guard at the Palace."

"And have Vinny as my boss? No way. Plus, you would worry about me too much." I elbow him.

He pouts. "I thought I was the boss?"

Do I want a future in security or the military? I only started this routine because of dad. But I do enjoy it. I shake the idea from my head as we ascend the stairs. At the sound of voices, I stop short and see Ryan and Cherie arguing in the hallway.

Christian looks over to them, then places his hand on the small of my back. "Ann, you look pale. Are you feeling okay?"

"Why wouldn't I be okay? And even if I wasn't, it's not like I have much of a choice in the matter."

I brush past him and slam my door. Then I peel off my sweaty shirt and throw it at the offensive photo of Ryan and me at Christian's wedding. Behind me, the door opens and closes fast.

"Why in the world would you say you do not have a choice?" Christian spits out, his eyes blazing.

I put my hands on my hips. "Because Ryan never loved me."

"But *you* love him?" He crosses his arms over his chest.

"You know I love Ryan!" I throw my hands up in exasperation. "Just like I am sure you love Mary!" I let out a breath and look into his eyes. "Christian, we both have a history. But we may not have to worry about that, right? If they decide to have another selection, you could have a chance to meet another beautifully talented, *nonaggressive* woman come tomorrow."

"I do not want another woman."

"So, it's a man you are seeking?"

He rubs his face, then stares at my chest. "Where is your shirt?" I look at my sweaty sports bra and shrug. "I was changing before you decided to burst in here, demanding answers like a hot-headed dingdong."

Christian forces his eyes to meet mine and quickly changes the subject.

"Listen, whatever happens tomorrow after the vote, I want you to know you can continue to place your trust in me."

"I'm not worried about that. Besides, I have a fallback; I can join the guard." I smirk and add in, "We will take it one day at a time, right?"

"You are correct."

We turn as we hear arguing outside my bedroom door. I cringe as curse words fly around.

"Sounds like it may be a long night for Ryan."

"I'll allow them to battle it out on their own for now. Cherie is a convincingly resilient woman—she will have Ryan excusing her quickly."

Images of Ryan and Cherie rush through my mind, and I turn away from Christian, refusing to cry over this situation again. Soon I feel the warmth of Christian's chest against my bare back, as he wraps his arms around my waist and places gentle kisses on my neck.

"If you want her to leave the Palace, all you have to do is ask," he whispers against my ear. "Anything you want, I will give you."

His soft-spoken words send shivers down my spine while his fingertips graze my hips. I know his promises ring true. Anything I want *can* be mine. I can make her disappear, make her scrub my toilets with her toothbrush—but Cherie isn't the real enemy. She got caught up in this mess, just like I had.

"Ann, do you wish to discuss why you are so upset with Ryan and Cherie?"

"Do you want to talk about Mary?"

That kills the mood fast. He loosens his grip and takes a

step back.

"I am always available to you, whenever you need me."

Then I hear the door close softly behind him.

As I lie in bed, I stare at the dark ceiling, wondering where I went wrong with Ryan. What did I do to push him towards Mary? What does she have that I do not?

I wake before the rooster can crow and decide to have my coffee with the feathered ladies. When I open the gate, I tilt my head. In the corner is a new black bench. I glance around, wondering where it came from before lowering myself onto it.

I lean back and wait for the sun to make its appearance. The chickens eagerly sit with me, hoping for the treats stashed inside my pocket. I turn my head as I hear voices approach from behind. I groan inwardly as I see Ryan and Cherie strolling hand in hand through the adjacent gardens. I quickly turn away from them, but Ryan catches my eyes and waves.

"Hey, Ann!"

I muster an awkward nod towards the couple, then I turn back, hoping they pass me swiftly. I deflate once I hear the gate open. Then I see Cherie's perfectly painted face look around with a frown at the chickens.

Ryan sits next to me and strokes a white hen.

"So, Ann, have you named all the chickens yet?"

I shake my head as Fluffer Muffin settles into my warm lap.

Ryan pivots. "Why don't you sit down, Cherie?"

"No, thank you. Who knows what is *on* that bench?"

"King Christian *just* had it installed—it is brand-new."

I turn my head. "Christian did this?"

Cherie comes closer to us but refuses to sit. She pulls at her perfectly pressed lavender dress.

"Cherie, did you know Ann organized and set up this chicken pen?"

Cherie rolls her eyes. "Ryan, you told me this already. I'm feeling warm, can we go back inside? Please?"

"Yes, of course we can. Enjoy your coffee, Ann. Are you coming in for breakfast soon?"

"No, thank you. I have my coffee and that will fill me up."

"You should eat food too."

Cherie narrows her eyes. "Ryan, Ann is a big girl. Get off her case already."

Ryan looks from Cherie to me.

"You know, Ann, I bet Christian and mom would love to see you at breakfast too."

Then he stands and offers his arm to Cherie. She grins up at him before narrowing her eyes at me. I wrinkle my nose and stick my tongue out at her. I hear her gasp at my unladylike gesture before lifting her chin and sauntering off with her prize.

I attempt to enjoy the chickens pecking at the grass as the sun rises, but I can't get the idea out of my head that I *should* be at breakfast with my adoptive family. They care for me and yet, here I am, pushing them away.

But the chickens are easier to understand and love.

I turn as I hear someone approaching. "Thank you for the bench."

"Trust me, I bought it purely for selfish reasons. I don't want chicken feces on my pants every time I join you out here." After I am done giggling, he adds in, "I came to collect you for breakfast. I know Ryan tried, but let's be honest, he isn't nearly as captivating as I am."

I snort. "You mean he isn't as insistent as you are."

I give the chickens one more quick pet and finish off their treats. Then I walk over to Christian. He smiles brightly as he offers his arm.

"Thank you for the invitation, your *highness*."

"You are most welcome, *Lady* Ann. But again, if I am to be completely honest with you, this request was more for me than you. Because I do prefer your company over theirs."

I smirk, thinking how the tables have turned. I remember him always criticizing me. And now he favors me over the prim and proper?

"Why do you prefer me, Christian?"

He tilts his head as we ascend the stairs. "You are the strongest woman I know. The peace that you bring, because of your demeanor, is refreshing. Plus, I really adore you in those pants." He teases as he glances at my skinny jeans.

Once we are in the dining hall, I am relieved when the eggs, bacon, and biscuits are placed in front of me so I can shovel them into my scarlet face.

After we are done, we go about our morning routines. When I enter the office, I am surprised to find a bouquet of vibrant orange roses in a clear vase on my desk. I pluck the attached white card and squint at the pristine handwriting. *Smile more, that's an order.* Then he signed it: *your ruler, Christian.*

I snort. *My* ruler? Whatever. I smell the flowers and run my fingertips against their velvety petals.

I sit behind my desk and shuffle around some forms. If this is Christian's way of buttering me up, it's working.

The day drags on *slowly.* I twirl in my chair as I deal with another ignorant moron on the phone. As I roll my eyes, I smirk up at Christian smiling down at me. From my phone call, I hold up a finger to indicate one more minute.

When I finally hang up, I rub my temples. People are being increasingly annoying today. Every time I announce who I am, they have to blab about the current status of the Palace and ask me about my feelings for both Christian and Ryan.

I just can't take a breath.

I glance up to see Christian narrowing his eyes at his wristwatch. His gaze meets mine and he offers an impatient smile.

"What are you up to, Christian?"

"What do you mean, Ann?"

I arch a brow but he doesn't elaborate. I lean back in my chair as I continue to stare him down. Then I notice the room is too quiet. I look around the office and frown at the empty space. "Did I miss a meeting? Where is everyone?"

I stretch my back and lean forward on my elbows.

"Let's just acknowledge that I *know* you are up to something. I'm not sure what it is, but you have secrecy written all over you."

I stand slowly then point a finger at him.

"Wipe that look off your face right now, lover boy. Before I decide to change my mind and call a few more vendors."

He offers his arm. Then he guides me into the dining hall, and I am stunned to see the room filled with coworkers and dignitaries.

Finally, we reach our table and Christian pulls out my chair. I glance at him before I take my seat hesitantly. When we sit, Elizabeth clears her throat and addresses the room with poise.

"Thank you all for your presence at this momentous occasion. What I have here is the final vote from the people. Today, we will either be changing history and starting up another selection of women for our King to sort through, or sticking to tradition and welcoming Lady Ann as our future Queen."

My hands become clammy as I realize what's going on.

We are doing this *now*?

I could kill Christian! Why didn't he warn me?

Now I am sitting here like a deer in headlights. Before I can protest, Christian grabs my hand and squeezes it reassuringly. Elizabeth passes the envelope to Christian, who waves it away. "Mother, you may open it."

"Let's open this up and get our answers then!"

She rips into the creased paper, and her icy eyes skim the contents before she beams and announces, "Ninety-eight percent have voted to keep Lady Ann on as their future Queen."

My stomach drops. No, this is not happening.

Christian embraces me. I feel relief washing over him as he pecks my cheek and looks into my eyes. He never wanted another group of women. He knew exactly *who* he wanted. Christian kisses me softly and everyone claps louder.

The rest of the event passes in a blur as we celebrate and shake hundreds of hands. When everyone clears out and it is just the family, I fall onto my chair.

Ryan stares down into my eyes. "You can do this, Ann. You are an amazing woman, and we are here to assist you every step of the way."

I stare up into his dark eyes and feel tears burning. How can he act like we never had a relationship?

Well, fine. If he is okay with this, then I can be too.

Elizabeth envelops me in a tight hug. "Oh, Ann, my sweet girl, I am so happy for you! I always knew Christian would choose you."

Soon it's just me and Christian in the room. Why does it have to feel so awkward? It was so much easier when I was his friend and that was it. But now I am expected to marry him, to become Queen.

Mary's words sink into me again: *I am getting her leftovers.*

I will always be Christian's second choice.

"Come on, Ann, let's get some fresh air and speak."

We descend the stairs. He leads me to the familiar pond and I sit on the bench. He strides to the water's crystal blue edge, lost in thought. Then his eyes wander to the fish, while he taps a finger on his thigh.

"Do you recall the day I discovered you in this exact spot with Ryan?"

"Of course I do." I smirk at the memory. "You were so angry with me."

"I have never been so jealous in my entire life." He kicks a pebble, avoiding my eyes. "Here was a woman who was supposed to be here for me, and yet she was soaking wet and playing with my little brother. I mean, I saw the way you watched him, smiled, laughed, and it made me furious. Angry to know that I could never have you in that way, especially since father forbade it."
He kneels in the grass by my feet and grasps my hand.
"This is my second chance. An opportunity to get the woman I have always wanted but could never have. And I promise to make compromises with you, to try to be more considerate, to always make you happy, and to be there whenever you need me. Because you are the greatest thing in my life, Ann, and when I almost lost you, the pain I felt... I thought my life was coming to an end. You may be clumsy and outspoken, but I wouldn't change that for anything in this world, because it is who *you* are. And I love *all* that is you."

He stares deeply into my eyes. "I know our relationship has always been rough, at best, but I feel you are my best friend and one of the only individuals in this world that I can trust." He pulls out our original engagement ring and offers it to me. "Ann, will you make me the happiest man in the world and agree to be by my side?"

I stare, my mouth open and unsure what to say to follow that speech. I swallow the lump in my throat and push out the truth, "Christian, I am terrified."

"Ann, I am certain beyond any doubt that you can do this. And if I am completely honest, I am scared too."

"Yes, but Christian you were born and raised to live the life of a King. I was not. I am only a farm girl." My eyes glitter with tears.

"You are much more than a farm girl. Just look around you. Ann, you built a chicken coop, you rescued me from Mary, brought Cherie and Ryan back together, and pulled my mother out of her depression when my father died… I mean, the list is quite extensive. You are perfect for this life. And even if you feel inadequate, remember that *I want* you as my wife, as my partner, all before being Queen. You are my better half. I *need* you."

New Paths

I can't breathe or even blink, afraid that if I do, I'll realize this is all a dream. I scan over Commander Confusing and allow his words to wash over me.

I feel cold metal run up the length of my ring finger. The diamond sparkles as the light gleams off it. He didn't have to go through all of this. He already had me because of the law, but he did it *for* me.

Christian shifts and clears his throat as he watches my blank face.

"It is a beautiful ring and *very* familiar too." I wiggle my ring finger.

He releases a breath. "I petitioned Karen to recover and clean it for this special occasion."

"Wait, so, you knew the people would choose me?"

"I was always going to choose you. Whether they did or not," he says with arrogance only he can muster.

"Well, I don't know if I can see you without clothes on though... that may be a deal breaker," I tease.

His mouth falls open and I bite my lip to hold back the snicker. That brought Mr. Confident down a few notches.

"I'm sorry—it's sad but true."

He quickly regains his composure and stands, smoothing his invisible wrinkles out. Then he snatches my chin, pulls my lips close to his and whispers, "Believe me when I say this, you will be begging me to remove *my* clothes when the time arises."

His words flutter in the breeze as he tugs me to him. I'm caught off guard and place my hand on his chest to steady myself. My breath hitches as I watch his mouth. Instinctively, I run my tongue over my lips in anticipation. Christian emits a low growl, then he presses his mouth against mine, before I can come to my senses. Then he pulls away too soon with a smirk.

"I apologize. I couldn't catch your answer over the labored breathing. Was that a yes, or a no?"

I blink up into his eyes, trying to summon my composure.

"You do not play fair." I bite my lip. "My answer is yes, Christian. I will marry you."

We continue our kiss, enjoying the warm breeze and the sound of rushing water from the pond. My heavy breathing drowns out everything else as I press into him. He releases his hold on my hips and gazes into my eyes as he runs a fingertip over my flush cheek, all the way down to my swollen rosy lips. A slow grin forms as he takes in my hot mess.

"I look forward to the days when I do not have to hold back with you." I blush, not used to such bluntness. "I am sorry I didn't mean to embarrass you."

"I am just not as experienced as you are, Christian. But I will catch up, eventually." I grab his hand and we start walking back. Then it hits me, I'm going to be living at the Palace for the foreseeable future. "What am I going to do with my house?"

"What would you like to do with it?"

"Maybe I should sell it? You know, get rid of it."

"What about your chickens and farmland? Most importantly, what about all the memories that you shared with your mother and father? Surely you will want to keep it. If not for logical reasons, for sentimental ones?"

"I think it will hurt too much to go back there."

He pivots and stares into my eyes. "Ann, I do not require that you relinquish one life in exchange for another. I suggest we meld our pasts and create a brighter future. Wouldn't you enjoy sharing your childhood home with our children? You can show them where their mother, grandmother, and grandfather grew up."

I consider his words. Even though I hate to admit it, he has a point. If I sell the house, I will never get that opportunity.

He wraps his arms around me, and his warmth soaks my bones. "Take some time to think it over. Your decision does not need to be immediate. You know what? I have a wonderful idea. It has been some time since you last visited. Why don't we plan a trip to the house together? We can retrieve the important items and bring them to the Palace. I can even get your flock transported here for you. Would you like that?"

"I would love to have my girls close by, and Suzie wouldn't have to check on the house as often."

"Perfect, it is settled."

I nod as we ascend the stairs. Even though I love the idea of having my girls here, I wonder if traveling right *now* is a good idea.

"When is Mary and Max's trial starting?"

I regret the question instantly, as his smile folds down

at the mention of their names. I lose the sweet, carefree Christian and get the all-business, stoic brute.

"As soon as possible." His voice is clipped, and we are silent as he leads me into his office. "I want their trial to go swiftly."

"And *I* want them to die slow and painful deaths." I grumble.

He sits behind his desk and rearranges some forms, not looking at me.

"Let's not share that opinion with the nation, okay?"

"It is just eating at me that they are still alive."

"They are in a tiny cell with minimal food and water. Their lives are not alluring."

"They aren't even *apologetic*."

"I know… The situation is unnerving, to say the least."

The topic is turning the air stale, so I make a playful joke. "So, will it be a hanging, then a wedding?"

Instead of lightening his mood, my comment has Christian pressing his lips and avoiding eye contact. "Yes, that is my plan."

I excuse myself and stride to my area, eager to leave the tension-filled room. After we finish our work, we have a quick press conference on the recent vote then dinner.

I slide my peas and sigh. Soon I will be Queen and they will all be looking to me for advice. Am I ready for that?

I take a peek at Christian. Does he feel weird about this? Losing Miss Perfect Mary and getting stuck with me?

I watch Ryan as he talks with Cherie. And what about

Ryan? We were so close to being married. And now this. We will be in-laws!

My fork clatters to the table and echoes in the room, before I excuse myself.

As I turn the corner, I yelp as I fumble over an object at my feet. A high-pitched screech and ruffled feathers inform me that I wasn't looking where I was going.

"Oh, Snowball. I'm so sorry, girl."

She pecks at her pristine feathers, not making eye contact with her attacker.

"I was lost in my thoughts. Can't you forgive me?"

I kneel and offer her my open hand. She slowly turns from preening her feathers.

"Would you like me to bow for forgiveness, oh feathered goddess?" I tease. "Or can you find it in your heart of gold to accept my apology?"

"Are you seriously on your knees, begging to a chicken?"

My head shoots up, and I see Vinny standing with his arms crossed. Humor dances behind his eyes, as he offers me a hand up. Then he grabs her Feathered Highness and shoves her into the crook of his arm.

"If it was up to me, this little flea-infested renegade would have been tossed outside already. How the hell she keeps escaping is beyond me. And I don't have time for this."

Vinny tosses Snowball into Elizabeth's room with a narrowed glare at her fluffy butt. "Step one more polished talon out of this door, little girl. I dare you."

I can't help the frown as I watch him.

"What is going on with you, Vinny? You love Snowball."

"I never said I loved her." He runs a hand through his hair. "Karen wanted me to come and tell you she was put on bed rest."

"What? Oh no. Is everything all right?"

"Yes, they are all fine, but the babies are trying to come early and the doctor thinks Karen should stay off her feet."

I wrap my arms around him. "Oh, Vinny, I'm sorry. Are they making her stay in the hospital wing?"

He chuckles. "She wouldn't allow that. She is in her room downstairs, reading a dirty romance novel involving multiple men and one lucky girl."

I laugh, then rub the back of my neck.

"I have been so busy lately I have neglected to notice how close Karen is getting to her due date. We are running out of time, Vinny. You know, I have been playing with the idea of asking if a nursery can be set up for her here at the Palace. That way, you two can continue to be close by."

"Karen would love that."

"Really? You don't think she will want to return to your house?"

"Karen wants to be wherever you are, Ann. We both do."

"I will talk to Christian about it as soon as possible and take care of it."

"Speaking of the King, how are you feeling about the up-and-coming wedding with him?"

"Oh, you know, a whole whirlwind of emotions all at once. Anxious, unqualified, take your pick."

"You are perfect for the job. Plus, almost the *entire* country voted for you. Have faith."

"I agree with the other two percent," I grumble.

He laughs and pats my shoulder. "Well, I am going to get back down there and keep Karen company. I'll see you soon."

I turn to go into my room and pause as I notice Christian striding around the corner. I wave at him and he returns my smile.

"Ann, was that Vinny going down the stairs?"

"Yes. Unfortunately, Karen is on bed rest and he is going to cheer her up."

"I am sorry to hear that. Are the babies still healthy?"

"Yes, they are just trying to make an early appearance. Could I ask you a huge favor, Christian?"

"As long as it brings a smile back to that beautiful face, the answer is yes."

"Can I set up a nursery for Karen here? And before you say no, remember how important it is to me to be a part of their babies' lives. And traveling back and forth will take a lot of time away from you. So, you see, it'll benefit everyone," I rush out before he can deny me.

"I see no problem with that concept. I mean, we have the additional rooms, and the hospital wing isn't too far—they can assist her if she has anymore complications."

I let out a breath. "Really? You don't mind? Oh, Christian! Thank you, that is very generous of you."

He tugs me into his arms and kisses my neck. "It is generous of *us*, Ann. We are a team now."

Before I can respond, he lowers his lips and takes my breath away, warming me to my toes.

I love this side of Christian: strong, confident, and caring. This is who I always knew was buried deep down. I feel privileged to be able to bring it out of him. We look into each other's eyes and my insecurities get tucked away. I was afraid that this transition into a romantic relationship would be a hindrance on our friendship, but it feels like it is making our bond stronger than ever.

My fingertips trail his chiseled jawline and up through his soft blonde hair while Christian leans into my palm.

"How about a round in the training room?" I grin up at him.

"Will this be our new routine, Ann?"

I lean forward and whisper into his ear, "I plan on having much more *intimate* activities… after the wedding." As I pull back, I am graced with his blush.

He clears his throat and straightens his red tie. "I can meet with you in the training area soon."

"Afterwards, I am going to stop in and check on Vinny and Karen."

"I think I can manage that too. We can talk logistics for the nursery with them."

Once we are in the training room, we battle it out. We begin to learn each other's moves and it makes it harder

116

to land a hit, but fun. Sam even joins us and teaches Christian some techniques she showed me, and by the end of our session, we are tired and sweaty.

Nonetheless, Vinny and Karen are happy to see us when we stride into their room. We talk for an hour and agree on a location for the nursery—on the first floor and close to the hospital wing. Christian insists on paying for the renovations as a wedding and baby shower gift combo for them.

I elbow him as we ascend the stairs to shower and get ready for bed.

"Thank you for your help. I really appreciate it."

"Ann, do twins run in your family?"

I scratch my chin. "I don't think so. Why do you ask?"

"I would hate for you to be that large and uncomfortable for nine months."

I laugh as we reach the top landing. "Did you just call my best friend fat?"

He stops at his door and frowns down into my eyes. "I would never be that insensitive." He watches me carefully, then releases a breath. "You were joking, weren't you?" He sighs. "That sarcasm is definitely something I need to get used to."

I rise on my tiptoes and plant a kiss on his cheek as I answer, "Only if you plan on surviving hurricane Ann."

His chuckle rings out as my door closes. I pause as I pass my reflection in my mirror and my hand stills on the feather necklace my dad gave me. My lids flutter closed as I embrace the memories of his silly dad jokes, especially when he took me bra shopping for the first time. I was so uncomfortable, but he lightened the atmosphere by placing the fabric against his chest and asking if I thought the color matched his eyes. Even though my dad didn't know what he was doing, he took it in stride and hung on by the seat of his pants.

Would that be the type of parenting Christian and I take on? I snort at the thought. Our children are going to be spoiled. And I can't see Christian taking a little girl shopping for undergarments. He would pawn that task off on a servant. But the thought provokes the question: will we make good parents?

My days pass quickly. Everyone is preparing for interviews and reports while Mack and the legal team put together the case for Mary and Max. At times, the tension is overwhelming but, with our nightly training sessions and visits with Karen, it evens itself out. And, before I know it, I am grimacing at the date on my desk calendar one morning.

I feel tears sting my eyes as I realize my dad's birthday is coming up, and I haven't visited his grave since we buried him next to my mom.

I am a horrible daughter.

My lip quivers as grief swallows me whole, causing my head to fall into my hands in shame.

"Ann?"

I look up and see Ryan standing over me. Ever since the engagement announcement, he has been keeping his distance from me. I wipe my eyes. "How can I assist you, Ryan?"

He leans his frame against my desk. "What's up?"

It should feel awkward talking to him again, but it's the opposite. It's like my heart has been secretly waiting for this very moment. And now that it is here, I can't stop the words from spewing out.

"My dad's birthday is coming up."

"I am so sorry. I didn't realize." He runs a hand through his hair. "Did you want to go visit his grave? You could place some flowers down for him."

"I just want him here, Ryan." My lip trembles as I try to hold it together. "You know, here to celebrate with me, with his deep belly laugh as we make more memories." A tear rolls down. "Like... my wedding day." I laugh lightly. "The day he never thought would come for me."

Ryan hands me a tissue. "It's okay to miss your dad, Ann."

"I know that, but I shouldn't have to miss him. He should be here!" I yell as the dam breaks and tears flow.

Ryan collects me in a warm embrace, and I breathe in his woodsy scent as I bury my face in his shoulder. "Look at me. I am pitiful. What Queen cries wanting her daddy?"

He strokes my hair. "There's nothing wrong with you. Come on, you know nobody expects perfection. I mean, just look at me and how much I have screwed up. You can't do any worse, right?"

"What happened to Ann?" Christian asks as he tugs me away from Ryan, collects me into his arms, and carries me to my room, before Ryan can answer. He gently sets me on the bed and extends his pocket square. After I clear my vision, I stare into his eyes, but words escape me, and my lip starts to tremble again. He guides my head onto his chest, and I listen to his steady heartbeat. As the soft thumps resound, a blanket of calm washes over me.

"I am sorry, Christian. I did not mean to pull you or Ryan away from your work. I feel so stupid acting like this."

He kisses the top of my head as his fingertips graze my arm.

"You are far more significant to me than anyone or anything. Now, please, explain why you are so distraught."

"It has been so hectic, that I forgot my dad's birthday is coming up. I feel like I abandoned his memory."

"You were kidnapped and almost perished. I'm certain your father understands. If anybody should be reprimanded, it is me. I should have memorized the date. I apologize, Ann. I will add it to my calendar so the day does not come up unexpectedly next time." He rubs my arms gently. "How can I assist you?"

"Well, removing your shirt may help get my mind off the pain."

The emotions that flash across his face are priceless, as he processes my request.

"You are such a handful. How about I send you and some guards to your house? You can collect some of your beloved belongings, check on your flock, and visit with Suzie and your family gravesite."

I snuggle into his strong chest and grumble, "Is there any way you might be able to bring my dad back from the dead. You know, swish your magic wand, curtsy in a tutu, and turn back time?" I sniffle.

"I am far from a fairy godmother, but if I could turn back time, I would. It breaks my heart to see you in pain."

"Christian, can you come with me?"

"I know we discussed a visit later in the year, but, Ann, is that what you require?"

I know he doesn't want to be away right now, especially with the trial coming up. But I don't think I can make this trip alone. So much has happened in such a short amount of time. I need his strength, even if he will be completely out of place.

I wring my hands together. "There are a lot of memories at the house, and it'll be an emotional trip. I know its bad timing, but I won't stay long."

"Let me clear my schedule and get Ryan and mom to pick up some public appearances for me. I am available to assist you, always and forever."

I stare into his eyes, wondering what I did to deserve his friendship. We got off on the wrong foot in the beginning, but now he is turning around full circle.

I bring my lips to his and kiss him tenderly, trying to express my gratitude in the only language he understands.

I need something to distract me from this horrible feeling of failure. I want to lose myself in this passion-filled haze. My fingertips glide to the buttons of his dress shirt. His breath hitches while his heartbeat quickens in response. As the desire for closeness has my body aching, I deepen the kiss and we stumble onto the bed. I undo the first two buttons but he gently collects my hands in his.

"Oh, Ann, I want *this* more than you know," he says

121

breathlessly.

My face is blazing as I step away from him. He kisses my knuckles gently, making the pain of rejection more bearable.

"Please, not now. When we do this, it will be done in *love*, not in grief."

I clear my throat, unable to speak past my disappointment, and rebutton his shirt. He grabs my chin. "I promise you, Ann. You will be loved until you are begging me to leave you alone."

"Oh, are you trying out my sarcasm? How does it feel?"

"Ann. You can be so mean at times."

I chuckle as I lay my head on his forehead while he runs his hand up and down my arm. We lie there for a few minutes, before Tim knocks on the door and asks for Christian.

"I should organize everything in the office. How about you take a stroll in the gardens? Or enjoy the weather with the chickens? I can get somebody to bring you some herbal tea?"

I wrinkle my nose. "Tea?"

"Well, you consume an immense amount of coffee." He tilts his head. "Maybe tasting another beverage wouldn't be so terrible?"

"I will try this drink you speak of." I roll my eyes. "But I'll make no promises."

"Ann, you will not be disheartened. And to show my appreciation, I will also send out some treats that you can share with the poultry."

"Okay, okay. That's enough butt-kissing from you." I shove him towards the door.

"I will take care of all the arrangements for our trip to your home, and by this time tomorrow, we will be on our way."

After walking the garden and clearing my head, I spend some time with the chickens and, as promised, Christian sends out some herbal tea and tea biscuits.

I smirk up at the handsome errand boy delivering my goods. "Well, looks like they have you multitasking today, Prince Ryan."

He lowers himself next to me, guarding the biscuits from the chickens while throwing sunflower seeds for them. "I volunteered to come out here because I was worried about you." He looks down at his feet. "It feels odd, having Christian step in and take care of you, when it has been my job for so long."

I stop mid bite. "But you have Cherie to think about now. And I am sure she isn't nearly as clumsy or emotional." I bump him with my shoulder.

The sun sparkles, making his dark eyes glimmer. "I miss *us*."

"Ryan, don't be silly. There will always be an *us*. But as friends and, soon... family."

"I guess, but I hate change."

"Don't we all." I quickly aim to shift the subject. "Did you warn Christian about my house?"

"There is nothing to warn him about, Ann. It is a nice

farmhouse."

"If by nice, you mean a shack compared to this place." I observe the ninja raptors chasing after their snacks. "It will be weird, having a King there."

He elbows me. "And a future Queen."

I chew thoughtfully as his words sink in. Maybe I am overreacting? I need to think positive thoughts. This visit is going to be *great*. We can talk and get to know each other more. I rub my arms. But why do I feel so insecure with Christian? It was so much easier with Ryan and Dan.

That night, Christian and I visit Karen and Vinny, and update them on our trip plans.

"I will travel with you and organize the security team." Vinny nods to Christian.

"I would not expect anything less from you. However, I assumed you would want to stay here, by your wife's side, while she is on bed rest."

Vinny swivels to Karen and she rolls her eyes. "Go. Get out of my hair for a while. We will be fine."

I slip a new romance novel into Karen's hands. "We can have Ryan come and check up on you while we are away, Karen."

"I would like that. And I think Cherie should visit me too. She looks like she is in it for the long haul, and I want her to be comfortable around me, especially since Ryan wants to be an uncle to the babies."

"I think that is a wonderful idea. Try to get some dirt on her while you are at it." I smirk before turning to Christian's scowl. "Any ideas on when Cherie will be returning home?"

"Cherie has not mentioned anything to me about leaving. I informed her that she is welcome at the Palace for as long as Ryan can handle her."

"Well, that's crude," I comment.

He shrugs, unshaken. "Well, it is true. That woman is very high-maintenance."

"Aren't we all?" I roll my eyes and giggle with Karen.

Christian leans towards Vinny and whispers, "Am I supposed to respond to that?"

Vinny shakes his head. "For your own safety, my King, no, I do not recommend it."

The Forgotten

The golden tendrils of morning wrap around my curtain, trying to entangle me in its alluring spell of false brightness. I groan as I stare at the ceiling. The anxiety of today's events weighs heavily on my heart.

I slide my fingers through Snowball's soft plumage as she hums at my side. I heard Elizabeth sneak her in last night while I pretended to sleep. Once the door closed, Snowball beelined to my treat stash and pecked at the drawer, until I got up and rewarded her for inconveniencing the royal hen; then we stayed up late talking. She fell asleep on my chest, well before my own eyes closed, and yet she is still dozing.

"Come on, Ann. Suck it up. You've got this," I chide myself as I try to breathe past the rock in my chest.

Snowball shakes and puffs out her feathers as she gives me the stink eye. "Don't give me that look. If you were a regular chicken, you would have been up *with* the sun."

She preens her feathers, obviously not entertained by my speech about her constituents.

I dress in my regular jeans and tee shirt then step out of my room and look around. The Palace is quiet and peaceful.

I breathe in and feel saliva pool as I smell fresh bread baking in the kitchen.

"Snowball!" I hiss as she bounces down the stairs on a mission, her bright red diaper swaying. "Crap!" I grumble before following the trail of plumage she is leaving behind. "You are going through an early molt, aren't you?

126

Poor girl, soon you are going to be so ugly with those bald spots," I blurt out.

Snowball stops, causing me to stumble before she glares up at me with her chin raised, daring me to contradict her beauty, no matter what season of change her body is forcing her through.

Taking the moment of pause, I snatch her and tuck her into my arm. I stare up at the door she led us to, and sigh before I push it open.

"Spoiled, spoiled, spoiled," I chant.

When I walk through the kitchen doors, the aroma that enticed me earlier assaults my nose, and I am suddenly taken back to my past, before my mom was sick.

I'd stir awake in the early morning hours and pitter-patter towards the kitchen. I would peek around the corner to see mom singing and kneading the soft, pale dough. Mom's eyes would sparkle with laughter, she'd turn down the radio, and pull out a stool for me to stand on. Together we would sing completely off-key as we dug our fingertips into the squishy material.

Then she would share her coffee and tell me stories while we waited for it to rise. Most of them were adventures of her and Sal, the wild-haired best friend she grew up with. Tales of them sneaking outside and playing flashlight tag for hours, before concluding their adventure by leaping into the ravine to rinse off the evidence.

Once the loaf doubled in size, mom would carefully slide it into the oven. Next, I would press my nose against the glass viewer and witness the white dough transform into a golden, delicious snack before my very eyes.

While I watched the magic, mom scrubbed the dishes

and tidied up the kitchen and eventually sat beside me. After she settled, she would set me in her lap, kiss my head, and whisper softly, "Patience is everything, Ann. Without it, we would just be lumps of dull, limp dough. Never to rise to the greatness we were created to achieve."

"Lady Ann, what a pleasure to see you again! What can we do for you?"

I blink away the memories and smile at the welcoming face of the head chef, Jock. Although he is my dad's age, he runs a kitchen with eight other chefs and is here every day, tinkering like a mad scientist. The dishes he expertly crafts are exquisite and fit for a King, while still being pleasing to common folk like me.

"Good morning, Jock. I am sorry to intrude on your morning preparations, but Snowball took off. And when I finally caught up to her, I smelled the fresh bread and was hoping for a sliver." Snowball wiggles in my grasp. "And I believe her Fluffiness would like a snack too, if you can spare it."

His eyes brighten as he strokes Snowball. "Of course, my Lady. Come, come." He ushers me to a counter and pulls out a bar stool. Then he slides over three freshly sliced pieces.

"Oh, but wait. I just canned a batch of fresh strawberry jam." He strides off to the enormous pantry and brings me a sizeable jar. "Let me know how it tastes, my Lady. I sweetened it with orange-blossom honey instead of sugar."

Jock sets down a bowl of stale rolls on the floor in the corner and places Snowball in front of it, while I spread the thick, fragrant jam on my slice and dig in.

The combination of sweetness and warmth melts in my mouth, and I groan as my taste buds explode.

"Jock, this is delicious!" I apply some to the rest of my slices, then I twist the lid and slide the jar over to him.

"You can keep it as a gift for being my guinea pig on so many of my recipes." He lets out a belly laugh before he grabs a wicker basket. "Here are some snacks for your trip home, Lady Ann."

I stare down at the fresh fruit, vegetable wraps, and my favorite monster cookies—all kinds of delicious smelling foods stored away with care. I look up at his smiling face. "Jock, this is above and beyond. Thank you."

"No problem, I'll make sure to have the guards pack it for your journey. Well, I must get back to breakfast prep, but if you need anything else, do not hesitate to let me know."

I watch him work as I finish my snack, then I make my way slowly up the stairs as the lack of sleep starts to wear down on me. When I get to the top, I run into Elizabeth as she comes out of her room.

"Good morning, Ann. You are up early, dear. Oh, and you found Snowball!"

"Yes, she somehow waddled into my room late last night."

Elizabeth collects the feathered menace out of my arms and offers a small white envelope. "If you wouldn't mind dropping this off at your dad's grave, I would appreciate it."

I blink at the small parcel and force down the lump in my throat.

"Are you sure you don't want to come with us and do it yourself?"

She pushes the burden back to me as her eyes glitter. "No, this way is better." She stands taller, swiping at her eyes. "Well, I am on my way to breakfast, care to join me?"

I look longingly towards my bedroom, wishing I had time for a nap. I give up and grumble at Elizabeth, "Sure."

We sit down as a butler offers us coffee. We are talking about the weather and timetable for the trial, when Christian turns the corner. Coffee spittle slips from the edge of my mouth, as I see him in the jeans and boots that I bought him for Christmas. They fit him perfectly, every curve and bulge. It may not be the first time I have seen him dressed down, but somehow, it doesn't lessen my appreciation. I tear my eyes away and dab at my drool.

The cocky grin spreads across his face as he lowers himself next to me and places his cloth napkin over one of his assets.

"Good morning, ladies." He sips from his cup slowly.

"I love the attire, Christian." I smirk over the rim of my mug.

He tugs at his baby-blue button-up shirt and Wranglers and shrugs. "I thought it would allow me to blend in at your homestead. And Ryan generously lent me his straw hat."

I pound my chest, trying not to choke. "He did?" I slide my cup away from me—it was just too dangerous this morning. "That was very generous of him."

I squeeze my legs together as I imagine Alpha Christian in a cowboy hat. Lord, help me.

"What's the matter? Do you dislike hats?" he says as he lifts his coffee cup to his mouth, feigning innocence.

"I love them. I just didn't think you did too." I bite my tongue, so it doesn't slip out.

He shrugs. "Well, I thought it was necessary to wear clothing options that were appropriate."

"That is very thoughtful of you. I promise you won't be sorry for deciding to wear them." I caress his palm.

The heated moment is short-lived as Ryan and Cherie come in giggling. They sit together, then look up as they realize they are not alone.

Ryan leans on his elbows, humor dancing behind his dark eyes. "Ann, did Christian tell you I am lending him my hat?"

"Yeah, thanks for that."

I nod as breakfast is served and we start eating our steak and eggs. I look around the room and smile as I chew thoughtfully. Even though I am going to visit my childhood home, it feels weird. This has become my home and these people are my family.

I pat my eyes dry again with my napkin. Christian lays a warm hand on my thigh, and I look up into his blue eyes. "Ann, are you feeling well?"

"Yes, I am fine. I'm just feeling overwhelmed with emotions, but in a good way for once."

We all look up as Elizabeth jumps up and runs out of the room. I blink and turn to Christian with a questioning eyebrow raised. He shrugs and continues his meal. As I roll my eyes at his lack of concern, I toss my napkin down and chase after her. It doesn't take long to locate her throwing things around like a mad woman in her room.

"Elizabeth?" I call out cautiously.

"They lost her!" Elizabeth screeches as she flings around loose clothing in her closet.

An exceedingly pale attendant pipes up, "I'm sorry. I just left for a moment, and I texted you the second I couldn't locate her." She turns her wide eyes to me. "Lady Ann, please. That hen is Houdini!"

I squeeze my eyes shut and pinch the bridge of my nose. "Don't worry about it. Why don't you go to the kitchen and ask Jock for some bread slices? Maybe that will bring her out of her hiding place."

Once they leave, I kneel by Elizabeth and rub her back. "Is this really about losing Snowball? Because that chicken is always up to *something* around here. And everyone knows she ranks higher than they do, so they won't harm her."

Elizabeth sniffles and shakes her head. "Of course it's about Snowball."

I'm not sure if she is trying to convince me *or herself*, but either way I nod and help her dig through her closet. If she's not ready to talk about it, I'm not going to force her. I know she and my dad had a relationship, and that losing him was difficult.

After we demolish the closet, I lean my head back on her dresser. This chicken is going to be the death of me. I glance down at my watch and cringe. Christian and I need to be on the road soon, and if he walks in and sees me on the floor, searching for Snowball, his attitude may be ruined for the entire day.

Suddenly a white blob catches my attention under Elizabeth's love seat. I get on my hands and knees and crawl over to it. I squint into the darkness.

"Well, you will be happy to know… I found her. But she is broody."

"Oh no, my poor baby!" Elizabeth reaches under the furniture without a second thought. Then she yelps and pulls out her hand. "She bit me! She has never done that before!"

While Elizabeth cradles her pride, I quickly snatch a handful of Snowball's tail feathers and yank. Her screeched commands can be heard throughout the Seven Seas.

"Calm down, you crazy lunatic," I say as I shove her into the crook of my arm.

"Ann, don't hurt her!" Elizabeth snatches the hen and kisses her growling head. "My darling, did she pull out your precious feathers?" Then she turns a scowl towards me.

"Elizabeth, I didn't hurt her. I was just grabbing her out. And if I didn't catch her that way, she would have bit me too." I point at Elizabeth's bleeding finger. "Trust me, when they get this way, they don't think straight."

The sound of the attendant's heavy breathing has us all turning towards the entryway. The poor thing lifts the bread victoriously before approaching her Feathered Highness with the peace offering.

"Mother, what has transpired in your bedroom?"

We each quickly go wide-eyed at Christian's sudden appearance, his attack mode activated.

"Oh, you know me, sweetheart." Elizabeth waves her hand around. "I lost my favorite gown and was searching high and low for it." She lets out a laugh as fake as her nails. "But the attendant just told me she found the dress in the laundry room." She pats the girl and nods. "All is well. Now, have a wonderful trip to Ann's house, dear."

"If that was *all* your attendant was doing, why does she look remorseful and have portions of bread shoved in her pockets?"

I take my cue and shove Christian out the exit. "Your mom is right. Come on, we have a long drive ahead of us."

When we make it past the threshold, I throw a sympathetic glare back towards the room.

Poor Elizabeth. She has no idea how hard it is to convince broody hens to stay off their nest. And of course, Snowball has no clue her eggs are not fertilized, so they will never hatch into baby chicks, only rotten stink bombs. I steal a glance at Christian. And I can guarantee Snowball would be outside for sure if she turned the Palace into a toxic gas zone.

As we stride out the Palace doors, I wave to Vinny as he stands by Sam and two other male guards in front of a dark SUV. Vinny nods my way while the driver grabs our bags and sticks them in the rear. Once I settle into the leather seat, I peek behind me and notice the basket Jock assembled for us settled next to a few bouquets of beautiful smelling flowers, some of every color, to place at dad's grave.

When we start our journey, the Palace passes, and the scenery morphs from lush green to dark grey as we merge onto the busy highway. I turn to Christian and watch him texting. I place a hand on his arm, and he glances up.

He offers me a half smile, and then looks back down at his phone. "Sorry, Ann. I am just making sure Ryan gets those reports filed correctly, or it will throw my whole system off."

"Listen here, Mr. OCD. It was *your* idea to drive out to the house instead of flying, so that you could get the full experience." I shake my head, pluck the phone out of his fingertips, and shove it in my day bag. "It will be fine. Now, let's enjoy the view and our time together."

A rare pout plays on his normally stoic face. "When did you become so dominant?"

"I have always been dominant. Now, come on, talk to me about anything. I'm an open book."

"Are you concerned about the hearing approaching?"

"I'm actually looking forward to it. They are finally going to get what they deserve. Are you anxious about it, Christian?"

"I acknowledge what Mary did was wrong, but at the same time, I cannot help but feel some sympathy for her."

My mouth falls open. I remove my hand from his and look away. I know I'm being immature, but I don't care. Mary doesn't deserve *any* compassion from anyone. Then I reach into my bag and toss him back his phone.

He glares down at it. "Ann, do not respond like this. I will do what is required of me when that time comes, but I wanted to be honest with you."

I look back out the window as trees and cars blur by. "I appreciate your honesty, Christian. But Mary deserves whatever she gets. The sooner, the better."

He clears his throat. "Ann, have you decided what you want to do with your residence?"

"No."

"May I make a suggestion?" When I ignore him, he sits up taller. "First, I propose that we gather up your flock and have a second chicken pen constructed at the Palace. That way, you can visit them when you want. And I give you my word that none of them will be butchered," he adds in quickly.

I let his words wash over me. Mr. Everything-Needs-To-Have-A-Purpose is going to allow my hens to stay at the Palace? Did someone slip something into his coffee?

I smirk. "That sounds reasonable."

"Next, I recommend hiring someone to take residence at your house, or possibly in a guest cottage, to take care of the property and the other outbuildings nearby."

I grimace at the thought of a stranger living in my home. It feels weird. "Maybe a guest cottage wouldn't be a bad idea."

"Excellent. I will discuss it with Dan and get him out there as soon as possible to build it. Then we can look through applicants to stay there full time."

At the mention of Dan, my ears prick up. Except for the occasional email, it's been a long time since we last spoke. "You are still in contact with Dan?"

"Yes, I keep tabs on all of your old love interests, Ann." He tries to hold back a grin.

"Very funny."

"I learned from the best."

"What about visiting my house after we pick someone to look after it?"

"You can stay whenever you choose. The employee would only be keeping up with the home maintenance and farm management. Maybe we can make arrangements to come seasonally? How about spring and fall?"

"You mean his royal highness is offering to return to the farmhouse, before he even looks at it?"

"Why wouldn't I? If it means that much to you."

I kiss his cheek. "Spring and winter."

He frowns. "Are you sure? It gets frigid in the winter."

"Oh, don't tell me you've never heard about this amazing invention. It's what we call heat, and it usually comes from a magical source like a fireplace."

He rolls his eyes. "Very childish. I know what you mean."

I elbow him gently. "Well, I learned from the best."

He gives me a long side-glance before we both laugh out loud.

"Can I run another suggestion past you, Ann?"

"I don't know about that, Christian." I lean towards his ear. "It looks like you are overheating with all this thinking."

My sarcasm has reached its limit with him and he carries on, "I was pondering about your morning ventures to the coop. And I would like to have a small cottage built along the back of the Palace for you. It would give you your own space, where you can have memorabilia, plus have the second coop attached to it. You could literally walk outside to your chickens every morning."

I tilt my head. "That sounds wonderful, but where would my adoring husband sleep?"

"Well, if you don't frighten him away first, I was planning on having him sleep right next to you in a king bed."

"So, we would go to sleep in a cottage surrounded by chickens? And you would be okay with it?"

He shrugs. "As long as the chickens, *all* the chickens, Ann, remain outside where they should be. Yes."

"That is a big sacrifice on your part. Are you sure? Because I am perfectly fine sleeping wherever, and with whomever my new husband turns out to be."

"There is only one man you are marrying, and that's me." He growls before he presses his lips against mine and kisses me deeply. "Ann, you have sacrificed far more than I ever could. If this is what you want, I will make it happen."

I smirk. "We are visiting spring and winter."

"You are a difficult woman to please."

"You have no idea."

"I don't mind a challenge, and trust me, I look forward to learning about *everything* that pleases you." He kisses my knuckles, sending tingles up my arm.

His ringing phone breaks our eye contact, and he barks his reply at the caller while shifting away from me. I tap my foot, waiting to see how long the exchange lasts. When he catches me staring, he pauses to apologize before he continues his string of curses.

I pivot and smile at Sam. "How did Vinny rope you into this trip?"

She shrugs. "I volunteered."

"Really?"

"Don't act so surprised, Ann. I do, *occasionally*, enjoy your company." Then she nods at Vinny and Christian. "Them, not so much."

"I agree. They are the worst."

Christian narrows his eyes at us while I giggle.

Sam sighs and leans back, looking lost in thought. "Do you have any siblings, Ann?"

"No, I don't. Do you have any?"

"Actually, I come from a big family with five kids total."

My mouth drops. "That is a lot! Do you miss them?"

"I miss them dearly."

"Do you keep in touch with them while you are at the Palace?"

"I wish I could."

"Did you have a disagreement or something?"

"No... They died in a house fire. The fire department said it was faulty wiring, and I lost my entire family in one night."

My face pales as I open and close my mouth. "I...

Sam… I am so sorry. I had no idea."

She swipes quickly at her eyes and nods. "Now I protect those in need." She frowns, looks back out the window, and whispers, "Because I couldn't protect them."

"Losing the ones we love… it's unbearable." I rub her arm gently.

"If anyone understands that, it is you."

I return her sad smile and look forward as we both reminisce over our lost family. I can't believe I never asked her about her family before. I glance towards Vinny and guilt rides up my spine. I know close to nothing about Vinny as well, only what Karen tells me.

Have I always been this self-absorbed? To not even ask questions about those closest to me? What a great Queen I'll make one day…

I am pulled out of my self-loathing as we finally park in my gravel driveway. I eagerly open the door, but Sam puts a hand on mine. "Let us do a quick sweep of the property and house first, to make sure it is safe."

Christian squeezes my leg. "Ann, do not be concerned. It is routine and for our protection."

I notice his phone in his lap and snatch it. "And this is for your protection." I squeal as he pins me to my seat. I hastily shove the phone down my shirt and smirk at him. He moves his hand towards my hemline, but I slap it away. "Nice try. Christian, you have been on your phone the whole way here. Can't you just relax and enjoy yourself?"

"If you allow me to retrieve it, I will be enjoying myself, *immensely*." He grins and leans in. I watch him carefully as my breath catches. He lowers his lips to mine, and then slowly moves his hand up my shirt.

I giggle and gently push him away. "You need to act like a gentleman."

"Come on, I will place the settings on vibrate for you."

I smirk. "Then I would have to move it to my front pocket."

His eyes glide over the front of my jeans as he processes my words. But before he can answer, Vinny opens my door and offers his hand. "My King and Lady, the house is secure."

I accept his hand and look around the small, brick, three-bedroom house while I breathe in the fresh country air. "It feels good to be back." My eyes sweep over the yard and land on Suzie's front door, waiting for her to emerge, like she always does upon my arrival.

Christian places his palm on the small of my back as he looks over the home. "It is an attractive place."

"It's definitely not a Palace, huh?" I wring my hands together and offer a forced laugh.

"It is your home, Ann. It means just as much to me as the Palace does. So, go ahead and give me the grand tour. What's the matter?" His eyes follow mine.

"Nothing, I was just looking forward to Suzie coming over and meeting you."

"I'm sure we will have ample time to meet your neighbor on another trip. We could even extend an invitation to her for our wedding."

Christian closes his hand over mine, and we step into

the quiet house. My eyes wander over all the ancient furniture and pictures. The memories begin to choke me, but I swallow them down as I force a smile and show Christian around.

As we move room to room, I purposely keep my dad's door closed and ignore the fact that he will never again grace this place with his presence. It was so much easier to pretend he was alive while I lived at the Palace. But now that I am home, the truth crushes me like boulders rolling off a cliff.

One by one, I remember the adventures we had and the many we've yet to complete. From the corner of my eye, I spot the tree house out the window in the field. Dad fixed it up every year, with hopes that someday my kids could have a fun spot to escape my craziness and chill with him.

I tear my eyes away and return them to the walls. Each photograph hanging up is another rock crushing me and threatening to level my sanity.

"You haven't shown me your flock."

Christian's words pull me out of my misery, and I blink past the memories and into his concerned gaze. Once our eyes meet, he steps towards me, pushing me against the wall with his body while his hand trails warmth up my cheeks to my scalp. I suck in a breath at the sudden closeness and my once-chilled body is ignited.

"I'm sorry about your father," Christian whispers. "If I could kiss away your pain, I would do it in a heartbeat." His thumb moves a tear off my cheek. "If you want to return to the Palace early, we can."

I plaster on a smile and lay a hand against his chest. "Thank you. But I'm okay. Really, I am. Now let's go meet

Dicky, Willy, and the rest of the girls."

I pull at his wrist, leading him towards the back door.

"Wait just one minute. Did you just say Willy and Dicky? What kind of names are those, Ann? Aren't they a little inappropriate?" he lectures.

"Oh, don't be a prude. We farm girls need some fun in our lives." I wink at him.

Once our feet crunch on the grass, the chickens rush over with their wings spread out. Christian arches a brow as he stares them down. I can tell he isn't impressed with our mismatched flock of Plymouth Rocks, Rhode Island Reds, White Leghorns, and mixed breeds.

"Ladies and gentlemen, I would like you to meet King Christian."

Christian turns to me, then back to the poultry. He kneels in the grass and offers his hand to them.

"It's a pleasure to meet your acquaintance."

The sight warms my heart and, at the same time, I can't help but burst into a fit of giggles. Soon I am bending over with tears.

"Well, how else am I supposed to speak to your feathered companions?" He pouts. "Ann, stop laughing at me."

"I wouldn't dream of laughing at you, your highness." I bow and start chuckling again. "I swear I am done." I swipe my face and stand straight. "Thank you for making me feel better."

Christian wipes his pants off in a huff. He turns and goes inside, but Dicky takes the opportunity to puff his chest out and charge Christian's leg, trying to spur him into submission. Christian jumps and yelps at the attack. He looks around quickly until his eyes fall on the feathery pimp. Dicky tries again but Christian sends him a glare and a warning kick. Dicky concedes and stalks off towards Fluffy, knowing he has been bested by the true King of the Roost.

Once Dicky is put in his place, Christian points a finger and narrows his eyes at me. "Do not even consider telling anybody about this incident. I mean it, nobody."

I press my lips together at his serious tone and can only muster a nod.

"Ann…" he warns.

He collects me in his arms and I laugh into his neck. It feels good being home again, and even better being here with Christian surrounded by my ladies. Even though he is completely out of his element, he is making an effort.

"Christian, you are King. Why do you care so much about what others think?"

"It is part of my obligations." He sighs at my arched brows. "I was born into this position, trained to represent our country's strength and unity."

"That has to be tiring, walking around with a stick up your butt all the time while having to please others."

"A stick? Really?" He sets me down. "My intelligence level is above average, so I don't tolerate others taking advantage of me, or shoving *anything* anywhere. If they can't recall what their societal position is, I am more than willing to remind them. Even if that means showing them a demonstration of my true capabilities."

His tone sends a chill up my spine.

I watch his clenched jaw and whisper, "Christian, are you telling me you have *killed* somebody before?"

"Yes."

I take a step back.

"What the hell? How can you say that so heartlessly?"

"Don't be such a hypocrite. You have been training to murder the individual who shot your father. What were you planning on doing once you met them? Having a tea party? I'll do whatever is required of me in order to protect my country. And yes, sometimes that means making enormous personal sacrifices."

I swallow. "Like marrying somebody you don't love?"

Even though I put up the front of a hard-ass, I am insecure, especially when it comes to Mary and her flawlessness. I don't expect an answer. I already know it.

He clasps my chin and tugs it upward. "Mary is an entirely different woman than you are. Her upbringing was extremely similar to mine, in more than one way." He searches my eyes for understanding. "And in some respects, crueler."

"Are you suggesting she was forced into the marriage arrangement too?"

Christian glances around and lowers his voice. "I do not wish to speak of this any further than to say: Mary's mother was not the warm and fuzzy kind you had. Nicole was abusive, manipulative, and demanded *nothing* but perfection from her daughter."

I have a million questions running through my mind,

but he releases my chin and rakes a hand through his hair as he looks around, and I know he will not say anything more.

"How about we go back inside before Willy tries to snatch you up next."

"Ann, why are some of your chickens thinning in spots? Are they ill?"

The change of topic makes me blink as I stare at the flock.

"They are shedding their dull feathers and exchanging them for new. It just signifies a fresh start, you know, a new season in their lives." I kneel and stroke Whitey on the head. "Although they are *supposed* to molt in the fall, you can't convince them this is *actually* spring, especially if the weather is tricky."

Christian's eyes twinkle. "It appears you are molting too, Ann."

"What do you mean?"

"While you are the same exact individual, you are shedding your previous ways of life and beginning a new season, by my side."

"Are you trying to say I was *dull* before?" I elbow him.

"If I answer honestly, I will be chastised, so I'll keep my mouth closed and pretend I did not hear your query, while I guide you inside for some refreshments."

I force down the urge to argue with him as I let his words wash over me. This is a new season in my life. And although I don't feel like my life was boring before this, it is definitely more complex. We hold hands as we walk back into the house, just in time to see the guards unload the snack basket Jock packed.

"When did my head chef start assembling picnic food?" Christian wrinkles his nose.

"Since you decided to fall in love with a plain girl from the country." I poke him in the chest.

The guards chuckle but quickly stop, as their leader shoots them an abrupt glance before returning to his plate.

After our snack, I wander back into the kitchen and eye the bouquets of flowers on the counter. The floral scent makes me miss our bounty of spring flowers from mom's garden. When she passed, we did our best to look after the delicate blossoms, but to no avail. The weeds took over and ruined her years of hard work and dedication.

Christian smiles as he watches me, his blue eyes glittering. "You do seem to love flowers. I think we should plant a flower garden around our cottage." Christian wraps his warm, strong arms around me and rests them on my stomach. "Just imagine it. A beautiful flower garden with butterflies and bees fluttering around. And every morning, opening up the windows to allow the fragrances in." He lowers his lips to my exposed neck and nibbles tenderly.

I ease into his body and hum softly. "Christian, that sounds breathtaking."

"Ann, this image of mine also has a barefoot, undressed woman in it."

"I wonder who that could be."

He turns me around gently. "She's a mystery to us all, this woman." He then kisses my forehead as I wrap my arms around him. My chest starts to ring, and I frown down at it while Christian smirks. "Would you like me to answer my phone?"

I reach down into my shirt and hand it to him with a glare. "Please try to keep it quick."

He gives me a peck. Then he answers it, walking into the living room.

I stroke the petals softly before picking up the flowers, along with Elizabeth's note.

Vinny comes around the corner with his all-business face on display. "We are ready to walk you down to the graves, Ann."

"I don't want a crowd for this, Vinny. I haven't visited since we buried him, and it will be hard enough."

He nods towards Sam. "It is me or Sam. You cannot go alone, Ann."

"I do not care who accompanies me. Flip a coin or something." I brush past them and find Christian sitting in my recliner looking through my books. "Christian, please keep those in order. I have a system you know," I say, narrowing my eyes at him.

"I would never dream of disrupting your hardcover harmony." He tilts his head. "Could you explain your sorting system to me?"

"It goes from my most favorite to least favorite."

"Ann, you are a complicated woman."

"Christian, I am going to walk down to visit my parents' graves before we lose daylight."

He stands but pauses. "Should I linger here with your books?"

"I just want some time alone, if that's okay?"

He crushes me to his chest. "Whatever you require, I'm here for you. But don't think I'm permitting you outside alone."

Sam walks up behind us and nods. "I will keep an eye on her, King Christian."

He arches a brow. "I would rather a guard with more experience assist Lady Ann." I elbow him and he grumbles, "But I suppose if you are vigilant, Samantha, you may watch over her." His eyes stare into hers intently.

She visibly swallows and bows. "Yes, Sir."

Christian kisses the top of my head before he returns to my chair. Then Sam and I walk towards the door. "Did Christian call you Samantha?"

"Yeah, it is easier for the guys at work to call me Sam, instead of Samantha. Because, I guess in their eyes, it makes me more masculine. But it's okay. I'm just glad to be part of the team."

I scoff, "Do they really think women are the weaker gender? Pfft. Who pushes out babies and bleeds for seven days out of the month *without* dying? That's right! We do."

She laughs and I soon join in. The world isn't perfect, not by a long shot. And the majority of men still view women as inferior. I raise my chin high. But that can change when I am Queen. I can make a real difference in more than one way.

At the sight of the weed overgrowth, I deflate. I brush off Pecker's rock and sigh at the fading paint. I can't believe how much time has passed since she died. My eyes tear up as I reflect on how far away Ryan feels from me, even after everything we had together.

I wish things could have worked out between us and fate would stop stomping on my heart.

Once I pay my respects to Pecker, we stride over to the many grey family gravestones. I walk slower, hoping to prolong the inevitable. Sam frowns and moves closer to my side, a hand on her holster. "Ann, is everything all right?"

"I just hate facing the truth that they are really gone."

She eases up on her sidearm, then stumbles on a rock with a grunt. "Isn't your neighbor supposed to be looking after this place?"

"Suzie is taking care of the house, along with the chickens, and is very generous with her time. I wouldn't dream of asking her to take care of the outside too."

"But wouldn't it be safer for the hens, and us, if it was at least mowed to a few inches instead of a few feet? You know to keep the snakes at bay?" She swats at a flying insect. "Stupid fluttering pests! I swear this demon has been buzzing by my ear since we left the house."

"Aw, has it been whispering sweet nothings into your ear? Maybe it likes you, Sam? You should bring it back to the Palace with you." I smirk at her scowl.

"No, thank you." She regains her professional stature as she pauses a few feet from the headstones. "I will be right here, Ann." She turns away from me.

I kneel in the soft, green grass in front of my parents' shared headstone and place the flowers down with Elizabeth's note. I settle cross legged in the tall blades as tears start brimming. I place my palm over the cold granite with their etched words and numbers. I take a deep breath and swallow down the massive lump.

"Oh, daddy, I am so sorry I wasn't able to be by your side in the end. Please forgive me." I wipe my hand across my face. "Mom, please take care of him for me. I know he can be a grumpy old man at times, but he loves you so much. And I know he is happy by your side, but I just can't help but feel selfish and want him here for everything: my wedding, my first born..." My emotions overwhelm me and I pound my fists on the granite platform. "It's not fair! Do you hear me?" I scream up at the cloudless sky. "Come back to me! Please?" I blubber out.

Sam kneels by my side and rubs my back. I slowly raise my head out of my hands, and look up into her green eyes as they shimmer with unshed tears. I wrap my arms around her, and she holds me until no more tears can fall.

My dad is gone and there is nothing I can *do* to bring him back, no amount of training, fighting, or words.

We gently pull apart, and I breathe deeply as I notice the sun sending bright orange and red hues in my direction. It feels like a sweet farewell painted just for me, and I silently thank my parents for the reminder that they are still watching over me.

"Thank you for coming down here with me, Sam."

She looks away from my tear-stained gaze and brushes a hand over the graves. "I am sure your parents are..." She pauses mid-sentence, then lifts up a single black rose resting beneath the grass. "Ann, is this one of the roses you brought with you?"

At her tone, I pluck the flower from her hand and inspect it. "No. I have never seen it before."

Once the words drop from my lips, there is an explosion and a chunk of my parents' headstone shatters and rains down on our huddled forms. Sam drops on top of me and yells into her earpiece, "Shot fired! I need back up," just as another shot rings through the air.

It splinters a sapling right next to me. I scream and flinch as the jagged edged bark cuts my exposed skin. Sam sits up against the headstone with her gun cocked. She peeks her head over the side as another shot is discharged. She yelps and leans to the side, holding her right arm and biting her lip.

"Oh no, Sam!" I crawl over as crimson soaks through her uniform. I rip a small strip of fabric from my shirt and tie it on her arm.

She slides the cold, metallic pistol into my hand and closes my fingertips around it. "I think our communication is jammed, but with all the gunfire, backup should arrive any second. I know you know how to use one of these, so if someone comes unannounced, fire. Do you understand me?"

The words can't register fast enough as the sound of crunching grass gets louder and louder. I peek over the edge and pull back just in time to hear a bullet whiz by my head. Sam waves to me silently while she points to my weapon.

You see, in all my training at the Palace, nothing prepared me for *this*. I thought I could do it, kill a criminal, but now that I am staring down the barrel...

The sudden stop of footsteps pulls me out of my

realization, and I hold my breath as I steal a quick glance.

Maybe I can just wound them? Or talk it out?

A man dressed in black with a ski mask glares down at me. I squeal at the gun pointed at my head.

Okay, so much for *talking* it out.

I take a deep breath and decide to use my head. *Literally*. I slam my skull into his stomach, knocking the wind out of him. Then we tumble around in the tall meadow until I hear yelling from above.

Is that Vinny? Just as I spot him, the shooter takes the opportunity to use my lapse in judgment and pins me down.

"Stop, we don't have to fight. Tell me what you want," I squeak out.

"We have tried to talk for far too long," the muffled voice replies.

When he squeezes me harder, I attempt to pull Sam's gun forward. Noticing my movement, he quickly collects his firearm and aims for my head.

I take a deep breath and squeeze my eyes shut, ready for my end. The gunshot explodes and my ears ring painfully. The ground beneath me vibrates. I lift my lids and see crimson everywhere. My gaze falls on the dead shooter as he lies at my feet, his eyes glazed over. I gasp and scurry back quickly before Vinny tugs me up.

"Ann, are you injured?"

I look down at my blood-stained clothes and shake my head, not trusting my voice. Is this what revenge feels like—numbness?

Once we get inside the house, Christian runs over, pale as a ghost. "Ann!" He leads me to a bar stool, and sits me down on it as his eyes wash over me. "You are covered in blood!"

He touches every part of me, trying to figure out where my wound is.

I blink, coming out of my stupor. "It is not mine," I whisper.

"Whose blood is it?"

"A man shot at us." The adrenaline suddenly wears off, and my body goes limp.

Christian scoops me up and strokes my hair. "Shh, rest easy. I have you. You are safe."

The front door flies open, and Vinny rushes in, carrying Sam in his arms before setting her on the couch. I pull away from Christian. "Sam! You are bleeding everywhere."

She smiles weakly. "I don't think they were aiming to kill—the bullet only grazed me."

I take off down the hallway to retrieve our first aid kit. I hear gunshots and my eyes go wide. "Are there more people out there? What is going on, Christian?"

"I am not certain. I have reinforcements in route, but for now, we just have to sit tight," he concludes as he guides me to the couch, right next to Sam.

I hear sirens and watch flashing lights bounce off the walls. Sam leans back on the couch as I finish bandaging her wound.

"Ann, you know I told you to shoot, not wrestle the

guy." She chuckles.

I purse my lips. "I wouldn't be complaining if I were you. Remember, I was the one who saved your life. By the way, you are welcome."

"You wrestled the shooter!" Christian blares.

Before I can clarify, men in uniforms rush inside and escort us out into a waiting helicopter. As we lift off the ground, I watch the world get smaller and smaller.

What the hell was all that? I shiver as the man's dead eyes swim behind my lids.

Christian pulls me out of my despair as he squeezes my hand.

I frantically look around. "Where is Vinny?"

"They are surveying the area to ensure there are no more gunmen."

"But that's too dangerous."

"Vinny is the best defense I have, Ann. He is more than adequate to handle a couple of low-life scum."

I lean my head back against the seat and close my eyes. Where did the shooter come from? Why didn't we see him on our way to the graves?

Christian wraps an arm around me and pulls me to him while he rubs my arm.

I peer at Sam, who has her eyes closed. She was willing to take a bullet for me. I swallow hard and shake my head at the thought of losing anyone else.

Soon we land on the helicopter pad on top of the Palace. As the door opens, I am ushered out quickly with

Christian pressed tightly to my side. Then a medic team wheels Sam to the hospital wing.

Christian helps me up the stairs and into the conference room, where Elizabeth and Ryan are waiting for us. While Christian guides me inside, Ryan topples his chair to the floor and runs over. Christian releases me to allow Ryan to embrace me.

"Ryan, I am in one piece. I promise. Not a hair on my head is injured."

As if I were a fragile baby chick, he leads me to the chair next to Christian. "What the hell happened? I thought this was a simple trip?"

Christian leans back and rubs his face. "Ann, can you tell us what transpired after you and Samantha went outside?"

I take in a gulp of air and explain everything, even the black rose Sam found.

"...a *black* rose..." Elizabeth says to herself as she stares at the wall.

Ryan looks to Christian. "Woah, wait a minute. I thought dad put an end to all of this?"

I jerk towards Christian as he shakes his head. "As far as I know, he did—although there have been accounts of insignificant quantities scattered around the country. But there is nothing to signify their ability to execute a coordinated attack."

"Who?" I ask.

They all look at me unblinkingly, then turn to each other. Christian explains, "We do not speak about them, because they are irrelevant outcasts. Very few individuals know of their existence, and if they do know, they are usually conspiring with them and are reprimanded. They call themselves the Black Rose. And they formed an uprising decades ago, but father flushed out their leaders and annihilated them."

"What are they fighting for?" I question quietly.

"A majority of them believe our Monarchy is an unjust dictatorship, while the rest are out for blood and are trying to gain power for themselves."

"Do they realize how hard the Palace employees work to run this country? It isn't easy, and you try to make it as reasonable as possible."

The door to the conference room swings open and Sam appears with her arm bandaged. "My King, I was asked to come to you immediately and provide my report."

Christian's eyes narrow, and Sam visibly swallows. "Samantha, explain to me why *you* insisted on strolling with Ann outside, and how *you* saw the black rose? In addition to all of that, why didn't you shoot first, and ask questions later?"

"Sir, the grass was extremely overgrown. It was hard to see the rose, but it caught my eye when I got close."

"This interrogation is far from over. Until further notice, you are off patrol duty." Christian observes my pale face. "Ann, why don't you have Ryan escort you to your room so that you can clean up. I will be in to check on you shortly."

Elizabeth rubs my arm. "Christian, maybe under the circumstances, we should keep her closer? After all, they did specifically target her."

"That is a valid point. Until we can collect more information, we will be especially cautious. Ryan, accompany Ann to my room while I get this subject matter resolved."

My mouth drops open as I look towards Ryan's outstretched hand, then at Christian. "Excuse *me*! But do I get a say in what I do? The last time I checked, I wasn't five years old, or your damn child. I'm a grown woman."

Christian runs his hands over his face. "Ann, please do not be challenging right now. We are attempting to protect you."

"By *excluding* me in all of your decision-making and locking me in your room? Is this how our marriage is going to be?"

Christian stands, slamming his palms on the table. "For the love of God, *listen* to me. I refuse to bury *you* next."

The air around us electrifies while Christian and I stare, each waiting for the other to blink, or back down. But this is one cock fight I'm not going to ignore. I need to know what I'm getting into, starting with this little boy band rebellion group.

"Could everyone please give me and Christian a moment *alone*?"

The tension is suffocating, and everyone is eager to escape. Once the door is shut, I close the gap between us. There's only one thing that can calm him down from his tornado of emotions.

I awkwardly wrap his arms around me. At first, he is unmoving, but with a sigh he relents. "I knew something like this was going to occur. That's why I intended to bring somebody else in as Queen." He pulls my chin up.

"You mean everything to me, and I *won't* lose you."

"Do not push me away, with the misguided notion you are saving me. We are stronger together, Christian. We need each other."

"But why can't I just safeguard you in a bubble?"

"Because, you see, there is a flaw in your plan. If I were in a bubble, how would you be able to touch me?"

"You make a valid point."

"Listen, we are both exhausted. Why don't we go to your room, change, and go to sleep? Then we can reconvene in the morning?"

"We should listen to Vinny and Sam's information first," he demands.

"We will wake up, *way* too early, and go through the reports *together*." I squeeze his hand and plead with him.

He runs his fingers through his hair and grumbles before stomping out the door. I am relieved when he advises the waiting group to get a good night's rest and meet for breakfast in the morning.

Elizabeth nods. "Great idea, son. And tomorrow, I will clear out Mary's old suite for Ann to stay permanently." She hugs me tight.

"Elizabeth, you do not have to do that."

"Do not be silly, Ann. The Queen suite will be yours sooner rather than later. And honestly, I really should have cleared it out for you a while ago." She turns to Christian. "Should I send Mary's belongings to her parents, or wait until after the trial?"

"Have the maids box her things up and send them out

to her parents as soon as possible."

"Good night. Sleep well." Elizabeth walks away.

Christian opens his door and ushers me through, but I drag my feet. "Christian, I am not ready for the Queen suite."

"It is the only adjoining room to mine. It was bound to happen."

My eyes roll at his possessive tone. I wander to his massive bathroom with some silk pajamas that were laid out for me. Before I can close the door, I catch Christian grinning in my direction. "What are you so happy about?"

"I just can't believe I finally get to have you in my room with *no* clothes on." Ugh, this man. I slam the door on his chuckling, hiding my red cheeks.

Once I start the shower, I let the steam build around my thoughts. How he can speak so openly about marital experiences is beyond me. I can joke around just as easily as everyone, but if I'm being completely honest with myself, I am beyond nervous. I suck in a breath as the realization hits me. I'll be getting married to Christian *soon*. What if I can't make him happy? What if I am a huge disappointment?

I step into the scolding water and focus on washing the day away. I clean vigorously to remove the dried blood. Once my skin is pink, I lean against the white porcelain and slide down to the floor. The steam of the shower creates a protective fog around me, while I lose focus on the present. And the bloody scene replays…

Could I have saved that man's life?

I put my head in my hands and sob uncontrollably,

remembering his unfocused eyes. I wonder if he had a wife or children? Could the consequences trickle down and have a domino effect? Did I just trigger the same pain Max caused when he shot my dad?

Why didn't Vinny ask questions before he fired? If Vinny hadn't shot him, could I have talked the man into putting the weapon down?

I was so ready to take a life for a life in the beginning, but now… now, I don't know.

"Ann?" I hear Christian call, but the darkness won't release its grip. I am suffocating within its confines, on the brink of a panic attack.

Suddenly, a white towel is pushed past the glass door and the hot water ceases to fall. I drape the cloth over my body, unable to muster the energy to stand and meet his gaze.

Christian steps inside. "Why are you weeping? Please, talk to me." He settles on the wet shower floor and pulls my head into his lap, while he strokes my dripping hair. "I cannot tolerate seeing you so distraught."

"I can't tell you, because you will think I am being ridiculous—as usual," I spit out.

"You must know me better than that. I might believe you are being *unreasonable*, at times, but I rarely speak it out loud." He smirks down at me, trying to make a joke.

I stare, my gaze unfocused at the wall. "He was shot because of me. He was trying to tell me something… I know it! But I'll never know what it was, because he is gone."

His hand stalls. "That man had a firearm aimed, with

every intention of killing *you*. I promise you... no amount of communicating would have ceased his actions."

I squeeze my eyes to force the tears to halt. "I would rather it have been me than him."

He collects me into his lap. "You don't understand what you are stating." He squeezes me tightly. "Your life is worth *everything*."

I look up into his icy orbs while my lip quivers. "But if he would have shot me, he would still be alive."

Christian grabs my chin, forcing me to look at him. "He would *not* have been living long *after*. I promise you that."

The intensity in his gaze sends a shiver down my spine. Before I can pull away, he crashes his lips to mine. The numbness ebbs as we kiss like there may not be a tomorrow. I feel a breeze graze my chest, as I wrap my arms around his neck and press my body against his.

A scream forms in the back of my throat when he pulls away and keeps his eyes closed.

"Please step out and get dressed before I take advantage of this situation."

I pull my towel up, step out of his lap, and exit the shower. I get dressed in the room, leaving him in the bathroom. Then I pop my head back through the door. "Sorry, crisis averted." I bite my lip as I notice his damp suit. "Christian, you are all wet."

He runs a hand through my locks. "Well, that makes two of us," he whispers softly, brushing past me and dropping his clothes as he gets into the shower. I turn away, shaking my head before I catch a glimpse of the full moon.

I meander around his meticulously organized room. I run my fingertips over the leatherbound books, notepads, and folders. This man works way too much. Does he ever take a break and do something he enjoys?

I pluck a frame from the dresser and reminisce. It was a photo I gave him last year of him scratching his nose, but to the untrained eye it totally appeared like he was picking it. I swore I would sell it to the highest bidder, but he stole the evidence before I could make good on my promise. I was furious that he went to such great lengths to destroy it. I accused him of caring way too much about how others saw him, and didn't talk to him for days. Then, one morning, I found this on my nightstand. No explanations were given, but I knew it was his way of apologizing.

I climb under the down comforter of his massive king bed and attempt to stay on one side, so he can have the other. I need to keep boundaries up, or things can escalate quickly.

As he enters the bedroom again, I pretend to be sleeping. But when he chuckles at me, I peek out.

"Could you possibly be any further away from my side of the bed?"

"Hey, don't look at me like that! I am just giving you your space." I wrinkle my brows at his chest. "I think you forgot your shirt."

"My space? Really? What am I? An elephant? You know what... do not answer that question." He shakes his head and climbs under the covers. "And, Ann, I never wear a top to bed."

"But... what if there is a fire?"

163

"Then there will be one less piece of fuel for the inferno." He drapes an arm around me and tugs me closer to his bare chest while humming softly in my ear. "This is all the room I need from you."

"Well, you *are* the boss," I tease.

He chuckles into my hair as he drifts off to sleep. "And you better not forget it."

Another Goodbye

After the day's events, we fall asleep quickly and wake up early—as promised. When we turn the corner, I gasp at the sight of Vinny. I squeeze him tight. "I am so glad you were not hurt." Then I pull back. "Are you okay?"

"You get shot and then question if I am okay? Classy broad you got there, King Christian." He shakes his head and follows us into the dining room.

Christian guides me to the table with his hand on the small of my back. Once we are all sitting and sipping coffee, Christian clears his throat. "Vinny, do you have any new information on the attack?"

"Yes, but I recommend we speak privately, after breakfast, Sir."

I bristle, but Christian holds up a hand, stopping the words before I spit them out. "It is safe to discuss here, Vinny."

"There were two more shooters—both worked under the Black Rose. One is dead and the other is here, awaiting further interrogation."

"Here?" I squeak out.

He nods. "Yes, I thought Christian may want to exchange *words* with him."

Christian's eyes darken. "Why didn't your unit see them during your security sweeps?"

Vinny glances my way. "They were inside the neighbor's house."

My mouth falls open and I stutter, "Suzie's house? But

then, where is she?"

Vinny looks from Christian to me, then back to Christian before he shakes his head slowly.

I leap up, knocking my chair over. "No! She must have just been away... visiting her children. Vinny, please, tell me she wasn't there," I beg.

"Ann, listen, I am really *very* sorry but she..."

"No!" I cover my ears.

Christian stands beside me. "Ann, please calm down. This is not Vinny's fault."

"You are absolutely right. It is all *your* fault! I should never have come here!"

I push past him and down the stairs, until I shove through the outside door and gasp in the fresh air. My feet have a mind of their own, and I end up on the bench inside the chicken pen. The girls look up at me expectantly, while a black and white hen hops into my lap. I glare at her, not wanting her pitiful stare either, but my heart soon melts as my fingertips glide over her.

"Life isn't fair. But of course, you know that, don't you, Henrietta?"

I hear the pen open, but I ignore the intruder as I keep my head down, trying to hide the tears as they silently plop on to the chicken's plumage. Ryan eases on the bench, and I let my head fall on his shoulder. He offers the hen the crust of his toast, and she greedily moves from my lap to his. Then she darts past her friends with it dangling from her mouth.

"I wish I could express my sympathy in words, Ann, but I can't. You do not deserve all of this pain and suffering."

When I don't respond to him, he frowns and places a hand on my leg. "Please do not blame anyone but those murderers. They are trying to isolate you, Ann. They are trying to get your compassionate heart to turn cold and vengeful... Do not let them win."

"It is so hard not to, Ryan." I look up into his dark eyes. "I feel like I have lost *everything*."

From the pen gate, Christian says, "Certainly not *everything*, Ann." He squeezes onto the bench on my other side and offers me a cup of coffee and breadcrumbs. The chickens perk up and surround us excitedly. I throw the crumbs and sip my coffee. "We will always be here for you, no matter what."

I clutch the mug. "Everyone I love is dying and I do not want you two to fall into that category."

We sit in silence as we watch the sun illuminate the darkened sky. Then Ryan squeezes my leg gently as he stands. "We are willing to die for you, Ann. You are part of our family now." He pauses at the gate. *"You can't go back and change the beginning, but you can start where you are and change the ending."*

"C.S. Lewis?" I question.

He nods before he walks away. I lean my head gently on Christian's shoulder. "Christian, I am sorry. I did not mean what I said to you in there."

"I know. You were disturbed by the news of Suzie's passing." He kisses the top of my head. "We have contacted Suzie's immediate family and proposed to compensate them for her funeral services and burial."

I tense as I imagine her children and grandchildren having to say goodbye—all because she was in the wrong place at the wrong time. "Is there any way I can be there for her services... to pay my respects?"

"We will send flowers and explain the unique situation, but my main priority is keeping you protected."

"I want to know how she died."

He shakes his head. "Let me keep this from you, Ann." Then he holds me tighter. "Please."

I lean into him and nod. It doesn't matter what happened to her. She is gone.

Christian squeezes my hand and pulls me back inside the Palace. Vinny is waiting by the door and watches me carefully. "I am sorry for snapping at you, Vinny."

"I understand. You are having a rough time. I wish I didn't have to tell you the bad news." He gestures at Christian. "The prisoner is in the interrogation room, whenever you are ready."

"Go see your wife, Vinny, and get some much-deserved sleep." He pats Vinny on the back and guides me to the staircase as Vinny heads to Karen's room. As we ascend the stairs, he turns to me. "I am going to speak with the prisoner. Do you want me to drop you off at the office, or your new room?"

"Why can't I go with you?"

He shakes his head. "It is not something I want you to witness."

"Why not? I need answers too! Wait. Are you planning on hurting him?"

"It depends on how cooperative he is with my interrogation."

I cringe at the thought. Then Christian walks me to my desk and I grin at the new bouquet. "These are beautiful."

"You will get new flowers every week for the rest of our lives. Among other pleasurable items." Then he bends down and kisses my cheek. "Ryan should be in the office soon. Do you want me to wait for him to return before I leave?"

"Don't be silly. No, go and be Mr. Boss-Man. I will be fine."

"I will return as soon as I can."

His face transforms into a dark mask, before he pivots on his heel and begins rolling up his sleeves as he goes. I would not want to be on the receiving end of that determined look.

Once he turns the corner, I sift through my desk for a piece of lined paper and a pen, then I begin a letter to Suzie's family. I offer my condolences and apologize for not attending her services. After I finish, I seal it carefully and press it to my chest to try to stop the ache.

Suzie was the stepmother I never knew I needed growing up. I'm really going to miss her.

I slip the envelope into our outgoing mailbox and frown as I look around the office for Ryan. When I do not see him, I decide to hunt him down.

"Oh, I am sorry, Elizabeth. I did not see you there," I say as I back-peddle into her in the hallway.

"Not a problem, Ann. Actually, you are the person I am looking for anyway, so you saved me from having to search."

"Oh, really?" I try to not whine out at her chipper tone.

Elizabeth ushers me inside the Queen suite, buzzing with excitement. "What do you think?"

My eyes trail over the brightly lit room with its wide-open balcony, queen bed, couches, mounted tv, dresser, gigantic bathroom with a Jacuzzi tub and shower, walk-in closet, and desk with stationery and a laptop. "It looks very big."

My hand reaches for one of the many frames hanging on the wall. A photo of me and my dad at Christian and Mary's wedding. His smile was so wide, his eyes glittering with pride.

"That picture is one of my favorites," Ryan says from my side. I jolt out of my memory and turn towards him, not sure when he came in.

Elizabeth stands on my other side and rubs my arm. "Jack really was a great man, Ann. And he was so proud of you." She dabs her eyes before clearing her throat. "Ryan has been helping me set up your room. Did we do a good job?"

"Thank you both. It is beautiful."

"Well, I should probably go, mom. I am meeting Cherie for lunch before she returns home," Ryan says as he hugs Elizabeth.

I tilt my head. "How are you two doing?"

"Good. But she has work and family she has to get back to."

"And are you two dating again?" I push out.

"We are giving it another try." He rubs the back of his neck. "And hopefully there will be no interferences this time around."

"Ryan, are you happy?"

He looks down at me and offers a sad smile. "As happy as I can be." He kisses the top of his mom's head. "I'll see you later." Then he goes out the door quietly.

Elizabeth turns to me. "How about lunch with your mother-in-law?"

I allow her to lead the way to my beautiful balcony, where a table is set up with some soup, sandwiches, and salad. "This is lovely, Elizabeth. Thank you."

She waves off my comment. "It is the least I can do for you, after everything you have done around here." I stare at the cloudless sky and marvel at the birds as they gracefully soar. "Ann, have you thought much about the wedding?"

"No. I have not."

"I was thinking it may be nice to lift everyone's spirits and do it *before* the trial ends."

"Either way, it doesn't matter to me." I stab at the lettuce.

"Wonderful! There is a lot of planning to do so we should get started on it soon."

"Just point me where to go and tell me what to do, and I will be happy with that. I honestly do not care about all the little details."

She pauses mid bite. "You are joking, right? What little girl doesn't daydream about her fairy-tale wedding with

171

her handsome prince waiting for her at the end of the aisle?"

I shrug.

"Well, I can plan it out if that is *really* what you want." She chews. "What about your guest list, or maids of honor?"

"I do not have many friends. So, the guest list will be small, just Vinny, Karen, and Sam."

"Are you sure you do not want to invite anyone else?"

"I would love to invite Suzie and my dad, but that is out of the question. And I doubt Christian would allow my chickens in the procession."

"Okay, I will take care of the guest list. And it looks like Karen and Sam will be your bridesmaids." She beams as she goes into planning mode.

"Oh, wait. I am not sure Karen can go because she is on bed rest."

"Well, I'm sure I can talk to the medical team and make some kind of arrangement, considering the situation."

"That would be great."

"Have you and Christian talked about where you want to go for the honeymoon?" Elizabeth asks.

"Not that I can recall, but with everything going on, I doubt he will want to go far."

"I am sure we can find a romantic place nearby for the two of you," Elizabeth sings as she swipes over her phone.

I slide my meal away and purse my lips. "I am going to excuse myself and visit Karen, so I can tell her the good news. Thank you again for your help and for lunch."

"Of course, dear. And don't you fret—I have everything under control."

I sneak out of my room, and as the weight of the world rests on my shoulders, I lean against the closed door. I take a deep breath and squeeze my eyes. What am I going to do? Everything is happening so fast. I didn't even think to ask how one goes about having a wedding... *before* the prior Queen is formally dethroned. Worse yet, I am not sure I care right now. I can't keep up. I suddenly get the feeling some creep is watching me. When I look over, I see Christian.

"Stop giving me that look, or you will gain more wrinkles." I push off the wall then pause as I notice his attire. "So, how did the interrogation go?" I gulp as I take in the blood splattered on his sleeves.

"Although he did say that they guessed we would be at your house for your dad's birthday, I couldn't encourage him to tell us who the leader of the group is. I put him on ice, and I am continuing the questioning later when he has had time to reconsider my generosity."

I don't dare question *the ice*. I clear my throat. "Is my dad's birth date public knowledge?"

"Yes, birthdays can be uncovered easily. Once they saw us pull up, they moved in on Suzie's house. Then they waited until they saw you head towards the graves."

"Wait, but why me?"

"I intend to dig deeper for more answers, but for now, how about we get something to eat?"

"Well, I ate already, but I was heading to Karen's room

to check on her. Do you want to come with me?"

"I should return to the office and complete the financial report. How about a raincheck?"

The door behind me opens and I falter as Elizabeth strides out. "Christian! Good! I have some questions about your wedding day."

He arches a brow at me, and I smirk. "Well, that is my cue! See you later." Then I kiss his cheek and sneak away as Elizabeth grabs Christian's arm and strolls with him into his office, chatting away about her arrangements.

I descend the stairs and make my way to Karen and Vinny's room. I knock lightly and crack open the door. I see Karen sitting in bed reading. She looks up and grins as she waves me in. I tiptoe to her and sit on the bed, making sure not to wake up Vinny on the other side.

She embraces me over her large belly. "I hate bedrest, I'm so bored all the time. I am so glad to see you."

"I'm sorry it has been so long since my last visit. How are you, Karen?"

"Bored to tears, but I have a good romance book to keep me warm. What about you?"

I lean back. "I am a mess, *as usual*." I update her on my recent events. "Oh, but there will be a wedding soon and you get to be my maid of honor."

"I am sorry, Ann. I wish I could be more help to you."

I smile. "You will soon, right?"

"Yes! As soon as I pop. And they gave me a steroid shot to help with the babies' lung development, in case they make an early appearance. Although the doctors are still trying to keep them in as long as possible, but when it happens, it happens."

"Then you can help me in my daily struggles again." I laugh bitterly.

"Ann, sweetie, I'm here for you now. What's *really* going on?"

My lip trembles. "I've just always imagined it would be Ryan and me, you know? We talked about everything. And now, it feels like he is miles away from me. I want my friend back."

She wraps an arm around me. "Of course you miss him." She rubs my back. "But these things are out of your control. Is Christian not making you *happy*?"

I blush as she draws out the word.

"Well, of course Christian and I have a connection, but it was supposed to be Ryan, you know?"

Karen waves my statement off. "Ryan is a wonderful guy, but he is young and he can be a little flaky. I mean, haven't you noticed? It's like he only wants you when another guy wants you."

"That's not true," I huff.

"Oh, come on. Christian, then Dan, and then Max." She counts on her fingertips. "But Christian, he has always loved you, girl."

I pout. "Christian was the same way. He only noticed me *after* Ryan and I started hanging out. Then he called out my name at the engagement party instead of Mary's because of his jealousy towards Kevin. So, you can't say that's just Ryan's flaw." I rub my face. "You are only saying that because you know I *have* to marry Christian."

175

She pokes my cheek. "The love triangle has to end sooner or later, Ann. Now tell me what I need to teach Christian so he can make you happy." She wiggles her eyebrows.

"Karen!" I turn scarlet. "We have only kissed."

"Oh," she draws out.

I wring my hands together. "My dad was old school and taught me to save myself for marriage. But what if I don't do it right? What if I suck and he divorces me because I can't make *him* happy?"

Karen grins and pats my leg. "Oh, girl, how much time do you have? I am here to give you all the tips and tricks." She slides her book over. "And when in doubt, read some romance novels. They are chock-full of useful information."

I bite my lip as I listen to her talk dirty. How she could be so open about this topic is beyond me, but she is very knowledgeable and I appreciate her honesty. Because, like it or not, I will be married and expected to give Christian heirs.

Then the topic morphs into pregnancy and about her labor and delivery plans.

"Ann, you will be there, right?"

I arch a brow. "Where, exactly?"

"Oh, you know, at the end of the tunnel with a baseball mitt."

"I am not that great at catching."

She erupts in a fit of giggles, then slaps her hand over her mouth as Vinny stirs.

"If you won't catch them, you can hold my hand while you take notes because, remember, you will be next."

My mouth goes dry as her fingers sweep over her large belly. "Karen, please let me enjoy my wedding night first."

"How many are you expected to pop out? Because for me, I am one and done, or at least these two and done."

"I never asked, so I am not sure. I guess two… at least. Or until I have a boy."

She grabs my hand. "I will be catcher for you."

"Thank you."

I yawn and lean my head on her shoulder, as she returns to her book, reading the dirty passages out loud as she goes. Eventually, I drift off to sleep until I feel someone lift me out of the bed.

"Christian, what are you doing here?"

"The King has come to collect his beautiful Queen."

I send a small wave to Karen as Christian carries me away. "Christian, I can walk, you know."

"But then I couldn't carry you like *this* and demonstrate how powerful and competent I am."

I nuzzle my face into his chest as he climbs the stairs. "Did your mom chew your ear off?"

"Mom has a lot of ideas for the wedding." He looks down at me. "Ann, I want to thank you for your generosity. Mary wouldn't let mom plan a thing for our wedding. And you are basically giving her free reign and letting mom do what she has always wanted, for the daughter that she never had."

Being reminded that this is *not* Christian's first wedding sends a stabbing pain right through my heart. The fact that I am so inexperienced is embarrassing as well. I always figured that *if* I did marry, the man would be just as inexperienced. "I see," is all I can squeak out as we enter my room.

He sets me down, and I feel his eyes on me as I walk to the unfamiliar bed and pull my shoes off. "Did I say something to upset you?" I shrug and stare at the wall, not meeting his eyes. "You can tell me."

"It still bothers me that you have been married before and this... well, this isn't going to be your first wedding night," I push out.

He arches a brow. "I am not sure I understand what you are saying."

"You are more experienced than I am!"

He smirks before he pins me to the covers as his lips trail my neck. "I can alter that really quickly. Just say the word."

I bite back my moan. "Christian. I am being serious."

"There is absolutely nothing wrong with you being inexperienced. It actually thrills me because I get to share these *experiences* with the woman I love, and we can experiment with new skills together." He kisses my forehead.

"You are only saying that to make me feel better."

"What can I do to make it up to you? I wish I could turn back the hands of time, but I cannot," he says into my hair. "Are you having second thoughts?"

"No." I swallow. "I can do this."

"That's my girl. Now, how about dinner?"

"I am actually exhausted. Raincheck?"

"Okay, well, I suppose I can see you in the morning if you want to go to bed soon."

"But you need to protect me. Maybe I should sleep in your bed, just in case," I tease.

"Yes, those terrifying closet beasts are loose and we can't be too careful, now, can we?"

"I wish it were just closet monsters," I whisper softly before gathering my chicken pjs as I get ready to dream the day away.

When morning comes, we have breakfast together with the family and then meet Vinny in the conference room for an update.

"I'm sorry, King Christian. The prisoner didn't give us any more information, and unfortunately, he didn't make it to morning."

I pale. "You mean he died?"

I fall back into my chair, feeling nauseated.

"We never obtained a name, but we are running his DNA through our databases."

"Keep me posted on the conclusions, Vinny." Christian shuffles a folder and clears his throat. "The trial date is scheduled for Max and Mary and it shouldn't be lengthy, especially with all the evidence built up against them."

We both turn as Ryan strides into the room. As he takes his seat, I can't help but notice his casual outfit and cute, pretty-boy grin, like he doesn't have a care in the world.

"You are late." Christian scowls.

Ryan waves his comment off, pulls out his phone, and taps an app. Next, he pushes it towards me without a word.

"What is this, Ryan?" I ask.

"My wedding gift to you and Christian."

I look up at Ryan. "You want to give us a house?"

He leans towards me and I take a deep breath. The calming, woodsy scent drifts off him in waves. He taps his phone and zooms out to the location of the house. It's within the Palace's massive walls but secluded by trees and a small flower garden.

"It is a nice getaway. It used to be an old maintenance shed." He shrugs. "I just redrew the plans and made it a simple, one-bedroom studio." After I nod my approval, he hands the design to Christian. "It is inside the Palace walls and near the rear for easy entrance. Plus, it has a fenced backyard for chickens, or maybe a little playground for children."

I can't breathe.

This can't be happening.

How can Ryan be so relaxed with all of *this*!

"Ryan, that is very kind of you. But I'm sure an espresso machine would have been a great present too," I push out.

"It should be ready for your honeymoon, if you want to test it out."

Christian tosses Ryan his phone and leans back. "Impressive architectural designs. You ought to take on larger endeavors around here, brother."

"If I do all the work, then what will that leave *you* with?" Ryan smirks.

"All I am stating is you have remarkable abilities, Ryan, and you should use them more." Christian turns to me. "I neglected to mention... your flock from your home will be arriving tomorrow."

"My chickens?"

"Now that there is no one available to look after them on the farm, we are moving them here. Remember? We've talked about this."

"Of course." I rub my temples. "I am sorry. I did not realize you wanted to do it *immediately*. We don't even have a pen set up for them."

"I am two steps ahead of you, Ann. I discussed this with Ryan and Dan, and they are working on it."

I clench my jaw at the name. Dan has been keeping his distance, and it hurts more than I care to admit. I figured it was because I chose Ryan over him. But Dan and I were still friends—at least *I* thought so.

We have emailed each other when he sent me his manuscripts to look over, but nothing more than that.

"*Dan* is here?"

"Yes, he is outside working on the cage now. He is confident that it will be done in time for their arrival. Then he will be working on our cottage with Ryan."

"Sounds like everything is taken care of."

"Not necessarily everything, Ann. We need to find a property manager for your farmhouse. I have some applicants on your desk when you are ready."

"That was fast. Suzie isn't even buried yet."

"I figured we would require assistance over there sooner rather than later." He shrugs. "I assure you it is a decent group of qualified candidates. Dan assisted in selecting them and even proposed to take residence there himself, if need be." He grabs my hand. "Ann, we know this is a challenging time, so we want to make this as simple as possible."

Elizabeth breezes into the room, waving around bridal magazines. Ryan and Christian use this opportunity to make their great escape while I resist the urge to beg them to take me with them.

"When would you like to try on dresses, Ann?" Elizabeth beams.

"Whenever you want," I push out the question as a statement.

"The seamstress will arrive this afternoon, and I plan on getting Karen and Sam fitted at the same time."

"Sounds good."

After the meeting, we go our separate ways. I beeline for the office exit, but Christian grabs my hand. "Ann, is everything okay?"

"Yeah, I just need some air and to stretch my legs, so I was going to go see the pen's progress."

"That's a wonderful suggestion. I'll go with you."

Once we are outdoors, the scent of roses eases my

tension. When we reach the area where the cottage will be, I see Dan's tall frame. He glances up from his clipboard and gives a charming smile.

"Lady Ann, King Christian, great to see you both again."

I look around. "This is some project you have going on here."

"Not as big as the chicken coop we worked on together."

I brush past him with my arms crossed. "Are you sure there is enough space for the flock?"

"Of course. They will be more than happy here." Then he arches a brow. "Did you want to look at the plans?" He places his clipboard into my outstretched hand while he rolls his eyes. "Women, can't live with them, but can't live without them." He elbows Christian. "Am I right?"

Christian shrugs. "Not all of them, just *this* one." He points his chin towards me.

They both chuckle as I flip through the papers and stick my tongue out. "You two are hilarious. Are you ready to stop acting like children? Dan, the pen needs to be larger."

I feel the warmth radiating off his chest as he steps behind me; his breath tickles my neck as he explains, "No, that's a good size. It offers about three square-feet per chicken." His arm skims my side before he points at the math.

I am rewarded with an "oof" as I slap the clipboard into his chest. "Is cannibalism, stress, and pecking acceptable also, *Dan*?"

The air around us fills with intensity, until Christian clears his throat and we both pivot towards his voice. "Ann, I am more than certain that Dan is intelligent enough to do his work, *without* making any severe errors." He turns a pointed scowl at Dan as he plucks me towards his chest. "Why don't we go back inside and let him do his *job*?"

"You can go inside if you have to, Christian. I need to straighten this man out."

Dan's eyes sparkle with mischief. "You heard him. Now get out of here and return to your desk job." I pout and grab for his papers, but he playfully holds them above my head. "Let me handle this while you obey your fiancé."

"Oh, please," I draw out. "Give me a break, Dan. You both have *no* concept of what the chicken coop requires. Just let me make some *minor* adjustments."

"Absolutely not, *my* Lady. I am the professional here; you may break a nail. Oh! Wait! Is that a hammer I see? Oh no! Is that a heel? Yes, you seriously need to move back, where it is safe."

My mouth drops, while my palm itches to slap his cocky grin. "Oh, really? Why don't you enlighten me on how many chickens you have raised in *your* lifetime?"

"Ryan is the one who organized the data and dimensions. If you intend to modify them, *he* is the one you need to communicate with," Christian informs me.

I purse my lips at Dan. "And here I thought you were the ringleader."

Dan throws his hand over his heart. "Lady Ann, are you angry with me?"

"Yes. You are bullying me," I fib, not wanting to admit his lack of communication with me is the real reason.

"Lady Ann, please do not be upset with me. How about a present to make everything right again?"

"You have nothing that I want."

He strides to his tool bag and pulls out a paperback book, before waving it in the air. "Really? Nothing?"

My eyes widen at the prize, but then I narrow them. "No, nothing."

"So, my third book, signed *and* not even on the store shelves yet, doesn't mean anything to you?" I shrug as he walks towards me and playfully sniffs it. "Hmm, it still has that *new* book smell. Plus, no creases or dog ears."

"Did you really sign it?"

He hands it to me. "I did even better than an autograph for *you*."

I cautiously turn the page and there, on the inside cover, is his signature. Then, a few pages later, the dedication reads: "Thank you to all my avid and encouraging readers, especially my favorite editor, Lady Ann." I try my best not to let the smile spread across my face as my heart warms. "That was very thoughtful."

"It is true. I wouldn't have caught all those comma splices without your vigilant eyes. Plus, I am hoping that adding in the future Queen's name will get me more readers." He winks.

I roll my eyes but hold the book to my chest. "Thank you, Dan. When I read through it, I will make my notes and email the results."

His genuine laughter warms my heart. "I wouldn't have it any other way." He turns to go back to his work but pauses. "I'm sorry to hear about Jack... and your kidnapping. It's good to see you smiling again, even after all the heartache." Then he continues his work.

I stare at his back as he puts more distance between us. "Thank you," I whisper softly, unsure what else to say and wishing I could read his mind.

Christian tugs me towards the Palace, and once we are inside my room, he leans on the door frame. "Ann, why didn't you inform me you and Dan were still speaking?"

"You didn't tell me you were still talking to him either. Besides, I know how controlling you are. You could have easily found out on your own."

He crosses his arms over his chest. "What did his note say?" I pass him the book, and he frowns. "*You* are Dan's editor?"

"*One* of his editors. He is a self-publishing author so he needs all the assistance he can get."

"Why didn't you tell me?"

"Because I did not think it was important—it is just business."

"So, Dan reimburses you for your editing services?"

"At first, no. I was editing for free, but now that he is making money, he insists that he pays me for my time."

A low growl escapes Christian's lips as he smashes me to his chest. "Ann, next time you are involved in another man's life, please inform me."

I shove off his chest. "Have you told me about all of the

women that you have been involved with?"

He narrows his eyes. "All of them that I have ever had a personal interest in, you've had knowledge of."

"Christian, we will inevitably be working around the opposite sex. We just have to trust each other."

"I do trust you, but I just got blindsided out there, because I never knew you were assisting him, let alone having time to read."

I laugh and pull him down to the couch with me. "Christian, I will always make time to read. That's like asking you not to be bossy." I smirk at his scowl. "If it makes you feel better, I do not edit anything but Dan's stuff."

There is a knock on the door, and we both turn to see Ryan pop his head in. "Dan told me you needed to see me, Ann?"

Christian grumbles as I reply, "Yes. Ryan, I think we need to extend the pen's length."

"We have limited space in that area, plus your flock has dwindled some since last year, so it should be more than adequate."

"Wait a minute. How many did I lose?"

Ryan pulls out his phone and looks at his notes. "Six."

"Why didn't I notice?" I whisper softly.

I am a terrible feather mama.

Ryan frowns at me. "I am sorry, Ann. I asked Vinny to do a head count when you guys went over there. I am sure the losses were due to natural causes."

"Then I guess that square footage is good." I can't meet his gaze, as I feel my eyes water.

"Are you okay?"

"Yes, of course I am." I rub my face. "Did Dan show you his new book?"

"Yes, but he wanted you to read it first, so I literally just *saw* it. Is it good?" He leans forward in his seat.

I smile, but then I notice Christian's narrowed eyes. "I can give it to you when I am done."

He nods, glancing towards his brother. "Christian, come on, stop pouting. They are just friends."

"I seem to recall you informing me that you two were just *friends* too," he grumbles. "And don't ask me to stop pouting, because if I remember accurately, *little* brother, you pilfered my helicopter to beat up Dan—when you believed he slept with Ann during the blizzard."

"Well, I'm glad you are following in *my* footsteps, big brother." Ryan stands. "Good luck with him, Ann."

I send a glare to Christian before I rise to my feet to walk Ryan out. I attempt to ease the tension by changing the topic. "How is Cherie?"

"She is doing great. Thank you for sending her a wedding invitation."

"Oh, well, your mom is handling the guest list. But I am glad she is including Cherie."

Ryan nods, not meeting my eyes. I shut the door and pivot towards Christian. "I need to meet with your mom and talk about wedding dresses. And you need to go back to work."

"Ann, I don't want to argue with you." He stands and readjusts his collar. "Please accept my apology, so that we can move past this."

I push out a breath. "From now on, I will tell you every aspect of my life, personal and business."

"That's all I ask." His lips quirk and his blue eyes sparkle. "Feel unrestricted in your level of detail — incorporate everything."

"I did sneak a Danish this morning that I forgot to tell you about. Oh, and I was planning on wearing my black lace underwear today, but I decided red would be more colorful."

The corners of his mouth twitch. "You are impossible." Then he lowers his warm lips to mine, as he glides his hands up and down my back. I shiver as soft tingles run up my spine. All too soon, he pulls back while resting his forehead on mine. "Do I have to go to work?"

"Well, you are the King. You can make up the rules."

"I wish I could *make up the rules*, as you say. Because if I could, we wouldn't have clothes on."

I push against his chest and tug him out of my room and to his office, then I give him a quick kiss and meet Elizabeth in the conference room.

We snack on finger sandwiches and flip through a few wedding journals as we wait for the seamstress to arrive. When she appears, the day passes quickly. We discuss all the different aspects of the dresses and even the suits, until my head is aching. We then make our way to Karen's room to get measurements and stretch our legs.

We descend the stairs, and I skid to a halt when I spot

Sam and Dan standing outside Karen's room, giggling. As we near, they look up, still smiling.

"Hey, Ann! Are we early?" Sam asks, glancing at her watch.

"No, we are running a little behind. I am sorry we kept you waiting."

"Not a problem. I found this handsome man to keep me company." She elbows Dan lightly.

Dan returns a warm smile towards her. "It was my pleasure, Samantha." He looks up at me and nods. "I will not keep you girls. Have a great night."

Sam watches him saunter off, then grins at me. "Oh my, Ann! Why didn't you tell me *that* was Dan! He is so sweet!"

I clear my throat. "Shall we get started, ladies?"

I push open the door, and Karen's eyes light up when we all saunter in. "Thank goodness! I've been rereading my pregnancy book because I've read everything else."

The seamstress starts getting Karen's measurements.

Sam pivots to me. "Dan told me about his books and that he would get me copies of them," Sam sings as she twirls her hair. "Actually, I confessed to him that I wrote a few novels too."

"Really?" I arch a brow at her.

"Don't act so surprised." Sam huffs.

"I just didn't think you would have time, with training and all."

"They aren't published, but I do love to write." She

smiles. "He said he would take a look at my manuscripts for me, maybe over dinner." She wiggles her eyebrows.

I nod as the seamstress tugs my arms out from my sides and runs her ruler all over my body. "That is wonderful, Sam."

"So, you are okay with Dan taking me to dinner?"

"Dan's a grown man. Why would I have a say in who he shares bread with?"

"Well, I know you two have a history, but I mean, you are moving on… so Dan should too, right?"

"Well, we have the measurements we need. Thank you for your time, ladies," Elizabeth announces as she and the seamstress leave us to our girl talk.

After the door closes behind them, Sam stretches out. "I need to grab some coffee before I fall asleep. I'll see you later."

Karen arches a brow at me as the door clicks. "So, are you really okay with Sam going after Dan?"

I lean against the pillows. "It is complicated, Karen. Of course, I want Dan happy and if things were different, I may have considered being serious with him. I mean, we have so much in common, and it is so easy to understand each other."

"Maybe, but I think you would be bored. Christian is different from you, so you have to work at your relationship. That makes it more of a challenge."

I snort. "That is an understatement."

We hear a knock and see Christian pop his head in. "Am I disturbing anything, ladies?"

I shake my head. "Just girl talk. Come in."

"We received permission from the doctor, allowing Karen to walk down the aisle as your maid of honor. The only stipulation is that she has to sit in the wheelchair during the surrounding events."

"That is great news!"

I turn to see Karen yawn and I offer her a hug. "I'll let you get some rest. Sleep well." I place a kiss on her belly.

Christian wraps an arm around my waist once Karen's door closes. "I hope you understand... I do trust you. It's Dan I'm hesitant about. I mean, I have complete confidence in his abilities as a contractor, but anything past that, I do not."

"Thank you for trusting me. And you will be happy to know Dan is actually having dinner with Sam."

Christian rubs his chin. "Really?"

"Yes, they seem excited to spend time together outside of the Palace."

Eager to move away from this conversation, I collect his hand and tug him towards the dining hall. Once we arrive, we eat and laugh together as we talk about the chicken coop progress. As I look around at all the smiling faces, I feed off their positive vibes and I am glad we decided to do the wedding early. It really does seem to ease the tension of the Black Rose rebellion breathing down our necks and lift everyone's spirits.

After dinner, Christian and I go to our separate rooms and I do my normal nighttime routine. Then I settle under the comforter with Dan's book. As I crack open the cover, Christian enters from our adjoining door. "Ann, may I come in?" I peek over the top of my book as he strides into the room. "Do you need to read that now?"

"Aw, are you seriously jealous of a book? Come on, I thought we were past this?"

He shrugs as he climbs under the covers and tugs me to him. I shake my head and start reading again. Soon I notice that he too is skimming the pages. Eventually, we start arguing over the fact that I read *too* fast. Christian claims that I need to slow down so he can catch up. Then he groans when I find errors and pause to make notes. After a few hours, we close the book.

"Does Dan constantly conclude his novels this way?"

"Yes, he enjoys keeping his readers wanting more." I set the book down on my dresser and stretch. Then I rejoin Christian in bed. He holds me close and kisses my head as he drifts off to sleep. "So, what did you think about Dan's book?"

"It was well penned," he mumbles into my ear.

I grin and fight the urge to say "I told you so" as we silently fall into a deep sleep.

Preparations

At breakfast the next morning, Elizabeth announces that she has dresses for me to try on and suits for the guys. So, we all take turns going into her room to change and get her approval. As I wait, I sort through the applicants on my desk that Christian left for me. All of them are qualified and very well versed in farming and house management.

"Lady Ann?"

When I focus on the speaker, I press out the invisible wrinkles on my shirt while avoiding his gaze.

"Hey, Dan. How are you?"

"I'm doing well. Thanks for asking. Oh, I see you received the applications." He points at the stack of papers.

"Yes. And now it is just more of an emotional task than a physical one... for me to pick."

"I can only imagine." He rubs his neck. "Is there anything else I can do to make the process easier?"

I rise to my feet. "No, I think this is something I should do on my own, but thank you for the offer." I arch a brow as he rolls my pen around on the desk. "Is there something I can assist *you* with?"

The pen clangs on the floor before he curses and bends to retrieve it.

"Could we possibly talk outside, privately?"

"Sure. I wanted to stretch my legs anyway."

194

I follow his lead down the stairs, and once we get outside, we walk side by side through the fragrant garden, while butterflies flutter around us enjoying the sweet nectar.

"Ann, I want to apologize for not being around when Jack passed away."

"You could have called." I kick a pebble.

Dan stops and grasps my hands in his. "Listen, I'm not perfect and I'll never pretend to be. I just want you to know... if I could have been here, I would have. But my family needed me, and they come first. I hope you can forgive me."

I pull my hands away. "Sam told me you two are going to have dinner together and talk about her books?"

Dan blinks. "Yes, that's true. I do want to take Sam out."

"Well, I hope you two have fun."

"Ann, you know, if things were different..."

I force a smile. "Don't be silly. Sam is a great woman and I'm delighted for you."

Dan pulls my chin and watches me carefully before he sighs and strides off, shaking his head.

Why did he have to date somebody I know... *and* at the Palace? I wish I was mature enough to let it go. But I'm not. I facepalm. Why can't I shake this stupid love triangle? Wait! This has turned into a wild love *square*! What is wrong with me?

Once he is inside, I glance towards the only things that make any sense to me—chickens. The flock from my house will be arriving today. And settling them in will be no easy task. I rub my arms and look around at the well-polished grounds. Tears spring from the corners of my eyes as I feel my façade splinter.

I hear footsteps from behind me and turn to see Ryan in a pressed grey suit.

"Ryan, are you spying on me?" I swipe at my eyes and stand straight.

He laughs lightly. "No, mom sent me. She has some dresses for you to try on."

I nod and look down at my feet. "What time are the chickens arriving?" I glance up into his dark eyes as mine start to tear up again.

He frowns. "They should be here before nightfall."

I sniffle. "And everything is ready for them?"

"Everything will be fine, Ann." He opens his arms wide.

I sigh as we embrace. Why does this feel so right? Why can't things be different? Then he leads me into the Palace, to Elizabeth's room.

"There you are, Ann! I have a few dresses I think you will absolutely adore!"

Ryan relinquishes his hold on me before he returns to the office, and Elizabeth ushers me towards three big white dresses hanging up in the corner.

The first one is white, skintight, and silk—which I *know* I won't be able to even breathe in. The second looks like it was made for a ballerina who loves wearing gigantic tutus (it reminds me of a loofah) and it's way too puffy for my good taste. But the third one… I reach out and trail my fingertips over the thin, V-shape top and pause on the floral embroidery.

It is stunning.

I follow the pattern down to the bottom and find it adorned with wispy feathers. I have never seen anything like this before.

Elizabeth touches my arm. "Why don't you try it on?"

It is a tight fit but not too unbearable. I walk out slowly, hearing the train ruffle behind me. When I turn the corner, Elizabeth throws her hand over her mouth as her eyes water. Then she guides me to her full-length mirror, and I stare wide-eyed. The dress is absolutely breathtaking, with its plunging neckline, beaded lace, and intricate embroidery. My hands instinctively go down to the feathers, and I run them between my fingers.

"Do you like it?" Elizabeth asks.

I only nod, not sure words could suffice at this point. "So do I." Elizabeth gestures towards the seamstress, giving the final approval.

Then it hits me. I'm getting married. In this very dress.

Adrie pulls me out of my panic. "Do not worry. You really do look lovely, Lady Ann."

I swallow back my terror. "Thank you, Adrie. Could you help me out of this before I ruin it?"

Later, I groan at the stack of papers piling up on my desk and the note about a press conference to discuss the wedding preparations. My hands begin to cramp just *thinking* about the time I will need to get it all done.

I stare longingly out the window as the sun teases me. I am not made to sit behind a desk all day.

I work until lunch, then I stretch before making my way to the dining room with Christian, where we eagerly receive our smoked salmon entrees. Soon Elizabeth graces us with her presence with a scowl on her face. When she passes Ryan, she hands him some money, which he pockets with a wink.

"What was that about?" I elbow Ryan.

"Just a friendly wager we had going, which I won."

"Really?" I stab my fish. "Wager on what, exactly? Nothing illegal I hope, because you know the King will have your head," I tease. Christian lifts his gaze from his soup bowl and narrows his eyes at Ryan.

Ryan clears his throat. "Let it go—it was nothing major or illegal."

Elizabeth rolls her eyes. "Oh, Ryan, just tell them so we can move on from this topic." When he ignores her, she continues, "I was having a difficult time trying to obtain a dress Ann would adore. And when I *finally* found two options, Ryan advised me that neither would be successful. So, I bet him he was wrong, because these gowns were perfect and it was two against one." She sighs. "Well, he cheated and went behind my back to speak with the seamstress about a custom-made option. And today, I set them *all* out for her, and Ann picked the one Ryan thought she would." She shrugs and returns to her meal.

"Wait just a minute… You made that dress?" I pivot to Ryan.

"No, don't be ridiculous. I just kind of *designed* one in my sketchbook and showed it to the seamstress; it was really no big deal."

"It is beautiful. Thank you."

Our eyes meet, then he returns my smile before clearing his throat and sipping his water.

Christian dabs his lips. "You just so happened to have a dress fashioned for Ann in such a brief amount of time?" Christian slams his napkin down. "You are delirious if you think Ann is wearing the gown that you made her for *your* wedding arrangements." Then he stomps out without a backward glance.

"Please tell me Christian is overreacting as usual. Ryan?"

"I never intended to cause a fight." Our eyes meet before he too storms out.

Elizabeth sets her spoon down with a clang. "These boys are going to be the death of me." Then she groans at her watch. "Well, we are out of time—the press conference is going to start in twenty minutes."

I shove my half-eaten meal away and nod.

After we scurry to freshen up our makeup and hair, we meet in the garden for the press conference. We play nice for the crowd of cameras and answer all the questions they have about the wedding. I plaster on a smile as I stand next to Christian. Afterwards, we do a few candid shots, shake hands, and return inside the Palace.

As we make it through the door, I pause to slip my heels off and massage my sore ankles. When I straighten, I see that Christian is already halfway up the stairs.

I huff and fight the urge to throw my shoe at the back of his pompous head.

"You can run, but you can't hide!" I grumble as he disappears around the corner.

"I wasn't trying to hide." A male voice calls from behind me. I pivot towards the voice. "Oh! Hey, Dan. I'm sorry. I didn't see you there." I throw my arm out in the direction of where Christian scurried off to. "I was actually talking to… you know what, never mind. What are you up to?"

"I was just with Sam, having a quick lunch. And now I'm heading outside to check the progress on the pen. Do you want to tag along?"

"Sure, as long as you don't judge me for going barefoot."

He laughs and shakes his head as he opens the door for me. "I wouldn't dream of it."

I run my hand over the sanded wood and breathe in the pine scent. It is definitely bigger than the measurements they showed me.

"It looks great, Dan."

He ushers me through the pen gate and points out the waterer, feeder, and nesting boxes. "Do you think it is ready for them?"

"It looks good."

He turns to me and his smile drops. "Usually, you speak with more than three or four syllables. Is everything okay?"

I force a smile. "Of course."

200

"It would be okay if you are feeling overwhelmed right now. I mean, it is a lot to take in." He looks into my eyes. "I am here if you need to talk to a friend."

"Thank you, Dan, I appreciate that. I am just processing everything while I try to keep my sanity."

We stand there in a comforting silence. It feels good to just take a pause.

Growing up on the farm, I learned that slow and steady won the race, but at the Palace, it is ass backwards—everyone is constantly shifting between events, press conferences, and paperwork. It is maddening.

Will it ever slow down so we can actually enjoy life?

"You'll get through this, Ann. You are the strongest woman I know." Dan lifts my chin. "Don't lose that, or your remarkable capacity to show compassion. Because the country needs it."

He plucks a white flower from the rose bush and slides it behind my ear, before he runs his thumb over my wet cheek. "Our hope for a better tomorrow rests in your hands." He kisses my palm, and then guides me back to the Palace, where we separate.

When I get to the third-floor landing, I twirl the stem between my fingertips as his words sink in. Why do the people need hope? Have I been so selfish that I've missed their suffering? Can I push past my pain to help them? I can, but first, I need to man handle the unruly cock.

I stomp into the office and knock on Christian's door, before I throw it open.

He looks up from a stack of papers and arches a brow. "What happened to your feet? Are you pretending to be

Cinderella again?"

"No, I took my heels off after the press conference. You would have noticed that, if you hadn't run off afterwards."

He frowns and then looks back down at his papers.

"What has gotten into you? You have been so distant." I snatch the document. "What are you working on, Christian?"

"I am reviewing the evidence for the trial."

"Is there a problem? Not enough proof?"

"No obstacles on *that* front." He watches me carefully, his dirty blonde hair almost touching his eyebrows when he looks down. "Your wedding gown, on the other hand..." he grumbles.

I clench my jaw. "Christian, it really is a lovely dress. You should see it."

"Ann, I can tolerate most incidents about our *situation*, but I have to draw the line when my little brother is inviting you to wear the gown he envisioned you in for your wedding day with *him*."

"Ryan never personally asked me to wear it; he was just helping your mom."

He rubs his hands over his stubble. "Ryan deliberately positioned it in front of your face, knowing you would select it."

I cross my arms over my chest. "Christian, please. You are overreacting."

He stands quickly, his face red. "I am not overreacting! You are being naïve! He still *loves* you, and this is a means to weasel his way back into your heart!"

I arch a brow. "Did you just say *weasel*?"

He grabs my elbow. "Please leave my office, Ann. I don't have time for your games. I have actual work to do."

"I'm not playing games! Ryan and Cherie are together, and he was just trying to contribute to our wedding. *Our* wedding! You and your mom have been planning everything, and the one thing I want you are trying to take away from me!"

"I'm not discussing this now—we can talk later."

I bite my tongue, cross the office to my desk, and plop into the chair. What a jerk!

Out of the corner of my eye, I see Ryan glancing my way. I swivel my chair in the opposite direction, but then my phone rings. "Yes?" I glare at him as I answer.

"Mom was desperate for ideas." His brown eyes stare at me. Then he looks away as someone passes between us. "Ann, I never meant for Christian to get angry," he says through the receiver, though we are feet apart.

"I know, Ryan, and I told him as much." I rub my temple. "But he is trying to sort out Mary and Max's mess and his trust level isn't very high." I start organizing my desk.

"Dan told me you went to go see the pen again. What do you think?"

I lean back in my chair. "I believe *somebody* listened to my recommendations."

"Or someone didn't have her reading glasses on when she read the measurements to begin with."

I stick my tongue out and we both burst into a fit of giggles before we hang up.

The day passes quickly as I finally finish my workload. As I stretch my limbs, I look up and see that almost everyone has gone for the day. The only thing remaining on my to do list is for me to go through the applicants for a house manager for the farm. I start leafing through them, and soon I am able to narrow the list down to two possible candidates. Both sound eager and able, but neither seem right for the job.

From the corner of my vision, I see Christian escape from his office and I wave. He lifts his chin in acknowledgment, and then he turns the corner. I rub my face with my hands and grumble as I stand.

Why does he have to make everything so damn hard? Why do I always have to be the one to sacrifice what I want?

I glance towards the dining room. I know he expects me to share a meal with him, but I can't handle the inevitable tension-filled dinner—not tonight. So, I go to my room, grab my workout clothes, and give Sam a call, asking her if she wants to meet up. But I'm disappointed when she reminds me of her date with Dan.

"Why don't you come to my room and help me pick an outfit?" she sings.

"Well, I really wanted to beat some of these emotions off."

"Come on! It will be fun! Plus, by the time we are done, Vinny should be there and you two can spar. I'll see you soon!"

I grumble as the click signals the end of our one-sided debate. I stare at my adjoining room door and wonder what Christian is doing. Can we really get married… with the history we have? I rest my head in my hands, wishing my dad was around to hug me and tell me everything was going to be okay. I take a quivering breath and stand up as tears fight to overcome me. With one foot in front of the other and a fake smile plastered on my lips, I walk out my door, through the halls, and towards Sam's room in the servants' quarters.

Before my hand can tap on the wood, she answers, her eyes sparkling and her hair sticking up. "I need help, Ann!" She yanks me inside.

I pull the soft-bristled brush out of her trembling hand and glide it through her hair. As I tug on a knot, she observes me in the mirror. "What should I wear?"

"Whatever you feel comfortable in."

"Ann," she whines, "that would be my uniform, and I doubt he wants to see me in *that*."

"Well, he saw it on you when he asked you out, so something about it must have turned him on." I smirk at her scowl. "Fine, how about a nice sundress or a skirt?" I wrap her hair into a tight bun, grab the hair spray from the dresser, and mist. "There."

"That looks great!"

"I learned everything fashion-related from Karen, because my dad was absolutely hopeless."

"Karen is a pretty amazing friend, isn't she?" She rubs an emerald ring on her finger. "I wish my family were still around." She pushes out a laugh. "My mom would fuss over me *just* meeting Dan and going on a date with him. And my dad and brother... well, they would not like the fact that Dan was a contractor. But my sisters..." She sucks in a sob. "They would squeal with delight and share embarrassing stories of how I sucked my thumb and picked my nose."

I hand her a tissue. "I'm so sorry, Sam. My dad once said to not be afraid to lose someone, and to relish the time we have with our loved ones... I never knew how true his words were until now."

She watches me in the mirror then pivots. "Are you really going to marry King Christian?"

My eyes widen at the bluntness, and I straighten my back. "Of course I am."

She grabs a skirt and a light blue shirt. "It's just... you and Prince Ryan..."

I hold a hand up, stopping her words. "He is happy with Cherie."

She watches me carefully, before she nods and shuts the bathroom door. I let a breath out and massage my temples. Then Sam emerges and twirls, allowing the skirt to flow out and frame her hourglass figure.

"You look beautiful, Sam."

As she dabs on her lip gloss, she watches me again. "Is Prince Ryan really not into you? And are you really over him?"

I let her words wash over me, and I almost spit out a lie to get her off my back. But as I look deep into her eyes, I decide to tell her the truth. "Does it really matter, Sam? We both have no choice. We might as well make the best of the cards dealt to us. I mean, you know what

I'm talking about—you lost your family and instead of drowning in self-pity and *what ifs*, you are protecting others and making the best of life."

She clasps my cold hands. "Look at me and my big fat mouth. I should not have brought it up. I am sorry. The amount of pressure you must be feeling right now—" She lets go, and then grabs silver hoop earrings. While she slides them in, she smirks. "At least the wedding night will be entertaining, right?"

I shake my head and turn as I hear a knock on the door. I get up to answer it, and standing in front of me is Dan, in nice black dress pants and a light-green button-up shirt. I notice the collar is messed up, so I reach towards him to fix it.

He tilts his head. "Ann? Am I at the right room?"

Sam steps out and his eyes glide over her. "Sam, you look beautiful." Then he offers his arm. "Ready?"

She nods as she accepts his gesture. Before they turn the corner, Sam throws a quick grin over her shoulder as she mouths, "Thank you."

I stare until they disappear around the corner, Sam's laughter ringing through the Palace.

When I enter the training area, it seems empty until I hear grunts coming from the back, and I spot Vinny and Christian. I groan and turn to leave before they can see me, not wanting to deal with Mr. Stick-In-The-Mud right now.

"Ann!" Vinny says as he waves me over. I drag my feet towards them, avoiding Christian's stare. "Sam told me you were going to stop by and work out." He tosses me gloves.

I silently complete some light cardio, and attempt to hold in my drool, while I watch the muscle show between Christian and Vinny. But all too soon my dirty movie ceases, as Christian stomps out without even acknowledging my presence.

Vinny stalks towards me, covered in sweat and breathing heavily.

"Well, it looks like you already had your workout," I tease him.

He chugs a bottle of water. "Nah, you know me. I am a hunky beast." He winks. "I am *always* ready to rumble." He pulls his gloves on and smirks at me. "So, your man just gave me a few bruises. Anything you want to talk about?"

I stumble. "Christian didn't tell you *anything*?" I regain my composure. "I mean, you two are like BFFs, right?"

He shakes his head. "When the King gets angry, he stays silent but enjoys punching off steam."

I throw my hands up in defense as Vinny offers a weak punch. Then I bring my right glove over, and he blocks the strike, pushing me back.

"It seems like you and Christian have some things to work out."

"Why do you say that?"

His grin throws me off. "Because when you are mad, you miss important details." He jabs and slams into my nose.

I yelp, step backwards, miss the mat, and fall. I land on my back and groan as I feel blood escaping my nose. Vinny throws me a rag. "See?" I snatch it and dab my wound, then I roll over and stand on shaky legs.

I return to the defense position, but he pushes out a breath. "Ann, get some sleep. You aren't going to best the master." I strike out and hit him in the jaw. As he rubs his face, he arches a brow before retaliating, but I block him. "That's my girl! You must channel your emotions, let them work *for* you."

We continue our battle for thirty more minutes before he finally holds up a hand for a water break. We lean against the wall and sip from our bottles. "As much as I love letting Christian and you try to damage me, I need to get back to my lovely wife." He grabs his bag, then stops. "Please speak to your fiancé. You guys need to work through whatever this is—preferably *before* the wedding."

I wipe my face as I stride off to the showers. After a quick clean up, I return to my room. I throw my bag in the corner and drop onto the bed. My body is *beyond* exhausted, but not my brain. I glare at Christian's door before I stomp over and open it wide.

Christian's eyes lazily lift from his reading with an arched brow. "Can I assist you, Ann?"

I cross my arms over my chest. "Yes, you can tell me what *your* problem is!"

He shuts his book before he sets it on his side table. "The only concern I have is with the volume and tone of *your* voice. Now, please excuse me—I am exhausted and I must be up early."

"Are you serious? We aren't going to talk about our wedding dress debacle?"

"Apparently there is nothing to discuss. I believe we decided that I am overreacting, and you are naïve." He rolls over and pulls up the covers.

I snatch one of his pillows and hurl it at his head. "We. Need. To. Talk."

He turns to me with narrowed eyes. "Let's just call it what it is, okay? A forced marriage between us. Let's just get it over with quickly, so we can push on with our lives." Then he rolls away from me again.

My throat squeezes as his words slap me. "What happened to love and compassion?" When he doesn't answer, I shake my head. "I thought..." I choke on a sob. "I thought you wanted this."

"I believed I did too, but now I see how much anguish my decisions are causing everyone, and I am questioning those choices."

I plop on the edge of the bed. "We need harmony if we are going to be running the country together." I grab his hand and squeeze it. "Please don't give up on our arrangement before we even have a chance to try. I am willing to attempt to make this work, but I can't do it on my own."

"If you are as willing as you say, you must choose another dress."

"No." His face falls before I have a chance to continue. "*I* will not select another dress, Christian. You will pick it for me."

"Me?" His eyes wander over my body in thought.

"Yes, because you are being so hardheaded. But under one condition." Before he can inquire, I push out, "You need to give Ryan an apology and fix your relationship with him—he was simply trying to help."

He plucks his hand away. "Absolutely not. My counter offer is that I can set up a meeting with him to discuss the situation, but I won't guarantee an apology because my reaction was justified."

There is a knock on the door, and we look up as Ryan pokes his head in. "Oh, sorry to interrupt. Ann, the chickens are here."

"Thank you for letting me know." I go towards the door and turn back to Christian. "Do you want to welcome the flock?"

He looks between Ryan and me, then he shakes his head before he turns off his lamp and settles back under the covers with a grunt. Disappointment radiates through me, but I swallow it down. "Good night, Christian."

As we descend the stairs, I feel Ryan's dark eyes staring. "Do I have a booger hanging out of my nose or something?" I rub my nose but regret it instantly as I remember Vinny's assault.

"Is everything okay between you two?"

I force a smile. "Yes, my nose and I are on excellent terms."

He taps his shoulder against mine. "I was talking about Christian and you."

"Of course. I mean, we aren't as tightknit as my nose and me. But there is some serious competition going on."

"You might be able to lie to everyone else, Ann. But I know you better. Now wipe off that fake smile and tell me what's *really* going on. And if you say your damn nose again, I'll be forced to tickle the truth out of you."

As we get outside, we witness the last of the sun's

rays lowering under the horizon. I cross my arms over my chest and kick a stray stick on the immaculate path. "Christian has just shut down on me, Ryan. I can't get him to stay in the same room as me for very long, he is angry with the world, and he won't let me try to fix things."

Ryan shoves his hands in his suit pockets. "As much as you want to, you can't fix everything for him. Christian needs to man-up and deal with whatever is going on in that stubborn head of his."

"But when will he, Ryan? The wedding is right around the corner!"

"Trust me, I *know*."

The silence stretches between us. I hate the hurt look on his face. I wish I could brush my fingertips over it and promise everything was going to work out for the best.

When we reach the pen, I arch a brow towards Dan, who is already unloading the chickens from the trailer in his nice clothes. "Dan, what happened to your date?"

"I figured you'd want someone familiar with the flock to welcome them."

As I close the pen, the chickens all run to me. I stroke them, before I chastise Dicky as he spurs Dan's boot. After I guide them around the pen, I show them their water, food, and their little hen house, where their nesting boxes and roosting nighttime area is.

"Thank you, Dan."

"No problem. Have you been through the applicants for the house?"

I pluck a blade of grass. "Yes, but I don't know for sure yet who I want to do the job."

Ryan and Dan exchange a look. Then Dan tilts his head. "Well, if you don't find someone by the end of the month, I will take it over for you until you find someone else."

I turn to him. "What about your contractor jobs? And Sam?"

He shrugs. "The pay is equivalent to my work now, plus I can focus on my books, and I can visit Sam."

"I will look through the applicants again."

He nods. "Well, I am off for the night. I hope you guys have a good evening." He smiles at the chickens as they peck their new surroundings.

Ryan shakes Dan's hand and I offer a lift of my chin. Then Ryan frowns down at me. "Are you coming inside soon? It's getting pretty dark out here."

"I am not wanted inside right now."

"Ann, come on, that's not true."

I lean back against the fence. "Good night, Prince Ryan. Thank you for collecting me."

I close my eyes and listen to all the hens as they cluck and scratch. Eventually, the yard is quiet except for the soft calls of the crickets. I yawn, stretch, and stare up at the full moon in the cloudless sky.

Having my flock here makes everything feel more real. Soon this will be my one and only home, with my husband. And right now, he doesn't want to marry me out of love, but out of convenience.

I stretch my palms up to the beams of sunlight as laughter rings from my crimson lips. I twirl in my pale wedding dress. I spin round and round until I fall dizzily to the soft grass. My

*eyes flit to the cloudless sky, then I tilt my head as I notice a
bouquet of flowers in my hand.*

*I sit up and finger the soft petals before I feel them evaporate
into multicolored feathers. I bring them to my nose and take in
their familiar, earthy smell.*

*The crowd is waiting, hundreds of faceless figures
anticipating my parade down the laid-out aisle.*

*Slowly, I place one heeled toe in front of the other, until I
hear gasps and watch guests point to the train of my gown.*

*My eyes trail theirs, and I notice the walkway has become
a puddle of blood. My smeared dress sloshes through, getting
heavier and heavier until my heels are cemented.*

Can someone lose this much blood and survive?

*As the question echoes in my head, dark shadows dance
around the room before they swallow me whole in a blur of
manic laughter.*

"Ann?"

I shiver as a cool breeze caresses my cheek. I pry my
eyes open slowly, confused to find twenty hens gawking
at me—plus two more in my lap. I rub the nightmare from
my eyes as I notice Ryan standing by the gate. I grumble
and reach up for his coffee.

"First, get on your feet and step out of the chicken pen.
Then, I will give you the coffee," he explains slowly as he
jiggles the mug, likely hoping to entice me.

I lean my head back against the fence. "Just give me
five more minutes."

I hear the gate open, and the chickens' warmth gently
moves off my lap. "Ann, take my hand and I will help you

up."

I roll my eyes and grab his wrist. "You are so bossy. When did you and Christian do a *Freaky Friday* move?"

He shakes his head and squeezes my hand. "Your fingers are ice cold." He gently grabs the other wrist and massages it. "No more sleeping out here. The cottage will be ready soon enough, then you can sleep ten feet away from the chickens, with your own bed."

I snatch the mug and greedily slurp, allowing the warmth to finish clearing the effects of the dream. He opens the gate for me and guides me out with his palm on the small of my back.

"What the—?" Ryan draws out as he fingers a blue cord dangling from a tall oak tree.

"Is that Snowball's lead?" I tug at the end.

Our necks crane as we glance up the long trunk, and sure enough, there is white fluff mixed into the greenery.

"Where is mom? Mom!"

"Maybe she went to get assistance." I grab the lowest branch and swing forward. "Give me a boost."

"Ann, no way. Mom will be right back with a ladder… or a tranquilizer," he mutters. "What are you… Get down before you break your neck."

"Oh, stop being a baby and give me a shove."

"Let me go inside and see what mom is doing. I'll be right back."

"Oh. My. Gosh. Okay, *Christian*. Always worrying about my damn safety, instead of asking me what I *want*," I grunt as I try to get my bearings.

"What did you say?" he pushes out.

"You heard me Mr. Stick-Up-The-Butt. Go *run* to mommy."

I feel a hand thrust me forward, and I easily grab the next few branches until I reach Snowball. I watch while she stalks a spider as it scurries up the thick trunk. I snatch the hen and place her under my arm before she has a chance to protest. When I start my descent, the eight-legged behemoth decides to take advantage of his attacker being held captive, and it scurries forward while laughing maniacally (internally of course)—or so I assume by the look in its beady little eyes.

I yelp as Snowball squawks at the offender, and my foot slips. I clutch her to my chest while we test our flying abilities. I squeeze my eyes shut and brace for impact.

"Ann!"

Instead of the solid ground, we are met with a squishier stiffness when Ryan attempts to catch us.

"Ouch, I think you broke my back," he groans from underneath us.

I begin laughing, and soon he joins in until we have tears springing from the corners of our lids. We stop at the same time and gaze into each other's eyes. He runs his fingertips through my hair and sighs. "Why don't you ever listen?"

"I'm sorry… what did you say? I wasn't listening?"

"Oh no! Snowball! Are you okay?" Elizabeth collects the chicken in her arms.

"Don't worry about us, mom. We're fine," Ryan mutters.

"What? Oh, Sam help them up while I go get Snowball checked out."

Sam chuckles as Elizabeth dashes into the Palace with the unharmed feathery princess. Sam sets the ladder aside to offer me a helping hand.

"Sorry, I was searching for a taller ladder to grab Snowball down. Elizabeth was exaggerating the height of the tree."

"Thank you, Sam."

"No problem. I need to go put this back and return to my actual job. I'll see you guys around."

After she is gone, I clear my throat. "Thanks for catching us, Ryan."

"I'm always eager to be your cushion." He elbows me.

We go into the Palace and at the top of the third floor, Ryan smiles at me prior to striding towards the office. I watch him walk away, then I turn into my room to get changed.

I pause mid step as I see Christian standing there in his all-business attire. "Ann, where have you been?"

I brush past him, but he steps in my path. I narrow my eyes. "Does it really matter? I mean, you just want to get it done and over with, right?"

Christian plucks a blade of grass out of my hair. "I apologize for my outburst yesterday. I received the decision for Mary and Max, and it placed me in an unexpected mood."

"Why didn't you just tell me that? What was the verdict?"

He brushes mud off my butt. "How about you shower first, and then I can show you the report they sent over?"

I reach up to adjust Mr. Perfect's crooked tie, but he steps away from me. I quickly pull my hands back, as if he burned me.

"I'm sorry, Ann." He inches towards me.

I reach up again, slowly, watching him. Then I fix his tie. "It was a little lopsided."

"Thank you. I have been out of sorts lately, even my clothing is out of order."

I walk past him, but he grabs my hand and squeezes it, forcing me to look into his icy blue eyes. "I am sorry, Ann."

I nod, before I lift my chin and pull my hand away to go into the bathroom. Why is Christian tearing away from me all of a sudden? Was Mary found innocent? Are they going to get back together?

I welcome the scalding shower as I attempt to wash away my insecurities. Surely, Christian is just feeling vulnerable because of what Mary did to him. Does he think I will do the same thing?

When I step out again, I am perfectly composed and ready to take on the day.

I walk towards Christian's office. Before I can knock, he opens the door and ushers me inside. On the mahogany desk, he has Danishes and coffee, which he offers to me before he sits beside me with a file clutched in his hand.

"Thank you." I take a pastry and sink my teeth into its warmth. "I could live off these things." I sip my coffee and the sweetness complements it perfectly.

"I requested that Jock bake a fresh batch for you." He stares intently.

"Oh, I see. So, this is an *I am sorry* pastry?"

"Ann, I assure you I will be extra vigilant with my choice of words next time."

I slide my hand onto his as it rests on his lap, and squeeze. "Excellent choice in pastry."

He relaxes in his chair while he waits for me to finish eating, then he hands me the thick file. I take my time flipping through the evidence, transcripts, and finally the verdict.

I run my finger over the words as I breathe them out, "Guilty, with the penalty of death." I close the file and pass it to him. "What is done is done."

He offers a sad smile. "Well said, Ann."

"What is the next step in this process?"

"Max and Mary will each have a chance to petition for their last request, then we can put this behind us."

"Any ideas on what their requests might be?"

"They are devious, so it will be interesting to see what they ask for."

"When will that be?"

"They have a few days to make a decision."

"That fast?"

"The quicker, the better." He shuffles some papers, ending the discussion.

"I agree. Oh, and speaking of sooner rather than later... your mother will need you to approve a dress for me." I snatch the coffee off his desk.

He runs his hand down his face. "As if I have ample time for *that*."

"Thank you for breakfast and the update."

"And thank *you* for accepting my apology."

"Of course," I say as I turn to the door.

In two quick steps, Christian meets me at the entrance. He uses his body to press me against the wood, then he lifts my lips to his. Warmth fills my body as he slowly deepens the kiss and wraps his arms around my waist. He tugs me closer, and I lock my hands behind his neck. Our bodies meld together, and he moans softly against my mouth before he pulls away. "I despise arguing with you, Ann. I've missed you."

"I've missed you too," I say in a whisper through parted, swollen lips. I open my eyes and see him staring at me as he strokes my cheek.

"I love you, Ann."

My heart skips a beat, and I freeze as he watches me expectantly.

"Christian, dear, are you ready?" Elizabeth barges in just in time.

He sighs softly. "Yes, mother, come right in."

I take the opportunity to sneak out and scurry to my desk. Why couldn't I reply right away? I am a mess.

I stop short as I see a bouquet of fresh flowers welcoming me to my desk with a sweet note from

Christian. I run my fingers along the soft, colorful petals. Then I grab my to-do list and push aside the aching questions in order to stay busy—*and sane.*

Awkward...

When I enter the dining room, I slide in next to Christian, who is frowning over documents.

I lean towards Ryan. "What did I miss?"

Ryan sips his water. "Trust me, Ann. You do *not* want to know."

"Ryan is right, you should stay out of this mess." Christian nods.

I arch a brow at Christian. "Are the peasants demanding you undergo a gender change again?"

Ryan smirks as Christian looks up with narrowed eyes. "Ann, please, let's act our age, particularly at dinnertime." Christian pauses his skimming and slams the papers down. "This is absurd! I do not see the need to hold off any longer."

Ryan shrugs. "I can see the request making *some* sense, Christian."

"Of course *you* would," Christian hisses.

"Now, dear, I am sure a pretty blue bonnet would look lovely in your hair," I continue to tease Christian.

"Someone, please get this woman some food!" Christian leans back.

Ryan elbows me. "I do believe a red bonnet would look better."

"Ryan, there's so much *more* potential to bring out his eyes with the blue one." Christian's face reddens. "You know, Christian, if you just tell me what is in that *pretty* little file, I will not have to keep guessing like this." I bat my eyelashes at him.

He finally shoves the folder in my hands as the food arrives. I sift through the pages and my mouth drops. "What! They demand that we have the execution first before we can have the wedding. But all that planning!"

"That's what I said too," Christian blares. "What's the point of being King if I can't modify the laws as I see fit?"

Ryan turns to us. "The reigning Queen is alive. You cannot assume a new one with the current one still here. No matter how much you attempt to change the rules to benefit your selfish ambitions."

"But Mary has been tried and is going to be executed." I pout.

He shakes his head. "I understand that, but she is still alive."

I stab my roast and grumble. "Why can't we just kill her sooner."

"I suppose we could do it sooner rather than later. Mary and Max turned in their requests today." Christian shrugs, eating a potato.

"Really? What were their requests?" Christian coughs on his potato, then dabs his mouth with his napkin before shaking his head.

Ryan smirks as he leans in to me. "Mary's was simple enough. She wants to write to her family and say goodbye. But Max..."

Christian holds up a hand. "Ryan, stop! That is enough."

Ryan winks at me before he focuses on his mashed potatoes and gravy.

I arch a brow at Christian. "What size dress are you, dear?"

He rolls his eyes. "Ann, Max sent in three requests. The first two were denied and the third is being considered." He stabs another potato.

"Size six then?"

"I cannot deal with your childish antics right now." He shoves the potato in his mouth and chews fast, refusing to look at me. "Ryan, you tell her."

Ryan leans back, whispering so his mom can't hear. "Well, the first request was to have intimate relations with someone before he dies. When that was denied, his second one was to at least get some foreplay time."

"What a pig." I shake my head, and then I tilt it. "Why didn't Christian want me to know about this?"

"Guess who that *someone* was?"

I scoff, "His sister?" Ryan chuckles as Christian glares. "Well, he is a creep!"

"No, Ann, it was you," Ryan answers.

I blink a few times. "Me? But he knows…"

"Exactly. It's super awkward." Ryan attacks his peas.

"So, what's Max's pending third request? Lingerie pictures he can pleasure himself with?" I stab a piece of meat.

Christian growls. "I would not even contemplate that absurdity!"

Ryan leans in. "Unless Christian saw them first."

I chuckle with Ryan, then face Christian. "So, what is his third request?"

Christian straightens. "Max has requested to have dinner with you."

"Wow, so we go from kinky to simple. Something isn't adding up." I tap my fork to my lips.

"Well, it isn't that *simple*—he has some outfit suggestions…" Christian trails off.

"That man deserves everything coming to him." I chew my meat, then pause as I feel their eyes on me. I glance side to side and swallow. "What?"

Christian clears his throat. "Ann, is this something you are willing to do for Max's final request?"

"Well, it sure beats the other two ideas." Ryan snorts and looks away as Christian shakes his head. "Yes, Christian. I am willing to have dinner with Max. But he is stuck in his cell. And make him a sandwich or something that I can pass through the bars." I cross my arms over my chest. "And there needs to be a time limit, with a guard, and a chair for me to sit on so I don't have to stand."

Christian nods. "That is absolutely reasonable, considering the circumstances." He watches me carefully. "Are you certain? We can deny it as quickly as the other ones. You do not *need* to do this."

"Max is just trying to drag out the inevitable and I will not tolerate it," I grumble.

After dinner, I meet Christian and Ryan in the training room. Together, we warm up and by the time we are ready to box, Sam saunters in. We team up, boys against girls, and duke it out. By the end of the night, we are exhausted but amused at the stalemate in our friendly competition.

When I return to my room, sleep comes easily.

"Max! Stop! Please!" I scream through my tears.

But it's too late... the gunshot cuts through the velvety darkness of my dream and I jolt awake, yelling. My eyes dart around the room as I look for my dad's bleeding body.

"Ann?" Christian's sleepy voice calls.

"Christian, my dad, he was..." I cry. He collects me in his arms and kisses the top of my head. "I never should have asked you to agree to Max's request."

My body soaks in his warmth as I snuggle into his chest. "The sooner we get it done, the better. Once he is dead, the dreams will stop."

"But at what cost, Ann?"

I gaze into the darkness, and I wonder the same thing before drifting back into my nightmare.

In the early morning light, I watch Christian's sleeping frame. As I run my hand through his locks, I bite my lip. I do love Christian. He is my rock. My alpha protector.

I place a peck on his cheek before I sneak out of his grasp and make my way down to the chicken coop with my coffee, but I stumble when I see Ryan hammering on the cottage. After he meets my gaze, I offer him a sip from my mug.

He holds up a thermos. "Thank you, but I got the big boy coffee cup today."

I sulk at my cup, wishing I had thought to ask for a vat. I sip the hot liquid, then tilt my head at Ryan. He is wearing jeans and a plain white tee shirt that is already fashioning some dirt and saw dust. "Ryan, what are you doing up before sunrise?"

Dark eyes raise from his clipboard. "I could not sleep. So, I thought I would be productive." He presses his lips together. "I really wish you would reconsider meeting with Max. It doesn't feel right to me."

"What can Max do to me, Ryan? He is behind bars and he will die soon afterwards. Win-win." I open the pen and present the flock with a piece of bread. They eagerly accept my offering, but I notice leftover crumbs in the grass. "Ryan, are you giving them food too?"

"Maybe."

I laugh lightly. "We need to make a treat schedule. That way, we aren't overfeeding them."

"Man, I lost *everything* in our divorce." He fake pouts as he scribbles notes.

I try not to let his words sting me while I sit in silence, watching the sun peek over the horizon. I close my eyes and spread my arms out. "It will be nice to see this every morning from right outside my bedroom window."

"I am sure you two will enjoy it."

I peek at him. "Was this one of the gifts that you were planning on giving me for *our* wedding?"

His face reddens. "I made it for you either way."

"Ryan…"

"I need to go get more measurements and materials inside. I'll see you later at breakfast."

I groan and stare at the ground as Willy pecks my toe. I stroke him gently. "What are we going to do with him?" He chirps softly in response, then wanders off towards his ladies.

Once inside, I sit at the dining room table, staring down at my coffee as Ryan's playful banter repeats in my head. Soon Elizabeth enters, breaking up my thoughts.

"You are going to have huge bags under your eyes on your wedding day if you aren't careful."

"I am sure I won't even resemble myself on that day anyway," I huff.

Her movements halt. "Ann, that's not true."

"Really? Did you really see a farmer girl marrying your son and becoming Queen?"

She pats my leg. "No, I always hoped *you* would marry my son and become Queen. You are perfect for him because you balance each other out."

"But at what cost though? We may very well kill each other before then."

She opens her mouth but stops as she sees Christian.

"You left your bed early this morning, Ann. Is everything all right?"

"I couldn't sleep."

He kisses my cheek. "Well, soon all your worries will

be over. I have approved their requests, and Mary has already sent her letter out to her family, while Max's dinner will be tomorrow night."

"Speaking of family, what happened to their parents? Were they part of the scheming?"

Christian snorts. "Governor Patrick and his wife are out of the country for diplomatic purposes. Once they return, they will be thoroughly investigated. The message Mary sent was addressed to a distant cousin, who will make sure her parents receive it. Although, I wouldn't be shocked if they were *intentionally* away right now—they couldn't care less about their children. At least, that is the information Mary imparted... whether it is accurate or not is still to be determined."

I aim to redirect the conversation. "Did we check the letter to make sure there wasn't anything incriminating?"

"Yes, Detective Mack looked over the document and stated everything checked out."

I wonder what was inside the letter. Did Mary beg for prayers and mercy for her soul? Or did she try to manipulate her story in order to receive more sympathy?

Breakfast plates are served just as Ryan sits down. My eyes scan his outfit change. Now he is in a suit, twinning with Christian.

"Ann and Ryan, we need your final fittings completed," Elizabeth says.

"When do you need us, mom?"

"Now would be perfect," she sings.

I shuffle to my feet. "I'll do anything to keep myself out of the office."

Christian gives me a quick kiss before I follow Elizabeth to her room with Ryan in tow. When we enter, the seamstress passes us our dress clothes and ushers us around the room. I squeeze into the gown and grumble. Of course, Christian chose the tightest fitting dress in the entire country. He must be punishing me for making him pick it out. The top is lacey with flowers and an arrangement of pearls and diamonds. It is cinched at the waist, hugging my chest and hips, before it flares off my thighs to allow me to walk. The gown is very sophisticated and I am afraid to ruin it or fall flat on my face while wearing it.

I take in a deep breath and inch my way out to show Elizabeth. When I enter the room, everyone falls quiet as they observe me in the full-length mirror.

Ryan breaks the calm as he saunters around the corner, fumbling with his shirt. "Mom, I think the sleeves should be…" When his dark eyes lock on to my frame, the words flutter into a stunned stillness.

I wring my hands together as I feel heat climb up my neck. "It looks horrible, doesn't it?" I glance back into the mirror. The dress glistens and gleams, but it just isn't *me*.

Elizabeth steps forward, placing her arms on mine. "I think Christian picked the best dress for the occasion. Ann, you look stunning."

I glance up at her then turn to Ryan. "Well, come out with it. How bad is it?"

He closes his eyes and swallows. "I agree with mom—it is stunning."

The seamstress busies herself around me, making notes on what to do and where, while pricking me twice with pins. Finally, with a curt nod, she gives me the okay to change, and I tread carefully to my clothes and let Ryan take my place in front of the mirror.

I watch as she works around Ryan. He looks so handsome in his new suit. I catch his dark gaze in the mirror and scurry to change.

When I emerge again, I take a gulp of air then another, finding it hard to breathe. I lean against the doorframe with my hand on my heaving chest.

"Ann? Are you okay? Do you need a doctor?" Elizabeth rushes over with a glass of water.

Ryan frowns in the mirror as the seamstress holds out his arms and warns him not to move again, *or she will poke him.*

I put my hand on my forehead. "Everything is happening so fast. And not in the way I wanted it to. I mean, my dad was supposed to walk me down the aisle before giving me away." Elizabeth rubs my back. "I was a mess when I married Mark too. Don't worry, dear, this is a normal feeling. I know it can be hard to imagine yourself married, with kids, and of course, there's the anxiety of the wedding night itself."

My head shoots up as I blush. "Thanks. Well, I should really go to work."

I close the door on Ryan's laughter as I rush out, not wanting to discuss the wedding night with my future mother-in-law. Once I am outside the door, I lean against the wall and try to catch my breath again.

When I open my eyes, I see Tim smiling at me. "Lady Ann, King Christian wanted to speak with you once your fitting was done."

"Thank you, Tim."

As we stroll together, we catch up on the events of his life. Presently, he and his boyfriend are talking about adopting a child soon. I offer my congratulations before teasing him about when *he'll* be squeezing into a wedding dress.

Once we part, I push open Christian's door and see him on the phone. He waves me in and continues his conversation. As soon as he hangs up, he rubs his temples.

"The press wanted to send cameras to witness your dinner with Max, and I said absolutely not. But my counter offer was that they could visit during the execution, then of course, again, during the wedding." He sits forward on his elbows. "So, what did you think of your gown?"

"It is tight."

He chuckles. "Yes, it is, and I believe you will look absolutely breathtaking."

"Is that why you wanted to see me? To ask me about my dress?"

"No, I was hoping to have lunch together, if you are available?"

"Oh, you mean *more* time out of the office and away from my boring desk job? That sounds perfect."

We walk hand in hand to his balcony and enjoy our soup and salad in the bright afternoon sun. "They say this summer is going to be hot and miserable," Christian announces as he looks into the cloudless sky.

I take a bite of my salad. "I saw they are also predicting a drought again this year, possibly worse than last year."

"That will make things difficult around here. We should release a plan of action to keep the people from becoming frantic. With your knowledge, you are the ideal individual to compose a document educating farmers on how to conserve water, while also tending to their needs."

My heart warms at his compliment and at the notion that I will be needed for something other than my role as a paper pusher.

Suddenly, Ryan rushes in, his face pale. "Ann, hurry, Karen's water just broke and she is asking for you."

"Oh, wow. Already?"

He nods, patting his face with a handkerchief. "Obviously someone messed up with the due date," he says breathlessly.

"Babies come early sometimes, Ryan. Christian, thank you for lunch. Are you interested in witnessing a live birth?"

Christian coughs on his salad and dabs his mouth. "Ann, we genuinely need to work on your table etiquette." He sighs. "No, thank you. I have a press conference, which I guess I am doing without your assistance."

"I'm sorry. Why don't you ask your mom to help you?" I kiss his cheek. "Childbirth waits for no one. I will be there for the next press event, as long as no one else is popping out children."

Christian's fork clatters to the table. "You have ruined my appetite."

I walk out the door, and I am surprised when Ryan steps behind me. "Wow. You are coming, Ryan? I didn't think you could stomach something like this."

"Karen is a mess, and for some reason, she asked for us both—at least until Vinny is done overseeing the press conference." He sucks in a breath as we stop outside Karen's door. "Ann, I am scared."

I laugh and clasp Ryan's hand. "It is just childbirth. Plus, you aren't doing any of the hard stuff. Think of this as an educational experience for your future."

He rolls his eyes and puts on a forced smile as we walk in. "I brought backup."

Karen looks up. Her hair is plastered to her face, and dark purple rings line her eyes. "Ann! Thank goodness. Poor Ryan looked so faint."

I smirk in his direction while he scowls. "Hey! I'm still a virgin over here, and I want to do the fun stuff before witnessing the consequences." He crosses his arms over his chest as he sits down.

I grab Karen's hand. "How are we doing?"

"The doctor told me they want to airlift me to a hospital that specializes in premature infants, just in case. But I want to be close to Vinny. I don't want him to miss the birth of his children. Because I am not having any more!"

"The doctor knows what he is talking about, so I would listen to him. And I'm sure Vinny can take some time off to accompany you, Karen. If not, I will stay by your side, little sister."

She squeezes my hand. "You are right. Thank you, Ann, that would be great."

Ryan frowns. "Ann, you have that dinner tomorrow with Max, remember?" Then his frown shifts. "Or maybe we can change the dinner?"

I tilt my head. "I don't think Christian would allow that."

The doctor ceases our conversation as he walks in. "All right, Karen, it is time to check your cervix." Ryan pales and leaves quickly. I laugh and shake my head at his departing frame. "I'm going to check on him." I kiss her forehead. "Don't worry, we will figure this out. As long as you and the babies are healthy and *safe*, that is all that matters."

I spot Ryan on a chair in the small waiting area, around the corner, with his head in his hands.

I lean against the wall. "Ryan, are you going to be okay?"

"No, Ann, I cannot do this anymore."

"Most men can't. But you gave it a try. I am sure Karen understands."

He stands quickly, overturning his chair. "Not that, us!"

"*Us*? Ryan, you aren't making any sense. Calm down."

He pulls at his hair. "I can't sit here and *pretend* to be the happy brother-in-law! I can't watch you kiss him and… wear the most beautiful dress in the world on *his* wedding day!" He brings his hands down on his legs with a thump as he stares at me with a tortured expression. "I want to be the one waiting at the end of the aisle for you. I want to be the one to sleep next to you in the cottage. I… I even want to be the one sitting next to your hospital bed, waiting for *our* child to be born." He looks away from me as he whispers, "It was always supposed to be us."

I fall into a chair, staring at him with my mouth open.

Words refuse to form as shock wrecks my mind. "Ryan... forgive me... I don't know what to say." Silence blankets us while we are lost in our memories. I know how he feels. But there is nothing I can do to fix his pain.

He rubs his hands over his face, and then kneels. "I am sorry. I shouldn't have said all that." He gently pulls my chin upward. "None of this is your fault. Do you hear me?" He releases his hold. "I am such a jerk to say all of that to you. I will leave now. Tell Karen I couldn't handle it."

He steps away, but I stand and wrap my arms around his waist. "If I could change the events leading to this, or if polygamy were allowed..."

He kisses the top of my head. "Just forget what I said, okay. I am happy for you. My brother is the luckiest man alive, and I am grateful to be a part of your life still."

I watch his defeated form walk away and my heart shatters into oblivion. I cry into my hands until the doctor comes back out. I wipe my eyes and force a smile. "These events always hold a special place in my heart," I fib.

"I completely understand, Lady Ann. Karen would like to see you now."

He guides me into the room as Karen breathes through a contraction. Once she rests her head back, she frowns. "Ann, what's wrong?"

I sit beside her on the bed and stare at her hand with an IV sticking out. "It is nothing."

"Oh, come on. Please talk to me. Take my mind off the pain."

I take a deep breath as I tell her what Ryan told me. My

tears fall again as I recall his tortured expression and the agony laced in every syllable. "Karen, I feel so awful. My heart feels like it is breaking and I just can't put the pieces back together."

She offers me a tissue. "I love you, but what did you think was going to happen?"

"That we would both pretend we never had a relationship and go on with our lives. I mean, he is with Cherie!"

"You guys were planning out your future. You can't drop those feelings easily."

"Thanks for nothing." I dab my eyes. "Now I feel like a slut, being all lovey-dovey with Christian."

"Sweetie, you are making the best of the situation and so is Ryan, but it will take time. I am sure Christian still loves Mary… even with all this going on."

I groan and lean my head back. "Why is this happening to me?"

She breathes through another contraction before replying, "This is real life, and it will always have its ups and downs."

"Do they still want to airlift you?"

"Yes, I am just waiting for Vinny to pop in to get a quick hug before I leave."

"I can't tell you how sorry I am that I cannot be there with you. Do you want me to talk to Christian and demand he let me go?"

She waves off my request. "You can fly out tomorrow after you are done… and meet the twins."

Vinny sprints in, out of breath and with his hair sticking up. He beams at his wife before he embraces her. Karen hugs him tight with no intention of ever letting go.

"The King is permitting me to fly with you, Karen." Vinny turns to me. "The King would like to see you in his office at your convenience."

I offer hugs all around. "Be safe and I will see you *and* those babies soon."

They nod before returning their gazes to each other. I slip out quietly, because I'm confident Karen is in good hands. They have an amazing relationship, and those babies are so lucky to have them for parents.

I lean on the wall and stare at the ceiling. When the time comes, will I make a good mom? Can Christian and I have a good marriage, like Vinny and Karen? I force down my uncertainties before I walk to Christian's office. I open the door and smirk at Christian as he sits behind his desk sifting through papers. Does he ever take a break?

"Vinny and Karen offer you their gratitude for allowing Vinny to travel with Karen to the hospital."

"Vinny is the best guard I have. It was a difficult choice to make, but I know he won't be able to concentrate entirely if he is concerned about Karen and the newborns."

"How romantic."

"I am only being forthright. However, I am genuinely pleased he can be by her side."

"Christian, when we have kids, are you going to be by my side too?"

"I am prepared to, if that's what you require, but I

would prefer to see them all clean and ready to go."

I smirk as I imagine Christian attempting to be patient for our child's birth. He'll probably stand at my feet and demand that the child pop out immediately. Or maybe a baby will change Christian's entire outlook on life, and he'll become more understanding.

Christian collects me in his lap. "Do you intend to discuss what transpired earlier?"

"What do you mean?"

I look up into his icy eyes, trying to read his thoughts. But he is composed, as usual. He guides his fingertips down my cheek. "I heard about your dialogue with Ryan in the hospital wing."

"Oh," I draw out.

"You can't quarrel in the Palace without somebody eavesdropping. That's exactly how rumors circulate."

"Christian, I don't know what to say... I'm sorry."

"Don't be apologetic. I understand our situation is unique. Ryan *somehow* crept into your heart before I could." He lifts my chin. "But I intend to steal it back and keep it for the remainder of our lives."

As his words warm my heart, he presses his lips to mine and kisses me deeply.

When he pulls back, he furrows his brows. "I am going to discuss this situation with Ryan too. He needs to control his emotions. And if he can't, he *will* respect me and keep away from you. Or I'll find a job for him elsewhere—maybe overseas."

"Today was just an emotionally off day for everyone,

between the wedding planning and the babies coming early. I know Ryan respects you, Christian. He'll be fine. We all will."

"Speaking of emotional stability, are you still willing to have dinner with Max?" He watches me carefully. "I know the event has roused nightmares for you, and I am concerned about your wellbeing."

"Yes, I just want to put this behind us."

"That's my girl." We go over the menu, beverage choices, and the dress that I will be wearing. "Also, you will not be permitted inside the jail with any kind of weapon. *But* there will be an armed guard by your side the whole time, and he knows about your trigger-happy moment with Mary, so he will be vigilant."

"I make *one* mistake and I get a reputation? That's not fair! What about you and the whole choking me out incident?"

"You are a strong woman. You do not need any weapons—end of discussion. And I never choked you out. I merely gave your neck a tiny squeeze." He kisses my hand. "I appreciate you taking this task on. I know this isn't easy for anyone."

His soft-spoken remarks remind me of what Karen said earlier. I know I should just let it go, but I need to know. "Christian, do you still love Mary?"

"Why do you ask?"

"You two were married and talking about having kids."

He suddenly looks tired. "Ann, I appreciate your empathy. Like I've said, this situation is complicated at best. But yes, I do still care for her. However, I know she is a murderer, a liar, and a master manipulator." He looks away. "I wish I could be stronger and force the emotions away, but I can't."

I squeeze his hand, and he gazes into my eyes before I lower my lips and kiss him tenderly. We are both struggling with our feelings for our exes. But we are on the same page and we intend to continue forward, no matter how broken we are.

"How about we brush this under the rug for now and have dinner?" I ask before collecting his hand and pulling him to the dining hall, and soon Ryan joins us with Elizabeth trailing close behind. They sit down while in mid conversation.

"That is a real shame." Elizabeth pouts.

Ryan purses his lips. "Yes, mom, but it is done now. Can we please just drop it?"

Christian looks over his wine glass. "What is done, mother?"

Ryan sends daggers in his brother's direction. "It's none of your business. It's nothing."

Elizabeth places her napkin in her lap. "Ryan will need a date for your wedding."

I cough on my wine, my eyes watering. Once I can breathe again, I squeak out, "What about Cherie? I thought she was looking forward to coming?"

"Why is everyone being so nosey! We are dropping this topic, right now." He slams his open hand on the table, jiggling the water glasses.

There are very few moments when I see their father reflected in their actions. But right now, Ryan's body language feels identical. Even Christian looks taken aback by the outburst.

Thank goodness the servers get the hint and bring out dinner: roasted chicken, snap peas, and wild rice.

Once we pick up our forks, the tension subsides and Christian turns to me. "I spoke with Vinny, and as an additional safeguard, he is going to place a headset in your ear and a USB recorder on you."

Ryan narrows his eyes and opens his mouth to argue, but then he clamps down and shakes his head.

As it's placed in front of me, I take a slow bite of my chocolate cake. "Can I have a knife or something?"

Christian frowns at his dessert. "Ann, we discussed this, absolutely no weapons."

"How about a nail file? Or lipstick? I've read you can assassinate someone slowly but still effectively."

He chuckles as I make hand motions like I am slaying him with my imaginary arsenal. "I am sorry, but my answer is still no."

"How about the underwire of my bra?"

His eyes lower to my chest. "What about it?"

"Am I allowed *that*?"

"You are being difficult, as usual." He turns his full attention to my prattling. "You may have your bra. And if for some reason, you feel the desire to remove it and rip out the underwire to stab someone... please reconsider your decision."

I hear Ryan laugh into his napkin and I smile, glad to have lightened his mood.

"Christian, are you going to join me for a workout tonight?"

"I need to punch out some of this extra energy."

He kisses my cheek softly. "Raincheck?"

When we separate, I grab my workout stuff and make my way down the stairs.

"Hey, Sam, I didn't know you would be down here tonight."

"Hey, Ann! What time is it? Oh, crap! I need to change."

"I'm going to rat you out to Vinny for skipping out early," I tease.

"That's why I came in early, so I can leave in time to meet with Dan."

"Do you guys have *another* date?"

"Hey, don't give me that look. You have enough going on between the King and the Prince. Dan is all mine, sister." She waves me off as she exits. I start whacking the punching bag. I look up to see Ryan saunter in, and I wave my glove at him.

"Wow, Christian is slacking on his training again."

I shrug. "He said he was tired and taking it easy tonight."

He arches a brow. "Oh, is *that* what he told you."

"What is that supposed to mean?"

He jabs the punching bag. "It's just not what I heard."

"What did you hear, Ryan?"

"He is scheduled to inspect the area for your dinner tomorrow."

"Christian is going to the jail where Mary and Max are? Why wouldn't he tell me that? I could have gone with him."

"Maybe he wanted to be alone with Mary one more time." Ryan's words sting.

"That can't be it."

"Why not?"

"Because we don't lie to each other."

"Ann, come on, it wasn't necessarily a lie. He probably *is* tired and might have a light night, but he is going to see Mary too." I stomp over to the mat and wait for a sparring buddy. Christian wouldn't keep that from me. He has no reason to.

Unless...

I mean, he did say he still cared for Mary. Maybe he doesn't think I will be enough for him, and he needs to have one last fling with her.

When I refocus, I frown up at Ryan as he pushes his way through with his gloves up.

"No, let me fight someone else, please." I look around at the guards. "*Anyone* else."

He smirks. "Are you scared?"

"Ryan..." He swiftly brings his glove towards my face. I dodge and squeal. "Hey, you jerk!"

"Hands up," he lectures.

"I've got your hands right here!" I jab low and get him

in the thigh. Then I jam my shoulder into him, knocking him backwards before I land on top of him. "Why would you tell me all of that!"

"What did I say?"

"Why couldn't you let me believe Christian was going to bed early? I could have been oblivious!" I go to punch him in the face, but he blocks, grabs my arms, and pushes me off. I tumble on my back next to him, panting.

"Ann, I am not going to lie to you to make you feel better. The sooner you realize that Christian isn't as innocent as you think and start to see his darker sides, the better."

I hurl my arm and strike him square in the stomach. He groans as he brings his knees up and rolls away.

"Oh, stop pretending you are protecting me. Admit it—you were being mean and trying to get Christian in trouble."

He throws his gloves off. "Fine! I was!"

We stand, and I glare into his dark eyes as sweat rolls down his face. This is not the Ryan I know and love. I shove my hands flat against his chest and thrust him backwards. But this man is made of steel and he doesn't budge.

In one quick movement, he snatches my wrists. His pained expression glides down to my lips, and I break eye contact.

"You are right, and I appreciate the honesty, even if it did hurt my feelings." I look at my feet. "Thank you for always being here for me, Ryan."

He releases my wrists and runs his fingertips along my

cheek. "I just wish it was enough to hold on to you."

The words are barely a whisper, but it feels like he is screaming at me. My eyes water, and my arms circle his waist. Even though he messed around with Mary, he doesn't deserve *this*. We stand there until we hear voices and move to go our separate ways.

That night, I attempt to sleep, but with Karen in the hospital, Max's dinner on the horizon, and Ryan's sudden resolution, it doesn't come easily.

Unexpected

I lean back on the fence posts while I sip my coffee and wait for the sun to begin its ascending masterpiece. I stroke the hens' feathers as they cuddle up next to me. And soon the hues brighten and the world's orchestra awakens.

"Today's the day, girls. I'm saying good riddance to dad's murderer. Then tomorrow, after they end his life, I can finally be free from this heavy burden of vengeance." I look up into the clouds. "I miss you, daddy. Wherever you are, I hope you know I love you."

I swipe at my cheek as I hear voices approaching. "Good morning, boys. Looks like I beat you to the jobsite *again*. You are slacking."

Ryan frowns down at my puffy, red eyes. "Are you not sleeping well again, Ann?"

I turn away from his pity. "How was your date, Dan?"

"Sam is very kind, and it feels almost too easy, being with her."

"That's great to hear. I'm glad you are happy."

Ryan hesitantly follows Dan into the cottage and leaves me to my coffee. As the sun's rays wash over my face, I close my lids and allow my skin to soak in its warmth. Eventually, I slip into an easy sleep, surrounded by familiar things. I hear Ryan's voice and my eyes flutter open. "Ann, I am going inside for breakfast. Are you coming?"

"No, thank you. I am not hungry."

"You? Not hungry?" When I nod, he tilts his head. "Do you want to talk about it?"

"No, I don't."

"If you're sure, I'll see you soon."

I nod and continue to watch the bright colors until it gets too hot. Then I decide to be nosey and step inside the cottage. It is simple, yet elegant with its cozy bedroom, bathroom, kitchen, living room, and beautiful patio. The patio leads outside to where butterflies are fluttering around sweet-smelling flowers, and the chickens are scratching for insects more obtainable than those flying overhead.

Nearby is a towering, shady oak with a birdhouse and feeder hanging from its strong branches. My heart soars when I think about all the hard work and planning that went into this.

I breathe deep and release it with a loud huff of air, as I carefully walk out of the cottage. Even with losing my parents, I still have others that go above and beyond to take care of my every need.

Once I return to my room, I change into a yellow sundress and simple silver flats, brush my long chestnut strands, and do some light makeup to cover the circles under my eyes. Before I get to the office, my cell phone clucks. "Vinny! How are Karen and the babies?"

"Ann, they are beyond words. Healthy, happy, and just amazing," he says breathlessly.

"That is wonderful. Congratulations."

"And Karen is finally resting now, but, Ann, she was remarkable!"

"I am so happy for you two. I cannot wait to meet them. Do they have names yet?"

"Baby A and Baby B." He chuckles. "It is pretty catchy."

I roll my eyes and lean against the wall. "Have you labeled their diapers to tell them apart?"

"Well, they are different genders so that will help us tremendously."

"Make sure you get some rest with Karen. Are they keeping Karen there or moving her back here?"

"They want to keep her here for a few days, just to make sure there aren't any complications."

"That sounds logical. Thank you for the update. I will see you guys as soon as I can."

"Thanks, Ann. I am a dad now…" he says softly.

"Congratulations, again, Vinny."

We hang up and I stare at my phone. I wish I could be there to celebrate this event with them. But no… My obligations keep me from doing what I want, when I want. Am I being selfish with my desire to be there for my best friend, instead of here to give Max his stupid last wish?

"What are we celebrating?"

I jump and turn to see Sam in uniform. "Vinny and Karen had the twins, and everyone is healthy and thriving."

"That is great news! I can't wait to meet the bundles of joy!"

"What are you doing up here?"

She stands tall. "I have been promoted to the third floor."

"That is wonderful news. Now I can see you while I am caged in my office."

She rolls her eyes. "Yes, what a horrible cage to be in. Well, I need to do my rounds. I'll be sure to throw you some breadcrumbs later." She winks as she saunters off.

I sit behind my desk and add some water to my flower bouquet. Thank goodness my to-do list is minimal today, so I can finish it quickly. But before I get too far into it, my stomach growls, reminding me I skipped breakfast.

Instinctively my nose detects fresh biscuits in the vicinity, so I sneak off to the kitchen. I slowly open the door, peek inside, and spot a fruit bowl on the counter. They aren't my heavenly dough balls, but I make a beeline, not in the mindset for small talk.

"Ann, what a pleasure," Jock sings while turning the corner.

I pause mid bite, apple juice dripping down my chin. "Jock, it's great to see you again. I was just dropping in to grab a quick snack—if that's okay?" I add, as his brows raise.

He laughs as he sets down some onions and carrots and hands me a towel. "You are the only Royal who creeps into my kitchen. You do realize there are hundreds of servants to aid you?" He pulls out a bar stool and pats the top until I lower myself onto it.

"Yes, but there's more satisfaction in coming down here myself. Plus, I get to see you and the other chefs hard at work. It makes me appreciate you more."

"You are quite the charmer, Lady Ann."

I reach for a pear as Jock chops vegetables. He hands me a slice of carrot and I crunch into it. "Wow, this carrot has a lot of flavor. Did we get a new supplier?"

"These are all from our greenhouse out back. The compost from your chicken pens helps a lot."

"Yes, back home, it did wonders for my mom's rose bushes too." I pluck a stray thread from my shirt.

"If I wasn't so greedy, I would share some with the flower gardeners to boost their blossoms." He pats my hand. "It's okay to miss them. Just don't let your memories wear you *down*—mourn them and then drive on. Otherwise, you'll simply blink and lose the best days of your life."

"But it's so *hard*, Jock," I say softly. "The pain is so agonizing… it's suffocating me."

I don't want anyone to pity me, or worse, feel my anguish, but the words escape before I can catch them.

"Over time your emotions may dull, or you will simply learn to live with them and incorporate brighter memories to help cushion the hurt."

The moment he finishes, I catch the gloom as it contorts his normally sunny demeanor, and I realize he too has experienced loss. I reach over, squeeze his calloused hand and nod my sympathy.

"Thank you for sharing your words of wisdom with me, Jock. I'll try to remember that."

He nods to the back counter. "There is a fresh pot of

coffee if you want some. What am I saying? Of course, you already know this—I notice you grab a cup every morning."

"I'm sorry. I just don't want to bother anyone this early with grabbing me a mug."

"Oh, so you would rather *steal* my secret early morning stash?" he teases.

"If it makes you feel any better, Becky's Cafe doesn't have anything on your coffee beans." I wink before I slip out.

I hold the railing of the staircase and bite my lip. Jock has a point. Most of the trouble I have gotten myself into is because I didn't *just* mourn all the loss and move forward with my life. Instead, I remained vengeful and almost lost my life in the process.

I enter the dining hall and join the full table.

"Where have you been?" Christian says over his water glass.

"I went to the kitchen to get a snack."

"Ann, are you planning on explaining why you are avoiding me?"

"*Do* I have any reason to avoid you?"

"Why are you answering a question with another question?" He turns to his soup as it is placed in front of him.

"Why can't we ever eat greasy pizza?" I grumble into the pea soup.

"I second that motion. Pizza would be better than this," Ryan chimes in, poking at the green balls.

"Please refrain from complaining, you two. Our kitchen is staffed with the best cooks in the country. All you need to do is simply put in a request, and they will make you whatever you feel like," Elizabeth lectures.

I push the green goop away and pivot to Ryan. "Did Vinny call you?"

"Yes, he told me he is now a very happy father and that Karen is resting."

"Will Vinny be returning soon?" Christian asks as he sips his spoon.

"I think he is grabbing a quick nap, then he is flying back," Ryan informs us.

Christian nods. "Ann, are you prepared for dinner tonight?"

"As ready as I can be, for a dinner with a killer." I grumble. "You know what, I filled up on fruit in the kitchen. I am going to go to my room and read for a little bit." I purse my lips before sauntering out and heading to my suite.

I notice my novels from home are here, and in the exact order that I had them in previously. I pull out a worn spine from my bookshelf and tilt my head. Christian had somehow remembered my particular arrangement of the titles, and brought them back for me to enjoy. My heart warms as I slip off my shoes, lie on the bed, and enjoy reading in the sunlight that the curtains filter in.

I look up as I hear a knock on the door, and a butler strides in carrying a silver tray. He bows before he sets it down on my table by the couch.

"I'm sorry, but I didn't order anything."

"Prince Ryan ordered a pizza for you, Lady Ann. Enjoy." Before he leaves, he lifts the lid and I am assaulted by the wonderful smell of fresh vegetables.

My mouth waters. "Thank him for me, please."

I leap off my bed and sink into the plush couch. I moan into the gooey pizza while scanning my book. After I devour my meal, I stretch out. Soon my lids become heavy and my novel slips to my chest.

I stir at movement and glance up to see Christian. "Did you finally get rest?"

"I must have. Although falling asleep on a couch wasn't the greatest idea." I rub my neck as I sit up.

Christian plucks a green pepper off my chin. "Ann, I should have explained to you earlier... I saw Mary last night."

I rub my eyes and set my book down, trying to catch up. "Why would you want to see her?"

"I was seeking to obtain closure among us."

"And did you find it?"

"No, the woman I believed I married was only a deception. I apologize. I should have spoken to you first. But I was trying to lighten your burden. I mean, you haven't slept well and then you had this dinner to attend."

I put a hand on his thigh. "I know your heart was in the right place and I appreciate the effort, but tell me next time. I can handle it... I promise. Because the alternative is letting my imagination run wild with unrealistic *what ifs*. And that is normally worse than the truth."

"It's great that I employ a professional therapist for us,

huh?"

Christian has come so far from that stuck-up Prince looking for an impossibly perfect wife. His blue eyes sparkle with mischief. At this rate, his sarcasm will match mine soon.

I can't help the laugh that escapes. "We are *special* people."

He runs a strong hand through my hair. "We make an exceptionally special team." Then he kisses me softly before he rests his forehead on mine. "I wanted so much more for you. You know that, right? You were destined to soar *beyond* these walls, not be caged within them. Can you ever forgive me for restraining you?"

"Christian, how can you say that? I chose to stay at the Palace. I may not be thrilled with my desk job, but I am making a difference." I grip his chin. "We are making a difference, together. And I love that. I love *you*—cage and all." I smirk.

So many emotions flash across his face, before he collects me in his arms and spins around in a circle with a rare, childish grin curling his lips. I hold tight and squeal at the spontaneous movement as my legs fly behind me. Then he presses his body against mine and grins. "Should I assist you into your outfit for tonight?" His fingertips send goosebumps up my arms as they glide over my sides. And soon I discover it's difficult to breathe as they trace over my hips.

"No, thank you," I whisper, but I'm sure my eyes are telling him the opposite.

"Well, if you are sure... After you change, meet me in my office, and Vinny can instruct you on how to utilize the equipment you will be working with."

Once the door closes, I take note of the outfit laid out on the bed for me and change into the red silk dress, dazzling silver heels, and glittering crimson-jeweled crown. Before I walk out, I take one final look in my full-length mirror. I adjust the weight of the head piece and stand straighter, looking every bit the Queen they want me to be.

Tonight, I should keep my composure and have compassion for Max and Mary. I mean, this is their final day on this planet. Surely, they will have regrets and are afraid of the consequences of their actions.

I adjust my dress before I knock lightly on Christian's office door. When he answers it, his eyes eat up every inch of my outfit, and I swear I hear a low growl while he steps aside to let me brush past him. I stop short when I notice Ryan sitting in a chair. But before I can greet him or assess his scowl, Vinny places a device in my hand.

"Okay, pay attention, Ann. Here is your earpiece. You tap it once to speak, then let it go when you are done talking," Vinny says as he fits the cold plastic over and inside my ear. "Now you try."

I tap it and hold. "Hello?" Then I release.

"Perfect. I heard your voice crystal clear." He taps his own device before he passes me a small box. "When you turn this little switch, it will start recording."

I frown at the gadget and look down at my gown. "But I have no pockets for it."

Before I can finish my statement, everyone's eyes sweep over me, then at each other.

"Well, how about in your bra?" Vinny questions, but quickly clears his throat at Christian's glare.

I bat my lashes at Christian. "But then I can't get to the underwire."

Christian rolls his eyes as Vinny arches a brow and hands the recorder to Christian, who puts it back into his desk drawer.

Ryan watches me. "I am wearing an earpiece too. So, all you have to do is say the *word,* and I will be at your side."

I smirk. "Which word is that?"

His dark eyes grin into mine. "Underwire."

Christian steps between Ryan and me. "That's enough, you two. You are acting juvenile as usual. Ann, Vinny will escort you, the food is already there, and there will be one guard inside with you and two outside—all of them are armed if you need them." Christian collects me in an embrace. "No matter what vile nonsense they spew tonight, just disregard it and hold your head high." He lifts my chin. "Because, my *Queen,* tomorrow they will be executed, and then we can move forward with *our* future," he whispers before he kisses me, and my knees weaken.

I pull away slowly. "I will return to you shortly. Hold that thought until I get back."

I link my arm with Vinny's. "Shall we?" Once we are descending the stairs, I turn to Vinny. "How are the babies?"

"It is such a trip to imagine Karen and I *created* them. Their bodies are tiny, but they are breathing on their own and unbelievably loud." He chuckles lightly.

"Oh, come on! With Karen and her big mouth, you

should have known they would be deafening."

We both laugh and I look around, expecting the woman in question to jump me from behind for making a joke on her behalf.

"And before long, Christian and you will get to experience this." He wiggles his eyebrows. "*All of it.*"

"You guys move too fast," Ryan calls from behind.

"Ryan, what are you doing?" I call back.

"I'm making sure you get there."

I laugh. "Yes, I mean, I may trip over my heels."

"Hey, it has happened before."

"Not because I was clumsy—I stepped wrong!" I protest.

"Whatever you say, Queen Klutz," he teases lightheartedly, as he wraps an arm around my neck.

"Says the man who was terrified of a duckling?"

"Hey, if I recall correctly, I saved that duck's life! Even if I was scared it was going to bite me."

Our laughter bounces off the cobblestone walls as we descend into the underbelly of the Palace. When we arrive at the jail door, Vinny introduces me to the two guards, who each nod in my direction.

"Ryan, I don't want you stirring up Max or Mary—you wait for me out here." He turns to me with a sad smile. "Are you ready?"

I square my shoulders and readjust my crown. "Let's get this over with."

Vinny ushers me inside, and I let my vision adjust to

the gloom. My eyes take in the room with its four cells, two of which are occupied. There is a desk in the corner with a bored-looking guard sifting through a newspaper.

Max pops his head up from his squeaky cot and lazily takes me in. "Ann, you look absolutely *delicious*. Like a juicy red apple, ripe for the plucking."

Vinny narrows his eyes at Max and pulls me to him protectively. Then he scowls at the guard sitting behind the desk. "Joey, I will return in an hour to pick up Lady Ann. If there is any funny business from Max, radio it in and we will end this event immediately."

"Oh, don't you worry your pretty little head, Vinny my boy. I will be on my best behavior." Max grins widely. "Scout's honor."

Vinny ignores him and rubs a hand over my chilled arm. "Just eat and pretend to pay attention to him." He squeezes lightly and turns back to Joey. "I am sure I do not need to remind you of the importance of Lady Ann. So be vigilant." Then he stalks out.

Joey stretches and stands. He is abnormally tall and very well-muscled. He offers me a smile as he bows. "Right this way, Lady Ann." He ushers me to a tiny table by Max's cell. Then he passes Max a wrapped sandwich and a bottle of water.

I smirk at the irony of the meal. This was the same thing Max gave me before he drugged me. "Are you enjoying your new life, Max?"

His eyes darken as I cross my arms. "Well, I am now that you are here."

I follow his gaze and notice my cleavage. I uncross my arms. "You are a pig. I can't believe I agreed to sit here with you. You aren't *worth* my time," I hiss.

He sits on the edge of his cot and unwraps his sandwich. "You will be thanking me later."

"You are delusional, Max. Why would I thank you? For killing my father! Trying to murder me?" I stand and my chair clatters. "Or for ruining my day by making me watch you eat your last meal?"

Joey glances over as I pick up my chair. *So much for keeping my composure. Get a grip, Ann!* You only have fifty-five minutes left of this torture.

"Such an attitude from a so-called *Lady*," Mary purrs from her cell.

I offer her my middle finger. "Shut it, blondie."

Max laughs. "What a Lady indeed!" He winks at me. "And Vinny was warning *me* to be on my best behavior. I guess he forgot to school you too. But that's okay because I'm an excellent tutor."

I narrow my eyes. "Just shove that sandwich down your throat so I can leave."

"Say please," he demands.

"How about I give you a finger and a curse word?"

"Aww, all these broken promises! Just you wait until I am free... I'll force you to keep your word." I roll my eyes and throw my sandwich at him. He dodges the projectile. "Well, I see your aim hasn't improved since the last time you visited me."

"Why don't you just leave it on the floor. I am sure you will be hungry later."

He narrows his eyes before he shrugs it off and bites

into his sandwich. "You know what I love about you, Ann?" When I ignore him, he continues anyway. "You are not afraid to do what needs to be done. No matter *who* you hurt in the process." He licks his lips slowly. "You are a woman after my *own* heart."

I close my eyes and count to ten. "Max, I am sure you can consume your meal *without* speaking to me."

"But what would be the fun in that? Did your fiancé explain to you that my first two requests were denied?" He licks mayonnaise off the edge of his bread with his long tongue.

"You are disgusting. I am nothing like you."

"Oh, really? You think so, *sweetheart*?"

I freeze up as dark memories threaten to break through my facade. I swallow the bile in the back of my throat and shake my head. I'm determined to not let him win, and I glare as I lean towards him. "It's funny you are using pet names now, when you will be nothing but *ash* tomorrow."

"You are only offended because you realize I speak the truth. I mean, you hurt *Ryan* to step up and become Christian's... well, whatever you are now." He shrugs as he takes another mouthful. "Then you hurt your *dad* when you brushed aside his doubts about Mary and forced him to take matters into his own hands."

I hiss as I grasp the bars separating us. "Don't you dare talk about my father!" He ignores me and continues his tirade. "Then, who could forget poor *Suzie*? Dead, because you had to go home to visit your dad's grave."

"Shut up, Max! You are..." My face pales and I step away, his words echoing in my head as I recall the events of the day I traveled back to my house with Christian. My hands go to my lips. "How?" I swallow. "How did you know about Suzie? You were locked up when she died."

His grin is all I need to confirm my suspicions, and my blood runs cold. My hand instinctively goes to my earpiece. "Vinny?"

"What's wrong, Ann?" Vinny cuts in through the tiny speaker.

Max smirks through the bars of his cell.

"Vinny, did anybody tell Max about Suzie's death? Could he have overheard a guard talking about it?"

"No, why?"

"Because he knows about us traveling to my house and Suzie's death."

The silence is deafening. *I'm safe—he can't hurt me*, I repeat to myself in order to remain calm. When I get no response from Vinny, I force myself to look into Max's cold eyes. "Max, how did you know about Suzie's death?"

"The right question is: why would I give up my one last wish to have a miserable, tasteless sandwich?"

I run my fingertips through my scalp and tug at the strands as everything comes together. I tap and hold my earpiece. "Vinny, please come and get me."

"Hold tight, Ann. We are on our way."

"You are so clever, *sweetheart*." He winks as he holds the bars. "Unfortunately, you are too late. My plan is already set in motion and the Black Rose rebels are already hidden inside the Palace. And soon, each of my requests will be obtainable."

Dread crawls up my spine. No. This can't be

happening. My attention darts to Joey, and I plead with him to correct Max's threats. But he doesn't meet my gaze as he leaps to his feet to advise the other guards.

Joey slams the door and locks it. "Lady Ann, you need to get behind the desk and stay low to the ground."

My mouth hangs open and my limbs can't obey his commands. Once he clicks his magazine into place, I am snapped out of my stupor and go into fight mode.

This is not *how* this is going down!

I send daggers to Max. "How could you!"

"You should be *praising* me. I saved *your* life. That's why you are in here with *me* right now," he purrs, "and not in the middle of the bloodbath. I did all of this for you, for us."

"You really are delusional! There is no us, you *pea-brained lunatic!*" I turn to Joey. "I cannot just stand here and do nothing. Hand me your sidearm!"

"King Christian instructed me to keep my gun away from you."

Max's laughter rings through the room. "Smart man, that King."

I ignore Max. "Please, Joey, I need a weapon!"

He shakes his head. "I'm sorry, Lady Ann. Don't worry, we'll protect you if what he says is accurate."

Gunshots blast outside the door. *No!* I watch as Mary and Max grin towards the sound.

"They are coming for the prisoners. If they break through that door, you shoot them both in the head! You got it? They can't be freed. Especially Mary, she knows too much information about the Palace."

Mary narrows her eyes, but I can't hear her words as the shots get more deafening.

Joey shoves me behind the large wooden desk, before he returns to his stance in front of the door. I hear heavy footsteps, and I know they are not from the Palace servants.

I tap my earpiece. "The rebels are right outside the prison. Can anyone hear me?"

I slip my fingertips down my dress and reach for my bra's underwire, but it isn't as easy as the videos made it seem. I can't even get the wire to poke through to grab it!

"Ann, we are being assaulted here as well. Remain with Joey and we will reach you quickly," Christian blares. There is a thunderous blast, and I am hurled against the wall. I gasp and hold my ringing ears. I force myself off the ground; my vision is blurry and my body is on fire.

My scalp screams when I am pulled up by my hair by a large man dressed in black. Blindly, I kick as hard as I can and twist at the same time. My silver spiked heels sink into the man's stomach and he dumps me on the floor. The fall is broken by my arm, and I shriek at the lightning bolt of pain that shoots through my body.

I squeal when I stare into the eyes of my former guard, who now lies bleeding in my path, a chunk of wood jutting out of his abdomen. My fingertips shake while I glide them over his neck.

I pray that he is just injured.

No pulse...

Voices pull me out of my despair, and I crawl over

Joey's gore, apologizing along the way. Metal brushes my thigh and I pause to look down. Relief floods me and I snatch his sidearm before kissing it like a long-lost friend. Once I am able to climb over the fallen soldier, I slip past the doorway.

My relief is short-lived when I gape at the three rebels right outside the door. They aim at me with warnings to stay put, but I roll away before shooting two of them in the foot. They fall, screaming in pain, while the third man retaliates with his own bullets, missing me by mere inches. I shoot again and graze my attacker's thigh. Once he bends over in agony, I leap to my feet and make a run for it.

My heartbeat hammers in my ears while I blindly move fast and hard. Every muscle in my body screams as I turn a corner towards what I hope is the kitchen. I quickly steal a glance behind me for followers. Before I can turn around again, I slam into a solid torso and instantly aim the gun.

"Wait, Lady Ann!"

Breathing heavily, I peek past the barrel and let out a breath. "Oh, thank God!" I squeeze Jock. "I may have accidently put a target on my back. We need to move quickly before the rebels find us."

I blink down at his once white chef's jacket, now covered in black smudges and crimson droplets. He snatches my wrist, pulls me towards the massive pantry, and pushes me inside. Once my eyes adjust, I see that the kitchen staff is tucked along the shelves, armed with knives, pots, pans, and one even brandishes a lighter. I run a hand through my hair as I lean against the cool wall. When I pull my hand back, I frown at the blood splatters.

They've forced me to become a monster…

My ear rings with static and I squeak, remembering the earpiece. "Hello, is anyone there?" I whisper.

"Ann, is that you? Where the hell are you?" Ryan yells.

His voice rolls over my exhausted body and calms me. "What happened? Is everyone all right?"

"Ann, answer me! *Where* are you?"

"I am in the pantry."

"The *what!*" he hisses.

"The food cupboard, Ryan. I narrowly escaped the rebels and wounded a few with Joey's gun. But, Ryan, Joey is gone." I swallow hard as the image of the guard's body still haunts me. I look down at my gun. "And I am running out of ammo." I rub my temples, willing my tears to stay put. Will I ever see Ryan again? Is this the last time I will hear his voice? "Ryan, if I don't make it, I want you to know how much you mean to me. I…"

I suck in my response while heavy footsteps approach. I release the earpiece to ready my weapon. I hold my breath when I listen to the clanging and banging of pots and pans being thrown around. When the steps run past the pantry, I wipe the sweat off my forehead.

"Ryan, are you still there? Underwire!" I whisper into the earpiece, but no response comes through.

A sudden jolt of pain rides up my arm as Jock checks my injured limb. "Ann, your arm is swelling."

I cradle it away from him. "I'm fine. How is everyone else doing?"

I take in the small group. They are servants, not

soldiers. Their eyes are wide with terror, their hands shaking as they grip useless objects. Some are on the floor, crying as quietly as they can manage in their despair.

"There are safe rooms located around the Palace for these instances, but we couldn't make it to any fast enough," Jock says. I nod as I remember the training the Palace representatives offered before I came here. They had mentioned multiple safe rooms in cases of emergency, and this was definitely one of those times. They each held food, water, and first aid kits. As a member of the royal family, I should be heading towards the hospital wing, where they have the most secure and equipped rooms. That's where Ryan and Christian will be going with Elizabeth and Vinny.

"Do not worry, Jock. I can go out there and distract them, while you take everyone to safety." I place my hand on the doorknob.

He tugs me away from the door and shakes his head furiously. "Lady Ann, no, *you* are our priority. We will keep you safe."

"No, I am the highest ranking." I stand tall. "And you will listen to me, do you understand?"

"Lady Ann…"

I suppress my fear and hold my hand up. "I will guide you guys to the safe room before they find us. Then I'll meet up with Ryan and Christian." I slowly open the door and peek out. It is silent except for the gunfire in the distance. "Jock, you take the lead, and I will take the rear. Everybody needs to get to safety and stay there, *no* matter what. Understood?"

I usher Jock out and the other fifteen people follow

close behind. As we round the corner, Jock sways a beautiful portrait of a past Queen and a door swings open. I watch as he steps through and helps everyone climb inside. Then he turns to me. "Lady Ann, come with us."

"I need to assist King Christian and Prince Ryan and make sure Elizabeth and Snowball are safe."

"They are already in a safe room."

"I have a bad feeling, Jock. I can't explain it, but I know they need me right now. Plus, my flock is outside and I can't leave them unprotected." I turn to him and plead, "Go inside and lock the door, Jock."

We both know this is goodbye, because I won't just sit inside a bunker, waiting for help to arrive while *knowing* others need me. Even if they have feathers instead of clothes. They are just as important and my responsibility.

I pale as I hear boot steps approaching. "Hurry!" I hiss to Jock.

He shuts the door quietly and stands beside me. "I can't leave you out here to fend them off on your own."

I aim the gun down the hallway and hold my breath. I pray that whoever is approaching goes a different route. I jump as a black figure emerges and turns towards me. "Oh, *sweetheart*! I have finally found you!"

"Max!" I glare into his dark green eyes while gritting my teeth. I aim for his head, but before I can pull the trigger, he shoots at Jock. I watch in slow motion as my friend crumbles to the ground. I drop to my knees, rip a strip of fabric from my red dress and wrap it around the gushing wound on his leg.

"Jock! No! Please hold on!"

Max had initiated the distraction he was hoping for, because soon two other rebels stand behind him with their guns raised.

"It's simple, Ann. You have two options. Either come with me quietly, or watch your friend die." He shrugs. "It's *your* choice."

Jock shakes his head. I run a bloody hand over his worn face. "I will not let them kill you too. I would never forgive myself." I whisper softly, "Tell the Princes I love them, and this was not their fault."

I stand in front of Jock's body with my gun still aimed at Max. "Max, give me your word you will leave him here."

"Fine, I promise."

"You *and* your men." I narrow my eyes.

He smirks as he nods to his men. "You heard the Queen. No one hurts the cook. Leave him here to die, okay?"

They each nod, never lowering their weapons. I hesitate, not wanting to place my life in Max's psychotic hands. I soon put my shaking palms up in defeat. Max smiles wide as he snatches the gun and pockets it. "I have been waiting a long time to say this, sweetheart." He grins as he steps towards me. "Turn around." I cringe but do as he says, and I feel him wrap zip ties around my wrists. Then he pulls me roughly against his chest and whispers into my ear, "Thank you for willingly returning to me." Then he smells my hair and groans softly, "Oh, the fun we will have together." He shoves me forward towards the other rebels. "Looks like I may get *all* my requests approved after all, boys!"

269

Max narrows his eyes at my ear and abruptly stops. "One more thing." He seizes my device and places it in his own ear. "Whoever is listening, I would like to inform you that Lady Ann is now a hostage of the Black Rose. Say *hello*." He leans his ear to me. I clamp my mouth shut and he pouts before he snatches a fistful of my hair. I scream out as my scalp burns and my vision blurs. He licks my neck slowly. "Was that so hard? Why do you insist on testing me?"

"What are you hoping to accomplish, Max?" I spit.

"A new government."

"And you think killing and torturing people will accomplish this?"

"Why not? It worked for King Mark, didn't it?"

"This will only cause pain and suffering, then another uprising for revenge. Please, you have to see this. *You* can stop this."

"Pause your lecture. I have an incoming call." He pushes his earpiece. "Hello, Prince Ryan, how are you?... Oh, that is not very nice." Max pinches his nose and stops walking. "Let me tell *you* how this is going to go. You will bring me your brother and meet me in the office. See you soon."

Then he pulls out the plastic listening device and grinds it into fragments on the floor.

I glare up at the stairs as Max shoves me towards them. "Max, I need to remove my heels."

"Hey, you picked out this outfit, so deal with it. Not that I am complaining." I don't respond, though I'd love to remind him the heels were his suggestion.

I make it to the third floor but my left foot slips and I knock my knee hard on the wood step. Before my face hits the stairs, Max catches me. "Geez, I can't take you anywhere."

I blink away tears as pain shoots up my leg. He throws me over his shoulder, as if I weigh nothing, then he slaps my rear before we continue our climb.

I yelp at the assault to my backside and attempt to wiggle out of his grasp, but he holds tight. The normal hustle and bustle of the office has turned deathly quiet.

"What the hell?" Max pushes out.

In the corner of my eye, I see Snowball rushing over — wings out and screeching. The other rebels are just as confused by her antics. When she realizes she can't scare my captors, she aims to disorient them instead. She runs around their feet, pecking at their laces. Max easily bypasses her, but before he hauls me into Christian's office, I witness the white fluffball trip one of the soldiers and I listen to them tumble down the stairs. "Snowball, run!" I shriek, afraid of the rebel's retaliation.

I squirm, and Max scrambles to keep me at bay. I fumble to the ground and make a pitiful attempt to run down the stairs, but he catches me before throwing me over his shoulder again with a grunt.

Once we walk past the office desks, I gasp as I take in the utter destruction. My eyes fall on the glass vase that once held my beautiful bouquet of flowers. Now it lies shattered, broken beyond repair.

As soon as we are inside, Max sets me down in Christian's chair, and a rebel reports to the group. "Keep on guard, boys. When the detonators are set, we are out of here."

My head shoots up. "You are bringing down the Palace? Are you insane?"

The men ignore me as they shake hands and congratulate Max on his return. Then they split up before Max closes the door and starts removing his tactical gear. "You know, I am not big on modern weaponry. I was trained to attack the mind. I enjoy getting into someone's head and breaking them from the inside." Then he leans on the desk, studying me. "But enough about me. What about you? You know, Ann, you could have anything your heart desires—*anyone you want*—if only you would stop allowing everyone to make decisions for you."

"Says the man who let his sister give him orders that led to his imprisonment. Why don't you take your own advice?"

"Come on, this new government is centered on the *people* making up their own minds, taking freedom into their own hands, and not following a dictator blindly."

I narrow my eyes. "I want nothing to do with a government that is murdering *innocent* lives to get what it wants."

"They are *sacrifices*."

"Don't sugarcoat it. It's murder, Max. Cold-blooded murder! At least *your* army knew what they were getting into! And what they are fighting for." Tears well in my eyes as I see Jock's bleeding leg and Joey's limp body. "Your fantasy, your so-called government, can go to hell!"

"You care too much." He waves his hand at me as he stands and looks through Christian's desk.

"You care too little," I grumble.

Max uses a hammer to strike the keypad on the safe until it shatters. Then he grabs all the files and slams them on the desk, pulling out multiple documents and shoving them into his shirt. "Don't pretend your fiancé doesn't do the same damn thing, sweetheart. I can't even tell you the masses his bloodline has slaughtered." He opens another drawer before he looks up at me. "And I saved *you*, didn't I? Doesn't that count for something? I should get some Jesus points for that," he mutters as he snatches another folder.

"You only rescued me for your own sick pleasure!" I spit out. "And Christian has been aiming to clean up his father's mess, not make it worse."

Max slams the drawer shut. Then he prowls towards me and kneels at my feet. His green eyes meet mine. "You know, I got swept away with the mission and forgot... I *did* rescue you for my own pleasure." He slides a warm hand up my leg and rests it on my thigh.

I swallow down my nausea while I narrow my eyes. "You wouldn't dare touch me."

I regret my words instantly when his eyes spark with my challenge. "The cold-blooded murderer? The one who watched your father fall to the ground and bleed out? The one who poisoned you and left you for dead?" He glides his hand upwards and rests it on my underwear, then teasingly moves his thumb. "Try me, sweetheart."

I pale and kick him. "You coward! How about you untie me and we can battle it out?"

He jumps back, his laughter reverberating off the walls. "Ann, I want more than just your body. I want your supporters and your keen mind." He kneels again but further away. "I want *all* of you."

I narrow my eyes. "Then why did you ask Ryan for Christian."

He grins at me, his green eyes darkening. "I will use you to get Christian to sign a petition. Then, once it is signed, I will snatch you up and bring you home."

I suck in a breath as his words wash over me. No. I won't be his prisoner again. Our conversation is cut short as a tall man saunters in. He looks a few years older than I am, and his dark eyes are sharp as they scan the room before falling on me. Then he shuts the door. "What is the status report?" He removes some of his gear to wipe sweat off his face.

"Everything is on schedule, and I am waiting for the King's arrival. But he should have been here by now."

The stranger glances at his watch. "We need to progress quicker." He eyes Max. "We should consider that Christian may not value her as much as we thought. He may choose self-preservation over her safety. We need to test those limits if we want to be successful, and coercion *by any means* necessary is authorized, understood?" The man looks around again. "Where is Mary?"

For once, I see remorse cross Max's features. "She didn't make it out of the jail."

The man rubs his face. "She will be greatly missed, but let's make sure her death is not in vain." He places a hand on Max's shoulder before he walks out.

Max shakes his emotions off, then rubs his hands together as the door closes. He picks up the phone, hits a button, and his voice booms over the Palace intercom:

"Ladies and gentlemen, I am still searching for your King. Then all of this will end." He smiles as he sits on the desk, staring at me. "And if he doesn't appear on the third floor in five minutes, things will get hot and heavy between Lady Ann and me up here." He winks at me and then hangs up.

He jumps off the desk and wiggles another set of zip ties out in front of him. I narrow my eyes. "Don't you even think about it!"

No amount of training prepared me to fight with my arms bound behind my back, so I quickly lose the battle when he wrestles me—casually whistling to himself throughout the process. By the time he is finished, I am on the ground with my hands and legs bound.

"Is this really necessary? Were you really that afraid I would whoop you?"

He straddles me. "This is all your fault—you are not playing nice." He taps his watch. "Your beloved only has two more minutes left. Why don't we try to hurry him along?" He grabs the phone and puts it on the floor by my head. "King Christian, you have just two minutes left," he sings over the intercom. His eyes meet mine as he strokes my cheek. I bite at his hand and growl. His fingertips dig into my chin as he clutches my face. "Ann is a spirited one. I see why you like her."

He buries his nose in the nape of my neck and gently nibbles. I twist away from him and he punishes me by digging his teeth into the sensitive skin. My scream of agony rings throughout the Palace halls, as blood trickles onto the white carpet. I muster all of my strength, and when he brings his head away from my neck, I thrust my temple up and knock him backwards.

275

He ends the broadcast, then wipes the blood from his mouth while chuckling maniacally. This man has lost his mind. If I can't find a way out of this mess, I must keep him talking, so everybody has enough time to get to safety.

"What the hell was that, Max!"

"I'm doing my job, trying to get your fiancé's attention." He rubs the egg forming on his head. "You are definitely stubborn."

"At least I am not a vampire."

"Stop being a baby. It was just a tiny *love* bite."

"I am bleeding! You probably gave me rabies, you lunatic."

"Well, unfortunately, your time is up." He strides over to me. "I really thought they would protect you. I mean, if they really, truly loved you, they would be here. At least one of them." He plucks a dagger from the sheath at his side and throws it into the air. The silver of the blade catches the light as it twirls head over end. Then he catches it and runs his finger along the edge. "Okay, so you have two choices." He tilts his head at me. "Ann, are you listening?"

My mind races as he nears me with the sharp metallic object. No, this can't be my end. I have more to offer the world. I swallow my terror and force my eyes to meet his. "I am listening."

"This is a once in a lifetime opportunity here. You can join the Black Rose, help us with our cause, and well… heck, be *my* girl. Or stay where you are, let me have my fun with you, and be left here to bleed out into the carpet."

276

I suck in a breath. Neither of those options are very promising.

"Are those my only choices? I mean, you could just let me go?" I twist away from him.

"Leave it to you to try to compromise—*very diplomatic.*" He runs the cold tip over my neck. "What's it going to be, sweetheart?"

His words slap me across the face. What am *I* going to do? Cower down and give in, just to live another day? Or can I rise up, accept my fate, and die while fighting like hell?

Christian's and Ryan's faces pass through my mind. I am going to miss them. But they will move on. I am just a feather in the wind.

"Do what you will with me. I won't help you *murderers,*" I hiss through my teeth.

"Even if you are free to make your own choices? Free to marry *who* you want? And do what you want in life? Come on, Ann! You are more than all of this!" he shouts. "You can accomplish amazing things with us!"

I lift my chin. "I *choose* to be here, with *them.*"

He frowns, taken aback by my refusal. "Is that your final answer?"

I squeeze my eyes shut and lean my head back against the plush carpet. "Yes, it is."

Max growls and stalks over to the phone. "Well, our fearless leader has *selfishly* decided not to show up in order to save his lady." He hangs up with a loud clang. "I wanted more than this, Ann." He slides his hand under my dress and up my thigh. "We could have ruled together. We are the perfect match. My brains mixed with your compassion and beauty. We could take over the world." He glides the blade along the front of my dress, exposing my skin. "You really are the most beautiful woman alive. King Christian is missing out." He gently places kisses down my collar, as his fingertips graze my chest. I squirm, trying my best to get out of his grasp. But my arms are numb and the zip ties on my legs are cutting into my skin.

Max laughs lightly into my ear as he nips my lobe. "You are more than I imagined. Who would have thought all of *this* lies beneath all of those fancy dresses? We can be civil about this, sweetheart. Choose me and the rebellion, or die *unnecessarily*."

"Just stop wasting your breath, Max! Man-up and get it over with already!"

My resolve is withering as his hands rove over my body. I bite my lip to hold back a sob, just as I hear the door behind Max slam open.

"You son of a bit—"

The weight of Max's body is suddenly thrown off me, and my eyes shoot open.

I turn my head and witness Ryan repeatedly slamming his knuckles into Max's face, until I am certain there is no life left.

"Ryan?" I choke out. "You came for me."

As the words echo in the room, his eyes slowly return to their normal shade. "I am sorry this happened to you." He removes his suit jacket and lays it over me. Then he lifts me up carefully and uses Max's dagger to cut me loose.

278

I groan when my hands are freed, but I feel like jelly as I try to put his coat on. "Ryan, I can't move my arms."

He assists me, fastening the buttons quickly. "Ann, we have to get out of here—it is not safe." He spots Max's gear and grabs it before he collects me in his arms.

My adrenaline drains and I feel an exhaustion I have never felt before, blanketing me down to my very bones. I breathe in his warmth. Ryan came for me. For a moment, I want to act as if we are back at the lake house, lying in the bed together with just our bodies and fireplace to keep us warm. But those simpler days are gone, and our lives are forever changed.

My eyes shoot open as I hear more footsteps, and I am shocked to see Jock limping by the office door. "My Prince, we need to get you to a safe room immediately."

"Jock, I am so glad to see you." I offer a weak smile.

His eyes wash over me. "She needs a medical kit. There are safe rooms nearby, but they were designed for a single individual."

We hear boots thumping and shouting. Ryan clutches me to his chest. "We will have to take what we can get."

Jock leads us to the first floor and around a few corners. I clutch Ryan's shirt, afraid he may drop me at the speed he is moving, but he never falters.

Jock opens a secret area and ushers us inside while whispering, "I am going to make sure we were not followed." Jock looks back once more with a sad expression before he seals us inside.

I intend to reach out, to yell for him to stay, but I am a coward and can't even push the words forward as I cling to Ryan like he's my lifeline.

My best friend, my hero, my world.

Safe Room

I am safe. I keep repeating the mantra.

Soon darkness envelops me, as the peace of Ryan's familiar scent lulls me to sleep.

I had forgotten how it feels to be held by him. Even with just my undergarments and his coat on, I feel secure.

I'm not sure how long I am out. But as soon as my body senses his absence, my eyes shoot open and dart around the unfamiliar area. The bleak room is tiny with a toilet, a first aid kit, water bottles, some food strips resembling jerky, flashlights, and a small cot, offering a pillow and a rough blanket.

I panic until I notice Ryan. He is leaning against the entrance with his eyes closed, breathing heavily and sweating. Maybe he is dreaming? Or just reliving the nightmare of the attack?

I rise unsteadily to my feet and reach for him. His lids flutter open, and for a moment, we gaze into each other's eyes. I nestle my head on to his chest and choke out a sob. My intentions were to keep it all bottled up and let my strength shine through for him, but again, I failed. Ryan wraps his arms around me, lifts me up, and sits on the cot before settling me in his lap.

I wipe my eyes and lean against the wall, observing his vacant expression. "Ryan, what happened out there?"

My words bring him to the present, and he blinks into focus. "When Vinny and I received your warning, the office atmosphere quickly changed into complete chaos.

We did the best we could to sound the alarm, but the rebels were quick and efficient. They somehow disabled the system."

As he speaks, the events of what happened—and the rebels' conversations—replay in my mind. "Ryan, there are bombs all over the Palace!"

"Are you sure?"

"Yes, Max was talking about them and how the Palace is going to blow—*and soon*."

Ryan grabs his cell phone from his pants pocket. "Vinny? Yes, I have her, and we are in one of the safe rooms near the kitchen. Jock should be heading your way... No, listen! We have bigger problems. There are bombs in the Palace." He looks down at his phone before he continues his conversation. "Not much battery left on my end, and there are no chargers in here... Will do... Okay, stay safe." He hangs up and leans back. Then he rubs his stubble with his free hand. "We did our best to get everyone to safety. Then we heard Max had found you."

"We? Where is Christian? Was he with you?"

Ryan closes his eyes and ignores my inquiry. "Jock and I had to fight our way to the third floor, but I am glad we made it in time." He opens his watery eyes. "We did make it in time, right?"

I blush and nod slowly. I reach a sore hand up to Ryan's face and run it along his jawline. "You didn't answer my question. Where is Christian?"

He gently guides me out of his lap and grabs the first aid kit. I sit up and scoot to the edge of the flimsy cot. He returns and kneels in front of me. Then he opens the kit and starts dabbing my ankles where the zip ties dug in. The pain shoots fireworks behind my eyes, and I bite back a yelp.

"I'm sorry, Ann. I think we have some pain reliever in here I can give you."

I move my legs away from his grasp and drop to the floor with him. "If Christian is in trouble, we *need* to help him! The Black Rose wants to corner him and make him sign a petition. He is in grave danger!"

When his eyes meet mine, I know his next few words are going to sting. "Christian said we could not risk saving you from the rebels. He thought the hazards involved were too great. That *we* must remain safe, to keep the country going and bring vengeance. He thought Max had a sick love for you, that he wouldn't hurt you... that he would only make a scene."

I watch his lips move, but it feels like Ryan is speaking another language. Christian told me he loved me—he said he *always* has. If you love someone, you don't abandon them to the wolves. You fight for them. Always.

"No, Christian said... what?" I stutter.

"I defied him and ran to help you, and Jock followed my lead." He rubs the back of his neck. "Jock said you saved his life?"

I push past my disbelief and whisper, "Yes, I traded my life for Jock's."

Ryan's eyes glaze over before he pulls me into his arms. "When I heard your scream over the earpiece, and then the intercom..."

"Thank you, Ryan. I owe you everything."

I can't meet his searching gaze. These last few months, I have been pushing him away from me, and yet here he is, taking care of me when everyone else has abandoned me.

"Don't be silly. You owe me nothing. Now sit still so I can clean these wounds."

I do as I'm told, still deep in thought, as he returns to tending my injuries. I am so numb. Christian was going to leave me in the rebels' hands... he left me to suffer. Maybe he only played the doting fiancé because it was his *duty*, and he felt obligated.

"Your knee is pretty swollen."

"I know. I had another run-in with the stairs. I swear I am never wearing heels again."

Ryan's phone rings and he pauses to answer it. "Vinny?... What!... How?... Yes, I dressed her wounds. But she still needs medical attention." He pales as he stands. "Yes, here she is." He passes me the phone.

"Vinny?"

"Ann, it is so good to hear your voice at a *normal* level," he jokes.

I smile weakly and lean back—only Vinny would crack a joke right now.

He clears his throat. "I have King Christian here, and he wishes to speak to you."

My back straightens. Finally! I can let him have it! I can get the answers I require in order to cut ties with him for abandoning me in my time of need.

"Ann? It is so good to hear your voice."

My body stiffens. There is no fire or assertiveness

behind those words, just exhaustion. This isn't the Christian I know.

My angry speech slips from my lips and I push out, "Christian, what is wrong?"

"Don't fret regarding me. I just needed to hear your voice. Now, allow Ryan to take care of you, okay?"

"I will see you soon, Christian."

My eyes water when only silence bounces back.

Come on!

Tell *me* it was a mistake!

Remind me that you still love me!

"Ann, we have the bomb squad here. Sit tight," Vinny blares.

As the line goes dead, I pass the phone to Ryan. When his hand glides over mine, I hold tightly to the receiver as I narrow my eyes. "Is Christian going to be okay?"

His face tells me all I need to know, as he shakes his head and tears form in the corners of his eyes.

"Ryan, answer me."

He releases his phone and resumes cleaning my cuts in silence. After a few minutes, he pauses. "Are there any wounds under the jacket?"

I glance at my chest. "No, I don't think so."

He sits on the cot as he dabs at the blood on my arm. "Did I kill Max?"

I look at his clenched jaw and swallow. "I think you did."

He nods and reaches towards my neck. "Good. That bastard deserved it. And what about Mary?"

"She is dead."

I squeal as the bite on my neck burns like hell.

"Sorry, Ann. This wound looks the worst."

He leans towards it again and I scramble away from him.

"Please sit still—it can get infected." He cautiously moves closer and touches me again. The searing pain makes me suck in a breath and hot tears roll down my cheek.

"I am trying to hurry." He snatches the antibiotic cream and his throat bobs. "I can't believe I killed a man today."

"We both did, didn't we?" I sigh as I wipe my eyes. Although I aimed for places that would heal, I did shoot them point-blank.

"We are murderers."

"But did we have any other choice?" I ask with big eyes. "We were defending ourselves."

He shakes his head as he puts up the first aid kit. "Does it matter?"

Those three words hit hard. Each syllable encompasses such agony as he forces the realization out. We will be forever changed after what we did tonight. And by what was done to us. To what extent, I am afraid to know.

Suddenly, there is an earth-shattering explosion followed by rumbling and crashing. The lights extinguish, and I can't help the scream that rips through my throat as darkness consumes me. Rubble showers down and I panic, certain that the room will crumble and bury me beneath it.

Just as suddenly, the shaking stops. I feel stray pebbles bounce off my head as I cough through the dust that blankets me.

"Ann?" A beam of light blinds me as Ryan clicks on a flashlight.

"Don't worry, I'm still alive, for now." I wave my hand at the floating powder. "What the hell was that?"

"I think it was an explosive from our Black Rose *pals*." He makes his way to the door and attempts to open it. "Well, that's just great." He pushes on it with his shoulder, but it only budges an inch. He flashes his light into the crack and groans. "It looks like we are stuck here until they can clear the debris."

"What if the whole Palace collapsed?"

"Then we would be dead under the rubble, instead of just trapped." He pulls out his phone and curses. "I have no service."

"Well, at least Vinny and Jock know where we are." I bite my lip as I watch him. "They shot Christian, didn't they?"

Ryan is quiet as he sits next to me on the small cot. "Christian... he is tougher than anyone else I know."

Ryan is trying to put up a strong front, to keep me from worrying, but I see the guilt and pain etched on his face.

I close my eyes as tears stream down and exhaustion floods my mind. "Ryan, I am sorry I took you away from your family." I put my head in my hands.

He collects me in his arms. "Hey, stop that. I have no regrets. I'm exactly where I want to be—with you."

I snuggle into his chest and listen to his heartbeat, strong and steady. We lie together and I start drifting off to sleep, but soon Max's voice haunts me... I clutch onto Ryan's arms to steady myself. I have always been strong, but I can't hide the panic carved into every word. "Ryan, please promise me you won't leave me."

He leans back, holding me to him. "Never."

That simple utterance is the sweetest lullaby as I drift to sleep. All too soon, I'm startled awake and look around, afraid of where I am. Thank goodness Ryan left the flashlight on to illuminate the room and keep us from enduring total darkness. As I catch my bearings, I realize I am lying on the cot with Ryan positioned behind me. When I rotate, I groan as a shooting pain runs up my neck and knee.

Stupid Max and his *love bite*. I swear if Ryan hadn't killed him, I would have. I endure the pain and go to the bathroom, then I limp over to grab a bottle of water, some jerky, and a pain reliever. I scrunch up my nose at the limited supplies. It won't last long between the two of us.

I sit on the edge of the cot and stare at the wall. What are we going to do? Will we run out of the essentials before they can rescue us?

My fingertips glide through Ryan's hair. At least I am in good company.

Ryan hums softly before his eyes flutter open. "Are you okay?"

"My neck and knee hurt, but I took some medication. How are you feeling?"

"I feel like my body was run over by a truck."

He groans as he lifts himself from the cot and grabs a snack. Then he lowers back down next to me.

"So, what do we do now?"

He pulls his eyes away from the exit and shrugs. "How about a game of I spy?"

I laugh but play along as I call out, "I spy something black."

He smirks and our game takes off. After an hour of this, we start to run out of things to name in our cramped space.

I tap Ryan with my toe. "Hey, it's your turn."

"Ann, we have mentioned everything already," he whines.

"Well, you can forfeit and let me win."

He rubs his chin then a sly smirk plays on his lips. "I spy something red."

I arch a brow and point to all the red things I spot, but I eventually throw my hands up. "Ryan, I give up."

"Think about what *you* are wearing." He looks at my chest.

I blink down and my cheeks turn scarlet. "Ryan!" I whack him and cross my arms.

"What? We ran out of items, so I thought outside the box." He elbows me.

"Oh, you are just *hilarious*," I grumble. "I can't believe a gentleman would look, especially under the circumstances. I thought you were better than that," I spit.

"I couldn't help it. But I gave you my jacket, didn't I? Doesn't that count for something?"

I narrow my eyes, unbutton the jacket, and toss it at him. "Fine, you can just take it back!"

He turns away with a chuckle. "Ann, please put it on before you get sick."

He tosses it back and the heavy material lands over my head. I snatch it off and glare.

"No." I raise my chin. "You already saw *everything,* so what's the point."

"You are being ridiculous. What if the rebels break in? Or poor Vinny?"

"Fine, but no more poking fun at my undergarments." I refasten the buttons.

"They were *very* pretty."

My mouth falls open and I grab the pillow and slap him in the face with it. "You weren't supposed to see!"

Ryan raises his hands to defend himself, then he grabs my wrists and pulls me down. We wrestle playfully and soon we are out of breath.

"Vinny would have us running laps, for how out of shape we are," I joke.

Ryan runs a fingertip down my nose. "You weren't made for combat anyway." He smirks. "Oh, look! Your makeup is running, my Lady."

"Well, allow me to go fix it for you, little Prince." I give him the finger before I try to wiggle free, but he doesn't move. I stare into his eyes again and see them darken.

"Ann, can I ask you a serious question?"

"What else do we have to do in here? Unless you'd rather I guess what you are wearing underneath your clothing?"

"A rainbow Speedo."

I burst out laughing at the mental picture and his serious expression that accompanies it.

"Stop it! My sides hurt!" I swipe my eyes. "As long as you stick clear of my underwear, go ahead and ask."

He avoids eye contact. "If Mary was never charged, would you have married me?"

Without pause, I answer, "Yes, Ryan."

"No doubt in your mind?"

"Although it would have taken some time to forgive you for messing around with Mary, there's no doubt in my mind that I would have *eventually* chosen you."

He lets out a breath. "That's good, because when we get out of here, I am going to marry you."

I blink, trying to catch up while he caresses my face. At first, my words can't form properly. How the hell can Ryan just say that? He knows Christian and I are engaged, and nothing can change those circumstances. Plus, there is no way Christian will share me or let me go.

"Ryan, did you hit your head during the attack?" I place a hand on his forehead.

"I have *never* felt better."

He removes my hand and kisses my knuckles.

"You do remember I am engaged to Christian?"

"I do not care what *he* wants anymore. I mean, we should get what *we* want, right?"

"Ryan, Christian is your brother, and I understand you are mad at him right now, but I know you love him, and you don't want to hurt him."

Ryan scoffs, "Are you sure about that? After what *he* did to you, you are willing to just overlook it all and marry that coward?"

I flinch as his words slap me. "You know I don't have a choice."

"Come on, Ann. Think about it. We will run away, travel, get married, and have tons of feathered kids."

I shake my head gently. "Ryan, but…"

"No *buts*. We are doing this. For *us*." He kisses my palm. "I have never fought Christian on *anything* before. But now I know why. I was waiting for the one thing worth fighting for. And that's you, Ann."

Of course, Ryan would wait until we are trapped to say things like this. I look around the small area and shake my head of his honey-laced promises.

"That is sweet. But you need to realize we might not be rescued."

"You can't think like that. We will be fine. *And* free to be together again. Christian will understand eventually." He kisses my shoulder. "Why can't we get what we want? *Why*?" he whispers.

His despair-tinged words break my heart. They are filled with so much regret and pain. I run my fingertips over his lips. It has been so long since we were together. Does he still taste the same?

Ryan watches me stare at his lips and he runs a thumb over my own. I gasp at the spark it sends down to my toes. I've missed his touch—so safe in a world that is crumbling around me.

If we never make it out of here, it is all my fault. I should have gone inside the safe room with the kitchen staff, and since I hadn't, Ryan came to my aid. He risked everything, including his relationship with his brother, to be with me.

If Ryan can risk everything, so can I. I want him—the one person who truly loves me. When he crushes his mouth to mine, I don't fight it. We embrace and suddenly passion overwhelms my logical thoughts. I wrap my arms around his neck, tug him to me, and deepen the kiss.

He tenses and I fear he may stop me, but then he emits a soft groan and turns us around, his lips never leaving mine. My fingertips glide to the buttons on his shirt, but he collects my wrist.

"Ann, I am not strong enough to say no to you. So, I need to know that this is, without a doubt, what *you* want."

I watch desire smolder behind his eyes before I pull my arm away from him. Then I feel his panic as I move away, but he doesn't fight me.

I slowly unbutton the jacket he gave me, slide it off my shoulders, and toss it onto the floor. His mouth is agape while he moves closer to my exposed skin.

I hold my breath as his warmth radiates towards me, beckoning me like a siren. My body aches for his contact, but then he stops a few inches away.

I can't help but whimper. "Ryan, I want this." I

grasp his wrist and hover it above my chest. He runs his fingertips over me, and this sets off a chain reaction. Before long we are intertwined together, taking from each other the *one* thing that was promised to the person we would marry.

Eventually we come up for air and lie in each other's arms, enjoying our newfound closeness.

And all is right in the world.

We are now taking the final steps to achieve our happily ever after. And our love story will soon be complete.

Ryan strokes my arm. "No regrets?"

I run my hand through his chest fluff. "No regrets."

I snuggle into the crook of his arm and listen to his heartbeat while we fall into a comfortable sleep. Then we are awakened suddenly, when his phone blares. Ryan tumbles off the cot clumsily and tries to answer it, but fails. He grumbles and redials. "Vinny? Can you hear me?" He scowls at the phone and sets it down. "Great. No service, and no battery." He rubs his face before he strides back to me and cuddles under the rough blanket. "How are you feeling?" he asks as he traces over my belly button.

"I'm a little sore, but good." I position my leg on top of his. "What about you?"

"I have never been happier." He places a kiss on my forehead. "Ann, you are hot."

I run my nose over his neck. "Thank you."

He chuckles against my ear. "I mean you feel like you have a fever." I frown as he gets up, then I shiver before bringing the blanket to my chin. He returns with food, water, and a pain reliever. "Here, take this."

I turn from him, feeling sleepy. "Ryan, I am fine."

He leans over me. "Please, for me." He kisses my neck tenderly. A tingle runs down my back and I turn towards him, taking in his serious expression.

I sit up, letting the blanket fall. "Fine, but you *owe* me," I grumble as I eat, drink, and take the medication.

"I look forward to owing you *every* night for the rest of our lives." He moves to kiss me, but he pauses and narrows his eyes at my neck. "Crap." He reaches for the first aid kit.

"What's wrong?" I pout.

"It's your neck." He dabs the alcohol wipe on it and I scream. "It's inflamed and looks green."

I shield myself with my hands. "Ryan, stop! You are hurting me."

"Ann, this is serious. It is most likely infected." He moves closer. I pull away, but I have nowhere to go. My eyes water as the wound stings. "I am sorry. I am trying to be gentle." He pats the open gash while blowing on it at the same time. He then applies ointment and bandages it. "I didn't realize it was that bad. Hopefully this will stay on."

"Well, Max has a dirty mouth." I itch at the bandage.

He slides his hands over his face. "Let's get some clothes back on."

"But you owe me." His lips twitch as he helps me back into my undergarments. "There will be plenty of time for that when you are feeling better."

"You just don't love me anymore," I tease.

Ryan snatches my chin. "I love you more than anything else in this crazy, upside-down world." He kisses me tenderly. When I try to deepen the kiss, he chuckles. "Please, at least break that fever first. Then you can have me all you want."

I feel my energy deplete as he puts his jacket on me and buttons it. Then he lays me down on the pillow and covers me. He places a kiss against my hair, and I slowly fall into a feverish sleep. When I wake up, I'm not able to recall where I am. I shriek and soon Ryan returns to my side. He holds me and forces me to drink water.

I can't tell how much time passes as chills continue to wreak havoc on my body. Whenever I wake up, Ryan is by my side, soothing me, but I can see the worry written all over his face. Even as he promises me everything is going to be okay, I know I am destined to die in here. But I am leaving this world happy, with my man by my side, and love in my heart.

"Ann, do you hear that?" Ryan wakes me.

I focus and hear voices outside the door. Ryan beams and jumps up, screaming out to them.

"Hey, we found Ryan," a male says.

I sit up slowly and hold my aching head. "Ryan, who's out there?"

"No one I recognize," he whispers before he swallows.

"Well, look what we have here. Prince Ryan is trapped

inside a safe room. How quaint! How justified!" Max rings out.

No! I must be hallucinating! He *died* in the office! I bring the blanket over my mouth to muffle my scream.

"You know what? The hell with him! Just leave him here and let them find his body." The footsteps walk away.

I let a breath out and lean back. Thank goodness. Let that lunatic leave…. who needs him? I am perfectly fine staying here with…

"Wait! It's not just me! Ann is in here too." Ryan looks from my sick frame to the door.

The steps stop.

I feel bile rise up as my heart pulsates in my throat.

"What the hell are you doing, Ryan!" I hiss.

He kneels and clutches my hands. "You need medical attention. If they can save you…"

"If? Max was going to rape and kill me! Do you think he's magically changed his mind?" I retort as I hyperventilate.

"How do I know you are not lying?" Max rings out.

"Max, please, she needs medical assistance or she isn't going to make it," Ryan pleads to the dark door.

"How dare *you*! You said you loved me and wanted to be with me forever! You are no better than Christian! Don't you realize I will never go with them! Ever!"

Ryan's eyes water. "Please, Ann! I do love you. But if you stay with me, you won't survive."

"I would rather *die* with you, then leave with them," I spit out as I shake uncontrollably.

"My sweetheart! I have finally found you," Max sings at the door. "All right, boys. Start moving these beams. My Lady is waiting."

We hear them grunt as they throw around heavy objects. I can't breathe. Ryan is abandoning me, just like Christian.

Ryan squeezes my hands. "Hey, look at me! I love you, Ann, and no matter what happens..." He runs his hand through my hair and kisses me gently. "No regrets."

The door slams open, and three guns are trained on us.

"Did you miss me?" Max strides in grinning. He looks me over before he glares at Ryan. "What have you done to her?" Max snatches my chin while anger burns brightly in his emerald eyes. Max pivots and his fist collides with Ryan's jaw, before knocking him to the ground. "First, you left *me* for dead, and now Ann! You selfish little prick!"

"Stop it, Max! Leave Ryan alone! Please," I cry.

My words drag Max out of his rage, and he stops mid swing. "Well, only because you said *please*." He turns and opens his arms to me. "Come on, let's leave this place." I frown at him and move away. Max pulls out his gun, cocks it back, and aims it at Ryan's head. "Don't make me tell you twice, *sweetheart*."

I look down at Ryan—his nose and mouth are bleeding. But he nods and offers a weak smile.

Ryan saved me; now it's my turn to save him. I swallow, look away from Ryan, and turn to Max.

"Put the guns down, and I will go with you without a fight."

Max tilts his head. "Are you making demands?"

I do my best to stare into his eyes. "Please, they scare me." I pout.

He arches his brow and signals his guys to lower their weapons, then he does the same. "There." I inch my way off the bed. That movement reminds me of my illness and when I try to stand, my legs are too shaky and I teeter. Max catches me in a strong grip and lifts me easily into his arms like a little child.

Then he looks deep into my eyes and forces a kiss on my lips. When he pulls back, he turns to leave, but stops in his tracks as he hears a gun cock behind him. He turns a grin at Ryan's bleeding face. "Well, look who finally grew some balls of his own. Are you *really* going to shoot me?"

Ryan smirks as he wipes the blood from his mouth. "No, I won't. But *they* will." Before Max can turn around, he and his men are shot by Palace guards. I squeal as I fall from Max's grip, but Ryan catches me before I hit the floor.

He lets out a ragged breath as he cries into my hair. "Please forgive me. I am so sorry."

I bring my shaky hand up to stroke his strong face. "You saved my life—again. No regrets," I say breathlessly.

I turn to see Sam grimacing at me. "Prince Ryan, we need to bring you to safety."

"Nothing happens until Lady Ann gets to the hospital wing." Ryan commands.

They help him maneuver over the rubble with me still in his arms. I squint as the bright sunlight burns my eyes. Ryan was right; it was a bomb that trapped us inside. And the rest of the Palace is in disrepair as well.

There are scattered bullet holes, broken glass, and blood smears everywhere. I lean into Ryan's chest and find myself drifting off as I hear his heartbeat against my ear.

Finally, I am where I belong—in his arms and ready to fight for our happily ever after.

Thank You

Thank you for reading *Molting!* What did you think of the book? Could you leave a quick **review** on Amazon and Goodreads? Reviews are so important, and I would greatly appreciate it. Just scan the QR code on the next page.

See Ann again, in all her feathered glory, as she continues her adventure in *Feathered Dreams Book 4: Split Feather* – coming in 2022!

Do we really *choose* our journey?

The world Ann thought she knew is spiraling out of control, and she's caught in its vortex. *Suffocating.* Pulled in every direction.

After a fierce battle, Native American warriors distribute eagle feathers to represent the conclusion. A split feather is indicative of a fighter who has been wounded but persevered. In this new chapter of Ann's life, the most devastating she has yet to face, will she persevere? Or will she succumb to the harsh truths and even crueler betrayals?

About the Author

Brittany Putzer was born and raised in Central Florida, so the need for sunshine (and coffee) is imbedded in her DNA.

Growing up, she turned to books to escape, because it was easier to pretend to be a wizard, vampire, or damsel in distress.

Her books are a wonderful blend of dark and light, with colorful sprinkles of sarcasm, twists and turns, sweet kisses and, on occasion, dramatic cliff-hangers...

She hopes her books can help readers remember how strong they really are... if only they keep moving and fighting the good fight.

Scan to chat with Brittany on social media, **review** her books, get signed paperbacks, check out merchandise, and join her newsletter.

Made in the USA
Middletown, DE
29 April 2022

64955611R00176